Books by Faith Sullivan:

REPENT, LANNY MERKEL

WATCHDOG

WATCHDOG

Faith Sullivan

McGraw-Hill Book Company

New York · St. Louis · San Francisco
Hamburg · Mexico · Toronto

1 2 3 4 5 6 7 8 9 F G F G 8 7 6 5 4 3 2
ISBN 0-07-062355-4

LIBRARY OF CONGRESS CATALOGING IN PUBLICATION DATA

Sullivan, Faith.
Watchdog
I. Title.
PS3569.U3469W3   813'.54   81-17163
ISBN 0-07-062355-4   AACR2

Book design by Roberta Rezk

For My Mother

Chapter 1

Six-twenty. He was late. Some last-minute emergency at the office—a sick dog or a mauled cat. Being married to a veterinarian had all the uncertainty of being married to a doctor, without quite the prestige. Last night at dinner there'd been a call from a farmer with a Tennessee Walker gone suddenly lame, and Jack was off. "See you in the morning," he'd told the children. "Wait up for me, honey, I have to ask you something."

Sometime after eleven he had bounded up the back steps and into the kitchen, whistling an unrecognizable tune—in nine years of marriage, she'd never identified *one* of his tunes—and locking the door behind him, a ritual she knew he enjoyed.

Wearing a thin white cotton gown sprigged with violets, Louise sat curled up on the living room sofa with a crossword from the *Falls Village Republican Leader*. The single lighted lamp on the end table spread a golden pool around her. Smiling as she listened to her husband's whistling mood, Louise set the crossword aside and looked expectantly toward the doorway.

He strolled in and threw his jacket over the back of a wing

chair. "Hi, Prom Queen. How about a glass of wine?"

"Fine."

Doing a snappy about-face, he went back to the kitchen. Behind him, the room remained charged with vitality. Athletic strength and high energy bred a force he had to suppress. The tension of it thrilled Louise.

"You should have been with me," he said, returning with a bottle of Chablis and a corkscrew. "It was beautiful in the country. Felt like summer."

"Well, it is almost." She waited for him to fetch glasses from the bar and uncork the bottle. "Rain's forecast for tomorrow."

"Damn. What about Saturday?" They were going to open the cottage at the lake Saturday.

"I don't know."

He sat down beside her, handed her a glass of wine and raised his own in a salute. "To summer."

The best part of any day was his homecoming, whatever the hour. There was still a restless anticipation as though he were a new lover.

A central core of mystery in him, growing out of his background, maybe, would always prevent him being a thoroughly known or knowable quantity. People were attracted by that and, like Louise, held by it. Wasn't she fortunate, she thought, to be the one among all of them who belonged to him?

She set her glass on the coffee table and lay down with her head on his lap.

"How was the horse? Had he fallen?"

"He'll be all right, I think. He'd thrown a shoe, but I don't think he's done himself any permanent damage." He looked down at her. "Okay, here's my question. Do you think Amy and Peter are old enough to take care of a dog?"

"A dog? That's unexpected. I thought you said you got enough of animals at work."

"I changed my mind. What do you think?"

"I guess so. If they do the work, which I know they won't."

"I've got one I'm going to bring home."

"What kind? How old? Big? Small?"

He ran a finger lightly around the shell of her ear and down her neck. "That's a surprise."

He liked to surprise her, and she knew she could trust his choice. He knew animals. "It might be fun for them to have a dog at the lake this summer." She reached up to play with a ringlet of his hair. It was silky between her fingers. "You win," she said softly.

"I'll bring him home tomorrow."

"Mmmm."

He was silent for a moment, his finger now tracing the neckline of her gown. "I'm going to start looking for a sailboat next week."

"Where?"

"I'm not sure. Minneapolis maybe." He cupped her breast.

"I thought we weren't going to get one until Peter could swim."

"He'll swim this summer."

"How can you be so certain? He's only five."

"He takes after his old man."

Whether that was true in this case, Louise wasn't sure but she wasn't in a mood to argue. Winding her arms around his neck and pulling herself up, she kissed him voluptuously. "I'm looking forward to summer," she breathed.

"Won't the boat be great?"

"Mmmm."

"I've always wanted a sailboat. We'll have to take lessons—all of us."

"Even Peter?"

"Yes."

"He's so young."

"He should learn from an instructor. There's only one way to do things and that's the *right* way."

"And the *right* way is *Jack's* way," she mocked lightly.

"You're learning, Louise."

"Mmmm," she murmured, unbuttoning the top button of his shirt.

"When you're shopping tomorrow, would you pick up a tube of silicone seal for the shower at the cottage?"

"Sure."

"If you think of anything else we need for repairs, go ahead and get it." He kissed her throat and, pulling the gown from her shoulders, kissed her breasts.

"I don't think we should push Peter too hard," she told him, unbuttoning the last button.

"I know what I'm doing. Don't worry." He turned off the lamp, and ran his hand along her leg and under her gown.

She unbuckled his belt. "Did you lock the garage?"

"Yes, ma'am." Pushing the coffee table aside, he slid down with her to the floor.

When they were naked and he'd thrust into her, hips twisting in a way she loved, she teased, "You're quite good."

"I practice a lot."

She smiled and arched acutely, contracting her muscles to pull him deeper into her as though she could draw some elusive secret of him into her body.

Reluctantly Louise coaxed herself back to the present. She stood at the stove idly stirring roast beef gravy while outside the kitchen windows, beyond the screened porch, the clouds which had held and dispensed the day's storm created a premature nightfall.

As predicted, the rain had begun in the morning, about half past seven. Throughout the day it fell monotonously as from a half-open tap, a depended-upon mid-May, after-planting rain, the tinny sound of it in gutters and downspouts.

The transistor radio on the refrigerator said the storm front was expected to move into Wisconsin during the night, leaving Falls Village and southern Minnesota with warmer weather and clearing skies for the weekend. Louise smiled. Perverse romantics, people who enjoy rain, she thought. With the storm moving east, she and Jack and the kids could drive out to the lake tomorrow, scrub out the summer cottage and give it a good airing.

She made mental notes for the morning. Get down the striped sheets she'd bought the previous January at Penney's white sale. Stop at the supermarket to pick up Budweiser and Ajax. Remind Jack, tactfully, to take a pipe wrench in case there was trouble with the plumbing again.

Six-thirty. Where *was* Jack? She walked to the telephone in the den. Brian, Jack's young assistant at the kennel, might still be there. Maybe he knew where Jack was. Amy, eight, and her five-year-old brother, Peter, played with Tinker Toys on the rug, heads bent intently together while a debate on demand abortion raged on the TV they'd failed to silence after the "Electric Company." Louise snapped off the television and picked up the phone.

From out of the early darkness a terrible thunderclap of sound—like a giant tree being felled by lightning—struck her. She caved forward clutching the desk and letting the receiver fall to the floor.

"Mommy!" the children screamed. Their faces lifted toward her were pinched by panic.

The awful, uninterrupted blare of an auto horn drove Louise out of the room and toward the front hall. Again Amy screamed "Mommy!" as she and Peter ran from the den following Louise. In stocking feet they raced to the street windows in the front room. Thrusting aside lace curtains the two children peered into the blurring wetness.

Louise rummaged hurriedly in the hall closet under the stairs.

"It's in front of the church, Mommy. A car crashed on the

church steps!" Amy cried.

"Can we go, Mommy?" Peter was asking. "Can we go help?"

"No. I'll go. You stay here in case Daddy comes. I won't be long."

Emerging with an old tan trench coat, Louise threw it over her head and shoulders and stepped out the front door, closing it carefully against the rain. Her heart pounded in her ears and her teeth were on edge from the continual wail of the horn. She ran across the wide Victorian porch and down the wooden steps, puddled where they sagged. The rain splashed over the tops of her sneakers and with each stride she felt the squish of it inside her shoes.

How could anyone crash on the church steps? Hit by another car? Drunk? Heart attack, maybe. She wished Jack were home. He was good in emergencies. If no one else came immediately, would she know what to do? She tried to remember what she'd learned about pressure points and shock in Red Cross First Aid.

Dodging peony bushes, Louise dashed through her own yard, then the parsonage yard adjacent, the stuck horn of the car spurring her on like a scream. When she reached the churchyard, she slackened, breathing hard, a stitch in her side. Peering into the downpour and pulling the coat higher over her head to shield her eyes against the rain, she recognized at once the blue van, caught in a bizarre position on the steps of St. John's Episcopal Church. VALLEY KENNELS JACK ANDREWS, VETERINARIAN

Chapter
2

The van was like a great mythical beast sprawled across the church steps. Though wounded, it nonetheless lived. The headlights were destroyed but the red hazard lights at the rear blinked pulsingly and the windshield wipers brushed away rain with seeming impatience. Inside, the radio played and, with professional enthusiasm, a masculine voice recommended Aunt Dora's bakery goods.

Someone was already on the driver's side trying to wrench open the door. Bent inward by the crash, it wouldn't budge. Louise pulled furiously at the doors on the passenger side. Someone else, a man, took her arm, moving her aside. "Let me try, Louise." It was Frank Pierson, rector of the church. He grabbed the handle, put a foot against the van, and heaved the door open. Louise slid past him into the front seat. "Jack, it's Louise."

His jacket in the dampness smelled of the disinfectants he used on the animals. His head, covered with light red curls soft as a child's, was thrown forward and to the side so that it rested against the window beside him. His right shoulder pressed against the horn. Louise pulled her husband's body toward her. As the sound of the horn was interrupted by silence, she heard herself whimper like an animal. Jack's head rolled limply back, blue eyes wide with captured surprise.

People were gathering around the van. Several cars stopped, headlights winking in the rain, the sound of windshield wipers blurring the questions asked by drivers. Dimly Louise heard Frank Pierson tell one of the gathered neighbors to call the police, another to locate her brother, Donald Coleman.

Inside the van, Louise locked herself stubbornly in the moment, unwilling to let time move on. Jack's body was warm, as if only the wind had been knocked out of it. She held him and kissed his neck below the ear where curls clung disorderedly.

"Oh, Jack," she whimpered. "Oh, Jack, please."

"Louise." She felt Frank grasping her arm, pulling her out of the van, she fighting him, then going limp. Putting an arm about her shoulders, he led her across the wet grass, under unslackening rain, past bushes nodding respectfully like quiet mourners. Around the van and along the walk, people she recognized, some with folded newspapers over their heads, stood as though to watch a parade pass by. Fearful they might trample some death etiquette, no one said a word to Louise.

She stopped and turned to look back. How could she walk away? A police car had arrived, its red roof light revolving, sweeping the downpour. Scattered across the churchyard were splinters of wood and glass from the bulletin board which normally stood by the sidewalk welcoming visitors and announcing the sermon.

"Jack . . ." How could she leave him there in the wreckage and confusion? She began walking back toward the van. It wasn't right to leave him there in the rain and all. What if, even for a second, he came back to life? What if by some magic he weren't really dead? What if she was not there? "Jack."

The trench coat she had carried over her head was gone. Like someone thrown into a pool with her clothes on, she was drenched and her clothes clung to her. Around her face her hair hung in wet strands and with both hands she skinned it back from her eyes as she headed back toward the van.

Frank grabbed her arm. "Louise, don't." Putting his arms around her, he held her close to him and spoke quietly. "Come in the house. Amy and Peter will be worrying."

Amy and Peter? She moaned and the sound was lost against his chest. She'd forgotten she had children.

Slowly he eased her around and with an arm supporting her, led her again toward the house. Making their way up the front walk, they hesitated before mounting the steps.

"Would you like me to tell the kids?" he asked.

She shook her head.

"I'll stay as long as you like."

The children waited in the open doorway, their figures silhouetted by the front hall light. Not until Louise put her hand on the screen door did either child speak.

"It was Daddy, wasn't it, Mommy? Is he hurt?" Amy held the door for Louise and the rector.

"Yes, it was Daddy." She looked from one of them to the other and they grew more anxious under her unseeing glance. Then she said, "Come in here," and led the way into the front room.

Amy and Peter followed. The room, recently bright and warm, felt cold and cheerless, the lights blinding. Louise turned off one of the table lamps before sitting down on the sofa between Amy and Peter. The children's faces turned toward her were pale. Sad-eyed and apprehensive, as if she were about to be punished, Amy smoothed her brown plaid skirt over scraped knees. Her fine red-gold hair haloed in frills around her face. Louise forced herself to focus on her daughter's eyes, almost black now with the shadow of impending grief, and was surprised and somewhat consoled to see there an understanding of what had happened and what must be said.

It was, in fact, Amy who spoke first.

"If Daddy was hurt, you'd be at the hospital or someplace.

Like when Uncle Donald broke his leg." She hesitated, determining the least shocking way to express her understanding. "That means Daddy is dead, I think."

Peter's round face was stormy and stubborn, hazel eyes brilliant with sudden hate. "That's not so, is it Mommy? Amy doesn't know, does she?" he demanded. "She doesn't know *anything*." He climbed on Louise's lap, took her face in his hands and turned it from side to side in a "no" shake. "That's not so, is it, Mommy?"

"Yes, it's so."

He began to scream and his arms were flailing at her. Amy helped hold him. Even at five he knew what death meant and felt a terrible frustration and betrayal. Were he older he'd be clever enough to reverse things. Now all he knew was that his father had died without telling him first. His mother, who'd always been kind, was telling him just as though she had no intention of doing something about it. Where could he turn? He wanted to hurt her. When he stopped thrashing, he cried.

Over and over between sobs he repeated, "I want Daddy." It was a litany finally carrying him, exhausted by tears, into a sleep full of twitching and muffled baby words. Sitting beside her mother, Amy lay her head against Peter's trouser leg and wept. Frank, in the wing chair opposite, gave her his handkerchief and she held it over her face.

The mantel clock struck seven and the three of them looked at it.

Finally, Frank stood up. "I think I should call Tom Benjamin."

"I don't need a doctor."

"He's a friend."

Louise lay Peter on the sofa and covered him with an afghan. She went to the kitchen, removed the roast from the oven, put the beans and salad in plastic containers and refrigerated them.

Frank came into the kitchen. "Tom'll come by when he leaves the hospital." He rubbed his hands together. "It's chilly in here. Where do you keep firewood?"

"Out there," Louise said, indicating the back porch. Everyday questions, everyday answers, a sizing to hold together the fragile fabric of their lives.

Frank called to Amy and took her with him. He loaded her arms as well as his own and they carried the wood into the living room and deposited it beside the fireplace.

"Help me build a fire," he told her. "Do you know where there's newspaper?"

When the fire was roaring and licking the dampness from the air, they sat before it, staring. They waited for Donald. For Tom Benjamin. For time to pass.

Louise thought of the hundreds of fires Jack had built on that same grate. She saw him bent over, back muscles taut against his shirt, a boyish smile turned to her when the fire caught well. He loved to build a fire, loved anything that made him feel comforted and safe, protected within a closed circle. The eighty-year-old house itself, Louise's house really, had provided that sense of protection, of past and future, stability and continuity.

Around her Louise saw the objects that in the past never failed to cheer and comfort her: the big, easy Chippendale wing chairs; the Queen Anne sofa covered in a plush grown soft and familiar, faded to an antique pastel rose; the fireplace of dark brick surrounded by massive, once golden, now darkened, oak, mantel and fretwork extending on either side into bookcases; the two large Oriental carpets which nearly covered the dusky floor, their colors dulled, gentled by the years.

She closed her eyes and Jack's face in dim light, pale and surprised, was before her. She opened her eyes quickly.

Despite the fire, Louise shivered. The high ceilings no longer conveyed graciousness, only remoteness and chill. It was as if the house were retreating from her, withholding itself in Jack's honor. But this is *my* home, Louise thought dully. Where *I* grew up.

All that was before she'd met Jack, however. Their first

meeting had been in this room. Perhaps she'd given him the house that December night. Maybe he'd simply taken it.

Chapter 3

She remembered holly and candles, the room dressed for Christmas, more than nine years ago. The party had marked the end of her and her brother Donald's formal mourning for their parents, Will and Genevieve Coleman. Will had drowned when the rowboat from which he was fishing capsized during a sudden early summer storm. Louise remembered the horror of that earlier death, police dragging the lake and divers searching for the body beneath icy, weed-snarled water. Thank God, it hadn't been that way for Jack. Two months after her husband's death, Genevieve Coleman, carrying a basket of soiled linens to be laundered, lost her footing at the top of the stairs and fell to her death.

That autumn had been the bleakest, loneliest period of Louise's life. Donald kept busy teaching his theater courses at the local university, and Louise teaching chemistry at Falls Village High School, but nothing could entirely fill the yawning emptiness.

At Christmas break they decided it was time for a party, the biggest one the house had ever held. For Louise it meant a great deal of running around, cooking, decking the halls, phoning and answering, but that was, after all, the point, wasn't it? To be very busy this first Christmas.

About five P.M. of the appointed day, Louise, still dressed in jeans and sweat shirt, got a beer from the supply in the kitchen, sat down cross-legged on the living room sofa and sighed deeply. Vague depression settled over her as the sky outside lowered toward evening. Maybe the party hadn't been a good idea after all.

"Here, Lulu," Donald said, handing her a paper plate with a ham sandwich on it.

"You probably wouldn't like it," she said taking the plate, "if I bought a ticket for Winnepeg and didn't come back till next Thursday. It would inconvenience you?"

"You buy a ticket for Winnepeg, Lulu, and you needn't come back at all," he hooted. "It'll be okay, kid." He patted her shoulder. "It'll be okay."

Bob Engstrom, who taught stagecraft at the university, arrived first, bringing with him two people unknown to Louise, one a plumply pretty dark-haired girl, and the other a tall, inconspicuously freckled red-haired man. As Louise took their coats, Bob introduced them.

"This is Delia Harper who works in the Registrar's office and is my date. And this is Jack Andrews who is new in town and has just bought Doc Bieber's animal hospital, and is *not* my date. As a fixer of cats, I can recommend him. He fixed Grushenka. As a date, I wouldn't know."

Louise led them into the living room. "Doc Bieber's retiring?"

"He was getting so blind, I don't think he knew a Great Dane from a Shetland pony anymore," Bob told her, settling Delia into a wing chair.

"The truth is, he retired to avoid the malevolent Grushenka," Jack explained to the company at large while his glance appraised Louise. She appraised him back.

The doorbell rang. "Bob, would you get Delia and Jack a drink?"

During the next couple of hours Louise intermittently located Jack Andrews, freshened his drink—he appeared to be a bourbon man—and introduced him to her friends. At first he was quiet and reserved, and Louise determined he should not, like the rose, blush unseen.

"This is a nice house," he commented, looking around appreciatively. Louise had tracked him to a window seat in the dining room. "I always wanted to live in a house with window seats. It's classy."

"I grew up in this house. Where did you grow up?"

"In an orphanage."

She was disconcerted. It wasn't what one expected. "I'm sorry. Where was that?"

"Madison, Wisconsin."

"I've never even seen an orphanage except in movies," she said apologetically. "What's it like?"

"Well, it's home, I guess. You don't have much to judge it by. But when you leave, you can't go back again the way you could to a real home. What I mean is, they don't have to take you back once you've graduated. You're on your own. Kind of scary." He took a drink of bourbon and water. "If you come from a regular home and you go out and make a mistake or get lonesome, you've got a place to go and get yourself together. If you come from an orphanage, *you're* all the home you've got until you settle down."

"Did you have brothers or sisters?"

"I don't know. I was a foundling." He paused. "An old-fashioned word, isn't it?"

"Dickensian."

"Right."

"I don't understand. Why didn't someone adopt you?"

"I never figured it out. Especially since I was always this charming."

Maybe he wasn't as shy as she'd thought. "May I get you something to eat or another drink?"

He stood up. "You stay here. Don't move. I'll fix myself another drink. What are you having?"

"Bourbon and soda."

"Good. I was afraid you'd say vodka and Coke. You look like a vodka and Coke girl."

"What a rotten thing to say."

"Sorry." He made his way gracefully through the crowded room, turning at the kitchen door to wink at her. She watched his curly head move through the kitchen toward the bar. He was a pleasure to look at and Louise wondered how long it would be before she could sleep with him.

Caught in speculation, she started guiltily when he returned with their drinks.

"Where did you go to college?" she asked.

"University of Minnesota," he said and resumed his place beside her.

"How did you end up in Falls Village?"

"I did time in the service after college. Figured I could save some money. A guy in my outfit was from here. Roy Anderson."

Louise nodded. "I know Roy. His sister was in my high school class."

"When he found out I was a veterinarian, he told me about Doc Bieber. Said I should look him up when I got out. Roy figured the Doc would be about ready to retire. I *did* look him up. That's it. What about you?"

Louise leaned back. "Boring, boring, boring. Born here. Grew up here. Went to college here. Chemistry major. I teach at Falls Village High School. My folks died a year ago. I'm an old maid and a pretty good dancer."

Louise found that although he spoke in a low, unrevealing voice, his words were unnervingly direct.

"So you're an orphan, too," he said. "Do you live alone here?"

"Yes."

"Do you like living alone?"

"I don't mind. Donald isn't far away, and I've got plenty to keep me busy. Besides, this house is a good place for me to be alone. It's full of my childhood."

They talked about skiing and ice skating. He liked both. She asked him to go skating with her one day. "There's a big public pond and warming house a couple of blocks from here in East Park. You needn't be embarrassed if you're a little rusty. A lot of older people skate there. Not many who do fancy stuff."

He leaned toward her, putting a hand on her arm. "You'll be sorry you said that. I'm not rusty. I'm terrific. Every girl there will want to do fancy stuff with me."

"Skating, you mean?"

He threw his head back and laughed, showing beautifully even, white teeth. Everything looked so good, Louise thought. Surely he must be flawed somewhere.

"You know," he said, gesturing out beyond the window where they sat, "if I had a yard as big as this, I'd flood part of it and have my own pond."

"A big skater on a little pond?"

"Listen, Prom Queen, I'm a big skater on any pond."

"We only have your word for that, don't we?" Enjoying this, Louise snitched a couple of ripe olives from the table and handed one to Jack. "My dad used to make a pond for Donald and me when we were kids. He flooded part of the yard on the south side. If you flood it, I'll let you come skating whenever you want at absolutely no charge."

"You're too kind, Prom Queen." He took a fair size drink of bourbon and considered. "Monday I'm driving up to Madison to take care of a couple of matters. I won't be back till the end of the month. I'll think about it and let you know."

"Fine. Give me a call when you're ready." She glanced around, "This is a nicer warming house than the one at East Park."

"But we'd be skating on a lot thinner ice here."

"My favorite sport is swimming. Do you like to swim?"

"Not only like it but I'm good at it."

"Gee, and you're modest, too."

"Well, I am good at it. In high school, I had a job after school so it was hard to get involved in team sports. The swimming and track coaches let me work out by myself a lot so those were the areas I got into. I'm a damned good swimmer and a fair cross-country man. The hell with modesty." He stood up and took her hand, "Now show me around. I like this house."

Louise didn't know quite what to make of him. He was alternately brash and reserved, someone who hadn't had a mother to hone the rough corners or a father to give him easy confidence. In the mixture, however, was something that beat Winnepeg in the winter.

She led him through rooms upstairs and down, identifying family pictures and pointing out favorite books, a particularly comfortable rocker, a quilt made by her grandmother and an antique vase brought from England by her grandfather when he came to the United States at the age of seventeen. The idea of a boy crossing the Atlantic with a Staffordshire vase in hand had always amused Louise. As they wandered through the house, Jack examined everything with thoroughness, picking up knickknacks, straightening rugs, testing the Lincoln rocker and, to Louise's discomfort, the bed in her parents' room. He even opened the door to the attic stairway and peered into the cold darkness above.

"Planning to move in?" she inquired, mocking him with her smile.

He laughed. "Maybe."

At eleven he excused himself. "Big day tomorrow—distemper shots for all the Christmas puppies." Louise walked him to the door where he shook her hand. "About the skating pond," he began, "what if I came over on the thirty-first and we talked about it? You could show me the most likely spots."

Louise was taken off guard. "New Year's Eve? How do you know I'm not busy?"

"Are you?"

"Maybe. But it's all right. You can come for dinner."

"What time?"

"Seven-thirty?"

"Seven-thirty." He looked beyond her shoulder at the hall, the broad, open stairway and the double doors leading to the living room. "If I lived in this house," he said, "I'd never leave." With that he was out the door and gone.

Louise stood for a minute staring after him, utterly puzzled and a little shaken. "Jesus Christ." She hugged herself, suddenly aware of the cold. "What an oddball."

The morning and afternoon of December thirty-first were spent in carrying out to the minutest detail preparations for seduction. Waking at eight Louise saw that the sky was portentously dark. She dressed and ate quickly, anxious to get the car out and begin the day's chores. Outside, the air was still, muffled and, for late December, almost warm. A sure sign of snow. Before she had pulled up to the second shop on the itinerary, Perrine's Meat Market, the snow had passed the initial fluttery stage and was tumbling down in feathery barrelfuls.

Louise had a list in her handbag. As the list grew shorter, the weather grew denser and Louise's mood giddier. It had been a long time since she'd met anyone she gave a damn about sleeping with. And what could be more seduction-promoting than a snowstorm? Right out of an old Doris Day movie. Emerson Florist would deliver roses to the house later in the day. After Harry's Value Market, she pressed on, pushing through small drifts, to the Cavern, the only one of Falls Village's four liquor stores specializing in wines.

Her mother's old friend, Stella Gordon, was behind the counter. "Big doings tonight?" she asked. "What can I do for you?"

"Well," Louise began, glancing thoughtfully at the beautiful and intriguing labels and the romantic-looking crates, "I need a straightforward, no-nonsense burgundy to go with steaks. Then, for midnight, a champagne capable of clouding men's minds."

Stella loved a scandal. "Sounds kinda serious. Anybody I know?"

"I don't think so," Louise told her nonchalantly. "Somebody new in town."

"Mmmm. Need any brandy?"

"No. I have some I've been saving. Oh, wait, I do need a small bottle of sweet vermouth for Manhattans."

"Take it easy on the Manhattans. You'll be flat on your can faster than you can say Muhammad Ali." Stella wrapped each bottle individually and put it in a heavy bag. "Want me to put this on your bill?"

"Please." Louise picked up the bag. "Happy New Year."

The older woman walked to the door and held it for Louise, sighing, "I wish I were dangerous again."

Louise laughed. "You never stopped, you vixen."

She drove slowly through the snow up the hills of Falls Village to Baker Avenue and around to the alleyway leading to the garage, a small barn. The alleyway was filling in with drifts. It looked like a serious storm.

For an hour that afternoon she tried on dresses before a cheval glass, settling at last on a floor-length ruby velveteen jumper and long-sleeved turtleneck silk blouse. Turning this way and that she tried to imagine how she looked to someone seeing her for the first or second time. Blonde, kind of skinny. Nice dark eye lashes. Blue eyes. Well, what the hell, she thought, it's all I've got. Take it or leave it.

Every twenty minutes or so she looked out to check the weather. The storm wasn't letting up. If anything, it seemed to pick up momentum as the day wore on, piling up drifts higher and higher against the lattice skirting of the front porch. The radio reported that the plows were out, but that traffic was at a standstill in many parts of town.

The florist's van arrived before Baker Avenue was cut off in the late afternoon. Louise arranged the roses in a Waterford vase and placed it on the end table next to the sofa.

The six o'clock news forecast a full-scale blizzard (no surprise there) with winds picking up during the night and snow continuing till midday, January one. Louise stood beside the radio worrying her lower lip and rocking back and forth on her heels. What if he can't get his car out or he gets stuck in a drift somewhere? Well, what if? I guess I'll kill myself or eat both steaks and go to bed with a good book.

She laid kindling wood and logs in the grate. When he gets here, I'll ask him to start the fire and make cocktails while I get the little mushroom soufflés and steaks going. Mustn't forget to take the Camembert out ahead of time, put ice in the bucket and open the burgundy to let it "breathe." Eat your heart out, Doris Day.

As seven-thirty drew nearer, she had begun pacing. She'd drawn the drapes over the lace curtains to make the living room cozy but now regretted it. Each time she peered out anxiously, she had to pull the drapes aside like an unhinged spinster lady with a basement full of empty fruit jars.

Louise turned purposefully away, marched into the kitchen and stood before on open refrigerator trying to recall what she was doing. Salad ingredients were ready to be tossed with the dressing, which was mixed and sitting on the counter. The steaks were out. The eggs had even been separated in preparation for the soufflés. He damned well had never given in under circumstances more splendidly prepared than these, she thought.

The doorbell rang. Louise found her lips sticking to each other, her hands were shaking. In her best Gracious Lady style she opened the door, then retreated a step to allow him to enter in wintery grandness. He stood in the middle of the

hall covered all over like Santa Claus with a thick layer of
snow, his eyes shining, cheeks flushed. Snow clung to his eye-
lashes and brows.

"I walked," he gasped, trying to catch his breath. "Do you
have a towel I can dry my hair with?" he asked, letting Louise
help him out of his coat.

"I'll get one in just a second. Let me hang this where it'll
dry," she said. "Here, give me your scarf and gloves. You've
got to be insane to walk all the way from Front Street in this,"
she gestured toward the storm outside.

Pulling off his galoshes and setting them carefully beside
the door, he looked at her from under thick wet brows. "We'll
see."

Jesus, she thought, you're a pushy bastard.

"Going to ask me in?"

"Of course. Come on in. I'll get you a towel from the downstairs bathroom. Hold on." Returning, she tossed him the
towel. "You must be a fresh air freak."

"Not exactly," he replied, wiping his face and neck and giving his short red curls a brisk rub, "but I wasn't going to take
a chance on not getting here. I figured the car would probably
get hung up in a drift. I knew I could trust my legs."

Lucky you.

Handing her the towel and looking much taller than Louise
remembered, Jack rubbed his hands to warm them after the
long trek. "Have you been thinking about the ice pond since I
saw you? I decided it might be fun."

"The ice pond? Oh, of course. Yes, I've thought about it." I
guess I thought about it a minute or two on Thursday.

"Well, do you know where you want it?" he asked, settling
himself on the sofa.

"Where I want it?" Louise clung to the back of a wing
chair. "Where I want it." You've said that already, Louise.
"No, actually, I thought you're more the expert so you ought
to choose."

"Sure. Fine by me. The sooner the better."

My feelings precisely.

"Would you like me to make you a drink? What can I help you with?" he asked.

You'll see. You'll see. "Help me? Oh, yes. Yes, I *was* going to ask you to do something. Well, first of all, would you make cocktails while I start things in the kitchen? I like Manhattans but make yourself whatever you prefer." There was something else. What? The fire. That was it. "Would you start the fire? I'm afraid I'm a little disoriented today. Barometric pressure or something."

"Or something."

Louise indicated the bar with a nod and hurried out of the room. A second later she poked her head back in the doorway. "I mean, a falling barometer *does* affect people's behavior, don't you agree?"

"Absolutely. I've known people who took to carrying an umbrella or wearing galoshes."

"I should have known you wouldn't understand."

In the kitchen she stood at the refrigerator, leaning her forehead against its cool enamel. How sweet is the refrigerator door to the fevered brow. Why the hell did I wear a *long* velveteen jumper and a *long* sleeved blouse? Well, one thing is certain. I'm not going to ask to be excused while I slip into something more comfortable. I'll sit there and swelter, she mumbled, turning the top oven to 350° for the soufflés and the lower one to broil. She opened the burgundy and ground fresh pepper over the steaks. That's enough for now, she told herself. No point in overdoing. After another stolen moment with head against the refrigerator door, she returned to the front room.

"Hey, you like ice in your Manhattan?" he asked.

"Not usually but tonight I think I will, thanks."

"Wait a minute," he said, setting the glass down again, "your cheeks are awfully red. Are you feeling all right?"

"I don't think so."

He put a hand to her forehead. "You're a little warm."

"I'll say."

"Well, come sit down and have your Manhattan. You'll feel better. You've been working too hard."

"You think that's it?"

They toasted the storm and Jack lit the fire. If this were a movie, Louise speculated, that would be symbolic. And there would be violins sawing away on Tchaikovsky.

"Have you seen any good movies lately?" she asked.

"No. I've been too busy with work. Would you like to go some night?"

"Yes. I love movies." Louise crossed to the stereo, riffled through a row of records, and removed one from its jacket. "How about some music?" she asked, settling Tchaikovsky's *Pathétique* on the turntable. "How was the trip to Madison?"

"Fine. The roads were good. I'm glad this weather didn't come a day sooner."

Me, too, she thought. "Mmm," she said.

"What have you been doing while I was gone?" he asked.

I spent easily thirty or forty hours planning and preparing this seduction, and that's not counting time at the hairdresser's. "Well, I went skating and to a couple of parties. And, of course, Christmas came in the middle." Where had he been at Christmas? In Madison, yes, but with whom? A girlfriend, maybe even a fiancée? What a helluva nerve.

"Who did you go to the parties with?" he inquired.

"Friends. Why?"

"Curious." He sipped the Manhattan thoughtfully. "Don't you want to know who I spent Christmas with?"

"Heavens, no. That's your business." Why did she have the feeling that he was running the show? He had stretched the hand not holding a Manhattan casually across the back of the sofa and as he talked he idly ran a finger along the shoulder seam of her blouse. Her eyes darted from ceiling corner to ceiling corner. She thought she smelled burning silk.

As the final notes of the New York Philharmonic died away, Louise rose again. "I expect I ought to get back out to the kitchen and do whatever it is I'm doing out there." That Manhattan had been awfully long on bourbon. Was she going to be flat on her can faster than she could say Muhammad Ali? Rushing into the kitchen, Louise took an ice cube from the freezer, wrapped it in a cloth and held it to her temple. What am I doing seducing a perfect stranger? It beats seducing an imperfect one, Louise. Stop that. I'm totally disorganized, not to mention out of control. Whatever happened to good old *sang-froid?* I'll never get this damned meal on the table. Julia Child can shove her *bon appétit* right up her . . .

"Let me help you with something out here," Jack suggested, putting his head around the corner. "What's this?" he asked when he saw the cold cloth, "you still feeling warm?"

"In a manner of speaking."

He kissed Louise's forehead and as she raised her face he kissed her again on the lips, first softly several times, then less softly. Sweet Jesus, what am I doing now? she wondered briefly, taking his hand and leading him into the hall and up the stairs. There goes respect. What the hell. As long as he comes back tomorrow.

"The problem is," she explained as they turned at the landing, "Tchaikovsky wears me down."

The steaks were medium rare and succulent. Jack broiled them while she watched the soufflés. At eleven-thirty they sat down, raised their glasses in a toast to barometric pressure, and ate ravenously.

After dinner he built a new fire while Louise cleared away the dishes, stacked them in the dishwasher and got the champagne from the refrigerator. When he had turned the sofa to the fire she handed him the champagne. "If you open this, I'll find Guy Lombardo on the radio."

"Do you suppose you could find the *1812 Overture* instead?"

New Year's morning she'd slipped out of bed before Jack

woke. The house was chilly. Shivering, she snatched a warm nightgown from the bureau drawer and pulled it on.

Pushing the curtains back from the window, she stood looking out for a long time. No one was about. No sound broke the early morning stillness and no footprint or tire track marred the whiteness. Everything was pristine and hushed. One could readily imagine (hope?) that the world had stolen away during the night and left only them to make footprints in the snow.

Behind her he stirred, the sheets making slithery percale sounds.

"Wearing that pretty nightie and with the lace curtains and flowered wallpaper surrounding you, you look like an ad for— what do they call it? Feminine protection?"

"Jesus, you're a sentimental bastard," Louise laughed, jumping into bed. "Get me warm. I'm freezing."

When they had dressed and eaten breakfast, Jack asked where the snow shovels were.

"Why?"

"Because I'm going to need one to dig your car out of the garage."

"Why do you have to dig my car out?"

"We'll need it to load up some of my clothes."

"To do what?"

"To get my clothes. What's the matter, are you hard of hearing? If we don't get started now, we won't be finished in time for the bowl games. I sure as hell don't want to be hauling clothes around while the Rose Bowl's on."

They were in the den, sipping coffee and cognac on the big soft couch, and watching a new and gentle snowfall.

"Wait a second. I must have missed something. You didn't mention anything about moving. I thought we could just lie around and enjoy ourselves today. Where are you moving? Can't it wait until tomorrow? This is supposed to be a holiday, for God's sake."

"Nope. Tomorrow I have to get up and go to work. If my luck runs out, I may even get a call today. I gave the answering service your number."

"Then I guess we're just lucky you haven't had to choose between me and somebody's Pomeranian."

"That's right, Prom Queen. Now, let's find the shovel." He stood up.

"Where are you moving?"

"Here!" he said spreading his hands impatiently to indicate the house around them.

"Here!"

"You like having me around, don't you? I like being here. What's to discuss?"

Indeed.

"Well, we'd better move into the big bedroom," she said, leading him to the back porch where the shovels were kept. "It has two closets."

"You know something, Louise? You're a goddamned romantic."

She knew that in those days he had never separated her and the house in his mind. She represented the house and the house represented her. A package deal. But she wanted him badly enough to accept that, she even found it touching. During the first year of their marriage she wondered once in a while what would happen if, God forbid, the house burned down. As the years passed she became convinced they could survive even without the house.

Chapter 4

Jack's house. How was she going to survive now—in Jack's house?

Donald arrived soon after eight. He didn't ring the bell but came directly in, head bare and shining wet. Throwing his coat over the newel post in the hall, he paused, smoothed back his hair and drew a deep breath. His face, ordinarily very youthful for forty, was mask-like with shock, his clear blue eyes old with pain.

Louise got up to meet him. He held her tightly. "Lulu." He used her childhood nickname. "Lulu, I'm so sorry." His body sagged with tenderness and grief. Louise felt unfathomably distressed by his suffering. Her darling Arrow Shirt Man, usually so cool and strong.

Frank got to his feet as Louise's brother came in and now Donald turned to him. "Jesus, I'm glad you were here, Frank."

"I am too."

The two men sat in the wing chairs opposite Louise, Donald taking Amy on his lap when she came to him. He touched her hair gently. "How's your brother?" he asked.

"Very sad. He cried a lot, then he fell asleep. We all cried but Peter cried the most."

"It's hard for him to understand. We'll have to help him, right?" His voice was nearly a whisper.

She nodded. "Reverend Pierson built a fire. It was cold."

He held her close and spoke over her head to Frank. "Has anyone called Tom Benjamin?"

"He's at the hospital. He'll be over when he leaves there."

"Lou, why don't I carry Peter up to bed? Maybe you can help Amy with her pajamas."

"Uncle Donald, I don't want to go to bed yet. I want to stay up."

"That's all right, but get your night things on and you can help me make tea." He set her down, kissing her cheek. "Now then, let's see about this old man," he said, lifting Peter and carrying him still wrapped in the afghan.

Frank pushed himself up out of the chair. "Louise, would you like me to leave now? I don't want to be in your way here." He looked at her with her hands folded in an uncharacteristically prim attitude.

She started, unfocused. "No. Please stay, Frank . . . I . . . if you don't mind?"

"I'll get more firewood while you put Peter to bed."

Later, pouring out tea, Donald informed Louise, "I stopped up the street before coming along here. Berwick's have taken Jack to the funeral home. Bud Berwick was along in the ambulance. I told him we'd come by tomorrow. The police said Slocum's would haul the car down to the garage. They were a little slow getting there. They've had a lot of calls tonight, stalled engines and minor accidents. The wrecker was arriving as I left."

Louise was staring into her cup. "Did anyone say what killed him?"

"Nobody knows yet. The ambulance driver said it looked like a broken neck. Bud thought so, too."

"But what caused the accident? I don't understand."

"I don't either," Donald admitted. "It doesn't make much sense. But someone may have seen it, or Slocum's may find something wrong with the car. We'll have to wait and see."

She looked up at him. "It really doesn't matter, I guess. What caused it, I mean. He's dead."

Before Donald could respond, the phone in the hall rang. While he hurried to answer, a heavy tread mounted the porch steps.

"I'll see who it is," Frank said, setting his tea aside.

Someplace out in the rain a dog howled mournfully.

Returning, the rector brought Tom Benjamin with him. Benjamin was tall, loose-jointed as a basketball player, his face carved to sharp angles by too much work and too little objectivity about suffering. For all that, he was earthy, ribaldry being a defense and escape.

"Louise, I'm sick about this," he said, crossing to sit beside her. "What the hell happened?" He looked around as though for an answer from Frank. "Rain probably had something to do with it. Brakes were wet, maybe. When I leave here, Louise, I'll stop by and have a look. Take him to Berwick's, did they? Maybe we can get some clues."

Donald spoke from the doorway. "Tom, thanks for coming. Louise, that was Betsy on the phone. Someone called her. She wanted to come over, but I told her there wasn't anything she could do tonight. She'll be over first thing in the morning and stay the day."

"Doc, let me fix you a whiskey," Frank suggested, noting the older man's exhaustion. He set the doctor's raincoat aside and poured whiskey into a glass.

"Thanks, Frank. Bring Louise some brandy if there's any there." He turned to Louise. "I'll call you tomorrow," he continued, "when I've got a little more idea what happened. Don, you're staying here tonight, aren't you?"

"Yes."

"Give her some brandy and warm milk when she goes to

bed." He took the whiskey handed him. Leaning back, he stretched his legs out under the coffee table, and tried to ease some of the tension out of his long body. It sure had been one son-of-a-bitch of a day. "Amy, school'll be letting out for the summer pretty soon. What grade'll you be in this fall?"

"Fourth."

"I can't believe it. Seems like you were just born a couple of years ago. How'd you get so big so fast?" He couldn't make himself talk about what had happened.

"I'm eight-years-old."

"Eight-years-old. You're old enough to take me fishing this summer. Would you do that?"

"Yes."

"You a pretty good fisherlady?"

"Pretty good."

"What about Peter? He know how to fish?"

"A little. We have to put the worm on his hook, though."

"Well, maybe we can take him with us. Don't forget. I'll expect you to help me. I'm possibly the worst fisherman in the world so you'll have your work cut out. I think the most I ever caught was an old hip boot and a rusty wrench and, even with tartar sauce, they tasted disgusting."

Amy smiled courteously. "I'll help you."

He stayed another ten minutes, swallowed the remainder of the drink and got to his feet. "Don't get up, Louise. Donald will see me out." He seemed to want to say something more, but shook his head. At the door he turned. "Talk to you tomorrow."

Nodding, Louise smiled as someone asleep smiles at a dream. Fleeing backward in memory, she pursued those moments in the past which might carry her through these unlivable hours of the present.

Early January of that distant winter when Jack had moved in, was glittering and arctic. By mid-month the newly flooded pond on the south side of the house was hard and smooth enough for skaters, and Jack wanted to initiate it with a small party. He invited Frank and Nell Pierson, the young Episcopalian priest recently arrived at St. John's, and his delicate and rather childlike wife, for a Sunday afternoon. They'd been pleased. Nell Pierson seemed particularly grateful for the diversion.

In addition to the Piersons, they'd asked Donald to join them, and he'd brought along a teaching assistant whose name Louise could no longer recall.

The afternoon, clear and diamond bright, rang like struck crystal with shouts and laughter and the clicking and hissing of blades on ice. As he'd boasted, Jack was a skilled skater and he waltzed each of the women by turns around the ice, flirting evenhandedly with all of them. Louise didn't see the necessity for such proportionate attentions. She said nothing, but as he grasped her mittened hand and whirled her away, Jack explained, "Mrs. Pierson's dying on the Episcopalian vine."

He was probably right. Nell did seem a singularly inappropriate candidate for a minister's wife. She was beautiful and shy and febrile. Her cheeks and eyes burned with unspoken thoughts. It gave her a romantic, consumptive look.

Frank Pierson, on the other hand, was both hearty and hardy, with a great rumbling laugh and easy, open cordiality. Having grown up in northern Minnesota on the Iron Range, he'd played hockey all his life, and within a week of the party he and Jack, dusty equipment retrieved from storage, were polishing old skills and forging a masculine bond.

As the afternoon spun away, Louise observed Jack beguile and win over their guests one by one. His seemingly genuine interest and the intense way he directed it at each of them, like a warming ray of light, opened them like spring flowers. It was almost frightening to watch his effectiveness. He ought to have been a politician, Louise thought. He could elicit devotion so effortlessly. As he had with her.

She had called Donald a day or two after Jack had moved

in. Anticipating something less than approval from her brother, she'd taken hold of her anxiety and explained unapologetically and without resorting to detail, how events had progressed. She wasn't soliciting permission or opinion, only bringing him up-to-date. But it unsettled her nonetheless. She and Donald were close and she didn't enjoy having to displease him.

"Pretty damned sudden, isn't it?" he'd asked, not injudiciously.

"A little."

"Have you been lonelier than you let on?" he pursued, his voice gentle with concern for a little sister who'd flung herself into a domestic arrangement with a stranger.

"No. It isn't that," she assured him. "It's Jack. I've never met anyone like him." She tried not to sound like a schoolgirl.

"Lulu," he'd continued patiently, "you hardly know this guy. What if he turns out to be a son-of-a-bitch?"

"I don't know a lot *about* him, maybe, but I *know* him, Donald. "It'll be okay. You'll like him, you'll see."

"Well, don't get carried away," he warned her paternally, meaning he didn't want to hear in their next phone conversation that she was married.

She'd laughed then. Now she laughed again, to herself, as Donald's misgivings melted beneath the warmth of Jack's shrewd charm and reassuring substantiality.

"Louise tells me you're directing *The Cherry Orchard*," she heard Jack tell her brother. "When does it open?"

"The middle of next month."

"Chekhov isn't one of my favorites," Jack admitted. "But Louise and I will be there."

"You don't like Chekhov?" Donald asked without surprise.

"Everybody spends his time sighing and regretting," Jack explained. "It gives me a pain in the ass." He smiled winningly.

Donald enjoyed a mildly adversarial conversation, particularly if the topic were theater. "Who *are* your favorite play-wrights?"

Jack considered. "Shakespeare. And Shaw." He paused. ". . . And Pinter. Yes, Pinter."

"It's hard to fault your taste. We'll be doing *Pygmalion* in the spring. That should please you."

"Yes. I've never seen it. Read it, but that's not the same. I think I'd like it. It won't be an evening of mooning and swooning."

Donald laughed, and Louise heard the note of inclusion and acceptance. Her brother liked Jack. She was relieved but not amazed.

The six of them played tag and crack-the-whip and other childhood games until they were exhausted and their extremities complained of the cold.

"I'll make Tom and Jerrys," Louise suggested.

They retired to the house and indulged in self-congratulatory discomfort, ranging from aching ankles to burning ear tips. While Louise prepared the hot drinks, Jack built a fire and they all lounged before it, content with themselves.

When Louise handed around the creamy hot drinks, a string of "skoals" and "prosits" followed. Jack, standing beside the fire, lifted his cup first to Louise and then to the group. He beckoned to Louise and she crossed the room.

"I have an announcement to make," he told her, slipping an arm around her waist.

"Oh?"

"Ladies and gentlemen and all others," he began. Conversation died away and everyone looked to Jack. "An announcement."

What on earth was this, Louise wondered. Was he going to propose parlor games? She waited expectantly, shrugging her shoulders at Donald to indicate that she didn't know what was coming.

"We would like you all to know," he told them, beaming

and holding her firmly, "that Louise and I will be married at the end of the month."

The room seemed to recede from Louise and the smiles and laughter and congratulations swam together in a sensory sea. Only Jack's arm at her waist prevented her knees from collapsing. The smile on her own face had turned to plaster of paris. She was thoroughly stunned and without words, without even thoughts. She felt fragmented and unable to pull her parts together.

The others were rising and coming toward her and Jack. They would be grasping her hand, bussing her cheek. What would she do? But no one seemed to notice her bemusement, much less find it odd.

"Louise, it's so romantic," Nell Pierson breathed, holding Louise's hand. "You must be terribly excited. Everything's happened so quickly. Jack is like a bold knight riding off with the princess." She smiled wistfully and moved aside.

Frank gave Louise a bear hug and told Jack, "Your timing's good, Andrews. I can use the extra cash right now." He laughed and grabbed Jack's hand.

At length Donald stood before Louise. He kissed her cheek and held both her hands, looking into her eyes for several moments.

"I'm glad," he said.

He *was* glad. Almost as much as Jack's announcement, this shook her. She couldn't understand it or quite believe it. Since their parents' deaths, Donald had become quite protective. Occasionally Louise was annoyed by this but for the most part she was touched, deeply touched. She recognized that his paternal behavior filled a need in both of them and that it was, after all, only a temporary role.

But here he was, suddenly handing her over to someone he barely knew, and only days after he'd warned her against rushing into anything. Of course Donald wasn't aware that Jack had never proposed to her or even discussed marriage.

Nevertheless, for the first time in her life she felt vaguely powerless, somehow bereft of prerogatives she'd hardly known were hers.

My God, Jack was good at having things his way!

When the others had left, Louise straightened the living room and washed the dishes, declining Jack's help when he offered it. He retreated to the den with the Sunday paper.

Turning out the kitchen light, she wandered through the house extinguishing some of the lamps and re-plumping pillows whose dents had already been removed. At last she chose a *New Yorker* from the coffee table and climbed the stairs to the big bedroom.

Soon after she'd settled into bed with the magazine, she heard Jack moving through the first floor putting the house to bed, as he called it. Checking back and side doors. Darkening each room except the front hall which was kept lit. Clicking off the front porch light and making certain the big oak door with its etched and beveled glass panel was bolted.

Every night since moving in, Jack had put the house to bed. He lavished concern upon it and relished the regimen of a householder. He usually whistled while carrying out the final routine of the day and mounting the stairs. Tonight he didn't whistle.

He stood in the bedroom doorway, leaning against the jamb and studying Louise. She glanced up but said nothing. He had pulled off his sweater and thrown it over his shoulder. A muted brown plaid shirt fit his shoulders and chest lovingly. His corduroy jeans were aged to a velvety softness of texture and color. Louise stiffened herself. She mustn't let him speak to her or touch her until she'd examined her roiling, conflicting thoughts.

For twenty-four years she'd been loved, protected and maybe spoiled, first by her parents and more recently by a doting brother. She'd been rather innocently smug. Then, only weeks ago, she'd met the man who watched her from the doorway. And, by God, how she had wanted him. She'd wanted to possess him in every way she could think of and any way that might exist of which she had not thought. But if you wanted a thing too much, it began to possess *you*. Before you knew it, you'd given yourself wholly and irrevocably away as payment to the beloved.

If she had not already spent all she was, she'd have spoken up this afternoon, she'd have protested being engaged without being asked. She felt she'd given up her soul to get him or to be gotten.

"Louise?"

"Yes?"

He threw the sweater across the arm of a chair as he crossed the room.

"Please don't be angry." Sitting on the edge of the bed, he took the magazine from her and tossed it on the bedside table. She didn't touch him but let her hands fall limply in her lap.

He picked up one of her hands, played with the fingers, put them to his lips and then, without letting go of her hand, put it on the soft corduroy that covered his thigh.

"Do you love me, Louise?"

She didn't answer. He repeated the question gravely as though the answer were in doubt.

"Yes. I love you."

"Do you want to marry me?"

"I don't know. I think so."

His face was close. She looked away from him. "I feel tricked and . . . trapped," she explained. "You shouldn't have told them we were going to be married. You hadn't asked me. What was I supposed to say in front of everyone?"

"I thought you'd get a kick out of being surprised. I thought I was being romantic, sweeping you off your feet."

Did he really think those things or was he being clever?

"Would you like to call it off?" he asked. "We can tell them you've changed your mind."

No, she didn't want to call it off and he knew it.

"Louise?" He kissed her temple. "Do you want to call it off?" There was more urgency in his voice as he whispered against her ear and kissed her neck.

She despised herself for having no part of her soul left to withhold. "No. I want to marry you." She hated him a little for making her admit it.

But then he smiled and the smile was so full of gratitude it tore her like a knife. For that gratitude, the gift of herself seemed suddenly inadequate.

"If you want to marry me, Louise, and I want to marry you, does it make so much difference whether it was your way or mine?" he asked simply.

She didn't know. Maybe he was right. Maybe it didn't matter. Her hand caressed the sensual softness of the faded corduroy.

Nine years later, clinging to the bannister, she slowly climbed the stairs to the bed on which she had been persuaded of so much.

Chapter 5

Saturday was a bloodless limbo hung in the space between death and burial. Louise woke with Amy and Peter on either side of her. Outside the bedroom windows the world was dazzling with sun and spring stirrings. Someone—Donald? Betsy?—had raised the windows to let in the warm May air.

The smell of coffee rose up the open stairway. Louise found she couldn't bear to think of drinking it. Now the pain starts, she thought. The idea of putting on a robe or brushing her teeth was paralyzing. The smallest act required more energy than she might ever have again. How can I care for the children or run the house when I'm not sure I can get out of bed?

The children lay peacefully unaware in slumber. If only they could sleep the grief away. First one, then the other began to wake. Peter, usually laughing and silly in the morning, inched over to take Louise's hand. Amy, delicate and self-contained, turned on her back, putting her hands behind her head, and stared at the ceiling.

No one wanted to be first to confirm the previous night. Finally Amy asked, "What will we do now? What will happen?"

I haven't any idea. "We'll go on living as much like before as possible. We'll still be living in our same house and you'll be going to the same school."

Though her lower lip shook, Amy controlled her voice. "But we'll have to do everything without Daddy."

"I don't want to do things without Daddy," Peter whined vehemently, squeezing Louise's arm until it hurt.

"I don't blame you," she told him, holding his plump hand against her face, "I don't either. I really don't."

Inside, everything ached—no, more than that—pained as though a vital organ had been yanked out. Outside, her body felt cold as glass.

"Will we see Daddy again before they bury him?" Amy asked, turning a thin, pale face toward her mother.

"Yes. We'll go to Berwick's Funeral Home later today or tomorrow with Uncle Donald. We'll see Daddy then."

"What about at the funeral?"

"Then, too."

"What's a funeral home?" Peter wanted to know.

"It's a place where they take dead people to get them ready to be buried," Amy explained.

Peter began to tremble and his eyes filled with tears.

"I think someone is making breakfast for us," Louise told him, wiping his eyes with a corner of the sheet. "We'd better wash our faces and brush our teeth and go see."

"I don't want any breakfast," Peter complained.

"You have to eat," Amy admonished as she took his hand, "or else you'll get sick."

"I don't care."

"You want to go see Daddy, don't you?"

"Yes."

"Then you better eat."

Yesterday morning she was eight. This morning she seemed ancient. For a second Louise hated Jack for doing this to them. Then she hated herself. She retched dryly with frustration, put her head in the pillow and ground her teeth.

Finally she went downstairs, leaving Amy to help Peter dress. Betsy turned off the flame under the coffee when she heard Louise. Her face, as she swung around to greet her, was red and swollen. Louise realized she'd never seen Betsy cry, supposed without thinking about it, that she never did.

They'd met five years ago, when Betsy had moved into the white frame house across the back alley. She was a tall, angular brunette, fresh from a divorce back east—Connecticut, Louise thought, though Betsy never discussed that part of her life. With the divorce settlement she'd bought a tiny red brick building on Main Street and turned it into a boutique, The Bee's Knees. The first year, Louise entertained a casual hope that Betsy and Donald might fall in love. It didn't happen. Lack of romance notwithstanding, they were friends. From Louise's observation, Betsy never seemed attracted to anybody but scoundrels.

The two women hugged each other wordlessly.

"There's stuff keeping warm in the oven, Lou," Betsy told her after a minute. "And I've set the table on the side porch." She cleared her throat, looked away, then rushed on. "I've got some gooey sweet rolls for the kids. I didn't expect they'd be hungry. Maybe the rolls will tempt them."

"Thank you for being here. I feel like I'm walking under water." Louise looked around absently. "Did Donald go out?"

"Yes." Betsy moved toward the stove. "Let me get you some coffee. Donald drove out to the kennel to talk to Brian. He said to tell you he'd be back about ten."

"It must be nearly that now."

"Bring your coffee out on the porch," Betsy told her, handing her a steaming cup.

Louise obeyed. "Poor Brian." She sat at the breakfast table and began worrying a frayed edge of the oilcloth covering. "I wonder what he'll do. What's going to happen to the kennel?"

"Maybe he'll buy it. He's been with Jack . . . what? three years? He must feel at home out there."

Louise let go of the tablecloth. "Do you think he might?" Her voice trailed off as she heard the children in the kitchen.

Betsy hurried in to them. Louise heard her coaxing them to have sweet rolls and milk.

Carrying their plates and glasses, Amy and Peter sat down at the porch table and nibbled disinterestedly.

Frank Pierson mounted the wooden steps and opened the screen door. His face was gray with fatigue, and he hadn't shaved. Drawing up a straight-back chair, he sat down beside Louise.

Betsy fetched another cup of coffee and a roll and put them in front of him. Frank stared at them blankly, his mind elsewhere. Finally, "The damnedest thing happened, Louise. Did Jack say anything to you yesterday about bringing home a dog?"

Remembering yesterday—except for those moments in the rain with Jack's body—was like reaching for objects in a murky pool. But, yes, Jack had talked about getting the kids a dog, hadn't he?

"This dog's a setter," Frank went on. "First we thought he was a patient Jack was delivering but your name and address are on the identification tag. They found him in the back of the van."

"A setter?" Louise asked, her voice barely audible. "I didn't know it was a setter."

Frank looked puzzled and at the same time relieved. "Then you know about the dog? This isn't coming out of left field?"

"Yes. Well . . . Jack said if it was all right with me, he wanted to bring home a dog." She paused. "I forgot. I forgot about it."

"This is the dog then." Frank reached for the butter. "He's at my place."

Louise struggled to understand. "You mean he's alive?"

"Not a scratch on him."

"What's he doing at your place?" Betsy asked.

Before Frank could answer, dawning realization struck Peter and he asked, "Do we have a dog, Mommy? Can I see him?"

Amy asked hesitantly, "Can we get him?"

Betsy interrupted quietly, "If you guys are going to have a

dog, there are things we have to do first."

"Like what?" Peter inquired, wary of grownups' delays.

"Well, what about food and a dish and things like that?" If those things had been in the van with Jack, she wasn't going to suggest it. Here was something to occupy the children.

"I forgot," Peter admitted.

"And a leash," Amy added.

"If your mother doesn't mind, the three of us can walk over to my place and get my car. We'll pick up supplies before we think about bringing a dog home." She looked at Louise.

"Of course."

Peter patted Louise's hand gratefully, kissed her and said good-bye.

Folding her napkin neatly beside her plate, Amy walked around the table, stroked her mother's hair and told her, "We won't be gone long."

They followed Betsy out the screen door and across the backyard. When they were gone, Frank's body slumped down inside itself. He studied Louise from under perpetually quizzical brows, eyes dazed and unbelieving. "What can I do for you, kid?"

"Nothing, really." Louise sat motionless like someone protecting a wound that reopens with each movement. "How *did* you get the dog?"

"Jack had the dog in the back of the van last night," he explained. "No one noticed it right away. It was probably dazed. After Berwick's ambulance left and the wrecker started towing the van away, the dog began howling. Scared the hell out of the mechanics."

Frank's housekeeper, it turned out, had been one of the onlookers in the rain. " . . . Hattie in her hideous gray slicker, watching, probably supervising. She told the police she'd keep the dog at the parsonage." He toyed with his cup, turning it this way, then that. " . . . fed him and put him on a rug. . . . Damned near fell over him . . . "

Louise's attention wavered in and out of the recitation. For several minutes she sat without speaking. Death wasn't a single kind of loss, a single kind of pain, but a continually changing kaleidoscope of pains and losses. How did you fit a dog into it?

Before she could change her mind about keeping the animal, she heard Frank urging, " . . . how good this will be for the kids . . . right now."

She sighed. "I'll keep it, Frank. Don't worry. I just can't think about it now." Her voice filled up and she cleared her throat. "Sorry."

"For God's sake, don't be." Pulling his chair closer, he grabbed her cold hands in his. Bending his head against her shoulder, he wept. He wept, Louise knew, not only for the loss of his closest friend, but for the wife who'd killed herself two years earlier.

Louise kissed the side of his face and wished she could be surrogate mourner for all of them—Frank, the children, Donald, Betsy, everyone. Seeing them in pain was worse than being in pain.

"Lulu? Where is everybody?" Donald's voice could be heard coming down the long front hall and through the kitchen. "Here you are."

He sat down across the table. "I'm glad you're here, Frank. I guess there are things we need to talk about."

Donald was keeping himself very tucked in, very together, though what it cost showed in the fine lines beside his mouth and in the muscles stretched beneath the elegant face, working, tightening, with a life of their own.

He's a remarkably good actor, Louise thought, touched by his performance. He's fashioned a role, "responsible older brother taking hold." His way of getting through. And why not? When our skeletons dissolve with pain, the role we play holds us upright.

"Is it all right with you, Lou? If we discuss arrangements?" Donald asked.

"It has to be done." She ran a hand absently over her hair. "Frank, last night after you left, Donald and I talked. We wondered if the funeral could be Monday."

Donald broke in delicately, "I spoke to Paul Berwick just now on the way in from the kennel. He said Monday is okay with them if it's all right with the church." He looked to Frank.

Frank hated getting down to the specifics, closing the deal. "What would you rather, Louise, morning or afternoon?"

"Morning, I think." She hesitated. "Frank . . ."

"Yes?"

"Jack hated funeral music. Any kind of organ music, in fact."

"That's no problem. We can ask the junior choir to provide the music. It'll probably be guitars if that's all right."

"Yes."

"Maybe there's some piece Jack particularly liked. Or I can make the choices if you'd rather. I should let the kids know by tonight so they can rehearse."

She nodded and pulled her shoulders up straight. "Donald or I will call you before dinner."

Putting his hands on the table, Frank pushed himself up slowly. He touched her cheek. "Betsy can come for the dog when you're ready." He let the screen door quietly to behind him and headed back toward the parsonage.

Beyond the screen, a languorous breeze stirred spirea branches. They shifted impatiently sideways like heavy, un- willing matrons. A woman's laughter, generous and musical, rode the morning air, disembodied, like a memory. Perhaps because Frank had just left, the laugh reminded Louise of Nell Pierson's. She had laughed so hard the day of Peter's christening.

Peter had been born in April. When he was two months old, he'd been christened along with three other infants at St. John's on a hot summer Sunday.

All four couples had carried their babies to the baptismal font at the rear of the church and one by one Frank laid dampened fingers on their heads until only Peter remained to be baptised. Jack passed the baby to Frank. Amy, who was two and a half, stood beside her mother, clutching Louise's dress.

Peter had fallen asleep during the buzzing somnolent morning but when he felt the water on his head, he woke astonished, howling and kicking. Frank completed the ceremony quickly and handed the baby back to Jack.

Peter was not to be quieted but continued loud and angry. Amy, imagining that her brother had been injured there at the font, began to cry also. When Louise's responses did not satisfy her, she stamped her feet and screamed, furious that no one understood the baby's plight.

The three other sets of parents began returning to their pews, anxious to dissociate themselves from the couple with the obstreperous children, but Peter and Amy's racket had upset the other babies, who contributed their unhappy voices to the pandemonium.

Frank returned to the pulpit but it was impossible for the service to continue. Nothing could be heard above the sound of five yowling youngsters.

Two rows in front of Jack and Louise, Mame Goodin, registrar of misdeeds for the congregation, slowly turned her head and torso as though they were bolted together and would not operate independently. First right, surveying all on that side, then left. One by one the young parents gathered bottles and blankets and bags and exited hastily with their offending offspring until only Peter remained of those baptized. Miss Goodin turned nearly the entire way around in the pew and rested an intense gaze upon Peter for seconds that seemed to Louise to stretch into years.

Louise looked imploringly at Jack but he only smiled piously and remained firmly put, Peter in his arms. Frank picked up the threads of the service. Amy was calmed by the offertory hymn. Peter fussed off and on until the recessional, which seemed to pacify him.

Leaving the church, Jack and Louise paused on the steps to remind Frank and Nell that they were expected for dinner to celebrate Peter's christening. Through the big doors, thrown open to release the congregation, Mame Goodin emerged with two blue-haired women who tittered and minced obeisance. Spying Jack with Frank, she made her way to them, hurling at Jack a smile mischievous and cold as a weapon.

Chuckling, she observed in a carrying voice, "I surely hope you're better with dogs than you are with babies, Dr. Andrews." The two blue-haired women crowded in behind, shocked and thrilled.

Close beside her husband, Louise could feel his temper surge. She picked up Amy and held her tightly.

"Frankly, Miss Goodin, my methods with both are quite similar," Jack explained measuredly, as though to someone who might have difficulty understanding. "I never hit a baby, a dog—or a woman—with a rolled-up newspaper unless they chew my slippers or piddle on the carpet. You're perfectly safe. Merely being unpleasant isn't provocation enough."

While she was stunned and brought to her knees, Jack delved into Miss Goodin's watered-blue eyes and located a rift through which he glimpsed her vincibility.

Louise and Mame Goodin each held her breath, waiting for Jack to deal a *coup de grace.* It seemed to Louise that immense energy and time were compressed into a few silent seconds, like the last moment before an awful crash.

Jack grinned then, a broad, boyish grin, not pressing his advantage, but holding the woman's frightened gaze with his smile, his body taut with unspent anger, yet entirely controlled. Finally, nodding graciously, he turned away and unhurriedly descended the steps, Louise at his side.

Mame Goodin at last expelled the breath she had held. She

was his. He had detected her secrets but had walked away without pillorying her. He had conquered without laying waste.

Later, on the screened side porch at home, Jack handed Louise a glass of white wine. Frank and Nell, seated in wicker armchairs, nibbled cheese and crackers and sipped cool white wine. It was a quiet, lazy afternoon.

Louise couldn't shake off the morning's events. Studying her husband, she felt pride and awe laced with formless alarm. What had Jack discovered in Mame Goodin's anxious stare? He had a quick comprehension of people that amounted to second sight. But why should that disturb her?

She shrugged and turned her glance from Jack to Frank who was lifting his glass. "To Peter. May his heart be a match for his lungs." He laughed and drank.

Nell looked at Jack and exploded in gay laughter that startled Louise. In the three years that she'd known Nell Pierson, Louise had never heard a sound so unrestrained from her.

"You were magnificent, Jack," Nell declared warmly. "Wasn't he, Louise?"

"He was . . . extraordinary."

Breathlessly Nell confided to Jack, "I felt as though you were fighting *my* battles."

Jack looked at her with bemused affection but Louise thought he understood quite well what Nell meant.

"Mame Goodin is a horrid old dragon and she can't stand me," the minister's wife exclaimed, eyes bright, "but you took the fire out of her. Here's to Jack." She drank. "You don't know how many times I've wished that Frank would do what you did today," she said with quiet intensity, twisting the stem of the empty glass. She glanced at Jack, then quickly away.

"I'll, uh, I'll get some apples to have with the Brie," Louise announced suddenly. When she returned, Amy had climbed onto Jack's lap and he was counting fingers and toes while the child giggled deliriously and hugged his neck.

Nell watched them. Her hand played discontentedly with a brooch she wore on her pale summer dress.

Frank, his face turned away from them, was looking toward the yard that lay between this house and the parsonage. "The spirea is beautiful in bloom, but I always seem to catch my sweater on it," he said to himself.

Another peal of laughter from somewhere on the block drew Louise out of the past. The spirea beside the porch curtsied its long green bows. It had flowered early this year. Already the lacy white blossoms were gone.

At ten minutes to twelve Betsy returned with the children. Louise asked her, "Will it be too much with the kids and all if Donald takes me for a drive? I'd like to get out of the house. I can't stand the thought of people telephoning."

"Go ahead."

Louise spoke to herself. "I have to stop at Berwick's." She looked at Betsy. "Donald was going to take Jack's navy blue suit over this morning but last night when we got it out, it needed cleaning." She thrust her hands deep into the pockets of her skirt. "You never die when your best suit is clean."

As Donald drove away from the house, Louise put her head back against the seat and closed her eyes behind dark glasses. She knew that whatever debris might have been left on the church steps, Henry Ellingson, the sexton, would have removed it but she couldn't bring herself to look. Monday would be soon enough.

Louise was uncomfortable with sympathy, so Donald didn't speak. He drove north out of town, turned right onto Swan Lake Road and set the Volvo on its tortuous route through a tunnel of trees, semi-dark with shade even at midday. He received an unequivocal "no" when he asked if she wanted to stop at the cottage.

"We were going to clean it out today and take the kids fishing. Stop at the Yacht Club, though. I need a drink before Berwick's."

He put a hand on one of hers.

Loving, protective Donald. Elegant. Like someone born rich and lucky. Pastel to look at: hair the color of new wood, light golden skin and gray-blue eyes. A Leyendecker man. Through a series of not unhappy circumstances, Donald had become head of the Theater Department at thirty-five. Summers he was artistic director of Lac des Cygnes Summer Theater in a defunct dance hall at the edge of Swan Lake. When the funeral was over, Louise knew, he had to start working on the first show of the season.

Beyond the trees on their right lay Swan Lake. It had a serpentine shoreline dotted with family cottages. Coming up was theirs, hers and Jack's. It had been her parents'. She peered through the trees to catch a glimpse of the second story as the tires hissed over wet gravel. No patch of white or windowpane was visible, however, and only the mailbox nailed to a birch tree indicated that this was the right driveway. The Volvo ignored the familiar turnoff and continued to snake its way around the lake.

They were almost to the wooden bridge just before Arthur Mack State Park. After that was Lac des Cygnes Summer Theater, Ginger Charlie's Drive-In, the Yacht Club, and a couple of boat rental shacks that sold bait and gear.

Donald pressed her hand. "I called the people on the pallbearers' list while Betsy was out with the kids. Everyone said yes so far. I couldn't reach Earl Jensen. Catherine hadn't heard about the accident. Earl is in Minneapolis on business. She'll have him call as soon as he gets in, but she says he'll be a definite yes. Jeanette Reed said to tell you that St. Anne's Guild is taking care of serving food at the house after the funeral."

Louise was relieved when they turned into the Yacht Club parking lot. Donald switched off the ignition, sat silent for a minute, then smiled ruefully. "What're you drinking, Lulu?"

Inside, they were the only customers. It was early in the season for lunch customers and early in the day for bar customers.

"Don. Mrs. Andrews." Art Christopher, the bartender and manager, nodded at them as they entered, the heavy door closing with a pneumatic whoosh behind them. Donald led her through an archway and into a room overlooking the lake.

Shards of brilliant sunlight, scattered on the water, kept Louise from removing her sunglasses. She and Donald sat in captain's chairs facing each other across a small table whose polyurethaned surface was mirrorlike.

"It's so bright," she said, putting her elbow on the table and shielding her eyes with her hand.

"Would you like to move?"

But Art Christopher was coming through the archway toward them and she didn't answer. Ice tinkled in heavy water goblets. He set them down and wiped his hands on a bar towel draped over his arm. He was a big man, youngish, perhaps thirty-eight or forty, with a kind face and restrained gentleness.

"I'm really sorry about the Doc, Mrs. Andrews."

She removed the sunglasses.

He continued. "My wife, Donna, is in St. Anne's Guild at the church. She heard about it this morning and called me." He looked at Donald. "It was a shocker. He was so young." Shifting his weight, he looked back at Louise. "I'd like to buy lunch for you and Don if you wouldn't mind."

"That's very kind, Art. Thank you." They ordered roast beef sandwiches and tap Michelob. When Art turned away, Louise put the sunglasses back on and sat staring out across the lake. No fishing boats were out at midday but a pair of carefree skiffs bobbed good-naturedly across the southern channel.

"I wonder why they ever called it Swan Lake," Donald mused. "I never saw a swan here, did you?"

"Wishful thinking on someone's part."

"And the Yacht Club. Doesn't it sound grand?" He gazed around the homely room. "A run-down steak house with a good bar." If he primed the pump, would her words flow? Probably not. She didn't have the faith in words that he did. "You should bring Betsy out to stay with you this summer. She might like living out here while she's working on the show."

"Mmmm. I'd forgotten. She's doing the costumes?"

"She's always threatening to buy a cottage. If she stayed with you and the kids, she'd get a taste of what it's like."

"I'll see." She glanced at him quickly. "You're going to be at the cottage this summer, aren't you?"

"Oh, yes." He folded and unfolded his napkin. "Louise?"

"Yes."

"Would you like me to get in touch with Ned?"

"Ned who?" She didn't know what he was talking about.

"MacRae. Jack's lawyer." He waited for her to assimilate that. "I kind of forget what legal things have to be done now. Would you like me to talk to him?"

She frowned, rubbing her hands together in a gesture of panic. "I can't . . . talk about that now. Please. If you want to see him, go ahead but don't tell me about it."

The sandwiches and beer arrived. "Okay."

Nibbling determinedly, Louise managed half a sandwich. She washed it down with beer which made her shiver but nonetheless tasted good. It was the first taste that had penetrated in the past twenty-four hours.

A country road crew spreading fresh gravel on Swan Lake Road stopped at the Yacht Club for lunch. The sound of their laughter and conversation came in staccato bursts from the bar in the larger room. Already Louise missed the maleness of her husband and resented that other women would have these men beside them tonight while she was alone.

Donald drove slowly back to town. He knew she dreaded Berwick's. A large, two-story frame house that rambled off in several directions, the mortuary stood on a big, tree-shaded corner. Except for the discreet sign in front, "Berwick and Sons Mortuary," in Old English script, it might have been a private home or a high-class boarding residence for senior citizens. A concrete drive circled into the immaculate front yard passing close to the portico. Donald parked in the drive. Walking up the two shallow, canopied steps to the wide porch with its dignified tubbed greenery, Louise glanced down at her hands. They were stiff and cold.

Donald took one, massaging warmth into the fingers. When they reached the massive white door, polished brass fittings gleaming at them, Louise hesitated. She looked at Donald. He squeezed her hand and promptly pressed the buzzer beside the door.

Louise started when the door suddenly swung inward and they were met by Paul Berwick himself.

Smiling sympathetically at Louise, he motioned them into the huge, hushed foyer, shook Donald's hand and then ushered them through a nearby door into his office, closing the door behind them.

Listening to Paul Berwick drone on about coffins and flowers, limousines and printed thank-you's, Louise wondered what it was about the man that she disliked, other than his presently being the keeper of Jack's body. With his prematurely silver hair and patrician nose, Berwick was handsome in a florid way. Yet there was something missing that ought to be there. He was standing up now and Donald, too, got to his feet.

"Would you care to see your husband now, Mrs. Andrews? It's often easier for the spouse to view the deceased alone the first time." He came around the desk. "We never know how these moments will affect us and it's best to spare the children our worst grief, don't you agree?"

"Our" worst grief, you ass? *My* worst grief. She did, in fact, agree with him. But his professional manner was horrible,

smooth, oiled by bone-deep indifference masquerading as so-
licitude. His physical presence made Louise uneasy. She
hoped fervently he wouldn't be beside her when she saw Jack.

He led them along a broad hallway to a set of wide, sliding
oak doors. Berwick pressed a button and the doors parted
noiselessly on their track revealing a room decorated in pale
green.

To prolong the moment of self-deception, an illusion that
Jack wasn't dead, didn't lie in this room, Louise concentrated
on the room itself, the deep, soft carpeting, the subtle damask
weave of the drapes, the suffused lighting. Eyes fastened to an
arbitrary point on the opposite wall, she moved forward, finally halted by the casket in her path. Louise forced her eyes
downward.

Involuntarily her hand rose to cover her mouth. The sight
of Jack's waxen face lying in a satin cocoon sucked the breath
out of her throat.

He was dead. No longer surprised, neither did he look resigned. Even in death there was an expectancy in the lines
and planes of his face. It had always held promises. It still
did.

Behind Louise, Paul Berwick's voice came from a great distance as though broadcast by a crystal set. "He looks very natural, don't you think, Mrs. Andrews?"

Natural? Oh, yes, the expression was very natural. Why had
she imagined that all people looked peaceful when they were
dead?

Chapter 6

It was nearly three when Donald and Louise returned home. Amy and Peter were sitting on the top step of the front porch. Sitting between them was a big Irish setter, its long plume of a tail slowly moving up and down, slapping against the porch floor. He rose languidly, tail still slapping, while Amy and Peter ran to the curb. When Louise opened the car door, the children were upon her, their words tumbling on top of one another. The dog watched from the porch, stately.

"He's *ours*, he's *ours*," Peter shouted incredulously. "Do you believe it, Mommy, he's ours?"

"Can you guess his name?" Amy pursued. "It's on his collar."

"Hey, kids," Donald put in, "give your mom a chance to get her breath."

Louise was unprepared for the light mood. The transition from Berwick's to this was jarring. Her nerves stretched taut as she attempted to summon patience. The kids shouldn't be made to feel guilty for what they found to enjoy during these long days. She must find a way not to be affronted by their enthusiasm.

She shrugged, allowing herself to be led by a child at each hand up the porch steps and into the house. Donald gave her a "what can you do?" smile and held the door for them. The dog, well beyond puppyhood, seemed relaxed and at home. He looked toward the street, as though lost in thought. Then he shook himself slightly, turned and preceded Donald through the door. Donald smiled at his imperiousness. "That's right, fella," he told the dog, "you're one of the family."

Thin afternoon sunlight pierced the lace curtains, casting swaying shadows around the room. Louise, lowering herself onto an armless Victorian chair, felt suddenly outside herself, an onlooker. Amy stood to one side of the chair and Peter was on his knees at the other. *Mrs. Andrews and Children*, luminous rendering in oil by the brilliant impressionist, whatshisname. Careful, Louise.

Amy moved around in front of her mother and held the dog by his collar so Louise wouldn't be able to read the tag.

"Okay, Mommy, now try to guess his name."

"Well, first of all, is it a he or a she?"

"It's a he."

"Hmmm. Let's see. Pat? Mike? Rover? Red?" To each of these the kids responded with a giggling "no."

"Caesar? Brutus? Rex? Prince? King?" Still "no" and more giggling. The dog patiently submitted to the game.

"I give up," Louise said finally. "I'm terrible at guessing games. Tell me."

Slowly, to heighten the drama, Amy turned the dog's tag over.

Louise put her head on the back of the chair and laughed soundlessly. "Fido! I don't believe it."

"It's true," Peter insisted, "and Betsy said it means 'I am faithful' in French."

"Not French," Amy corrected. "She said it means 'I am faithful' in Latin. She said Latin is a dead language that people don't speak anymore but we still use a lot of words from it. Is that true?"

"That's right. It means 'I am faithful.'" Louise ran her hands absently over the dog's fine-boned skull. "Donald, do

you think Jack named the dog? Fido doesn't sound like anything he'd pick."

"Beats me. Brian might know."

Fido stood before Louise, muzzle resting lightly on her
knees, eyes slanted up at her. He snorted softly, lifted his
head, then set it back as before, eyes never leaving her face.

"He's a handsome thing," Louise observed.

"Yes," Donald agreed. "He's quiet for a young dog, isn't
he? He won't need much training."

Physically he looked like a young dog, but Louise wasn't
sure. He seemed very self-possessed.

"Where will he sleep?" Amy asked.

Louise hesitated. "I don't know. What do you think?"

With her weight on one foot, hip thrust out in a pose she'd
picked up from Louise, Amy said, "Well, Peter wanted him to
sleep in *his* room and I wanted him to sleep in *my* room but
we thought *you* might want him to sleep in the basement."

Louise pondered, noting the dog's dignity, his seeming in-
telligence and beautifully groomed coat. "It does seem a
shame to put a sweet thing like this in the basement. I don't
want him sleeping on anyone's bed," she said with a mean-
ingful glance at Amy and Peter, "but I can't see any harm in
letting him sleep, say, in the upstairs hall."

"Those soulful eyes got to you," Donald told her. "He'll
end up sleeping on *your* bed." He leaned back and put his
feet on the coffee table.

"I'm going to put on a robe," Louise told them, bending to
pick up her brogues. "I'll be back in a few minutes." She
crossed to the front hall and started up the stairs.

Fido turned and followed, paws clicking wherever they
touched the floor. Up the stairs he padded at her side, matching his pace to hers.

"Come on, dog. You want to have a look around?"

At the top of the stairs he ran ahead down the hall and into
the master bedroom.

Away from the others, Louise felt suddenly overpowered by

exhaustion. She closed the door, lay down, and buried her face in Jack's pillow. It smelled of his cologne. Within minutes Louise was asleep.

The dog, his face resting on the edge of the bed, emitted a low whine. Then turning, he stretched out beside the bed, crossed his paws and placed his head on them. He didn't take his eyes from the sleeping woman's form, but lay watching the slow, steady rise and fall of her breathing.

Chapter 7

Louise woke with a start at five-fifteen, shivering and disoriented. Shucking off her sweater and skirt, she pulled on a warm robe and hurried downstairs, face flushed and puffy from restless sleep.

Donald was still on the sofa, lying down. Opposite him in one of the wing chairs Betsy sat, legs crossed, hastily scribbling notes on a kitchen pad. She looked up as Louise came in.

"I shouldn't have slept," Louise said, fidgeting with a loose button on her robe. "I've got to get ready for tonight." Glancing around she asked, "Where are the kids?"

"They're in the den going through an old picture album," Betsy assured her. "Sit down. You're making me nervous."

"Is there any coffee?" She looked from Betsy to Donald. "Hot coffee with brandy. I'm freezing." She shivered and pulled the robe more tightly about her.

Donald rose, stretching, yawning and talking through the yawn. "I'll get some coffee. Sit here. Bets, why don't you go over your list with Louise?" He indicated the pad she was holding.

There had been a steady stream of calls. Condolences, offers of help. "Brian called. Everything's under control at the kennel. He'll see you tonight at Berwick's and Monday, of course. If you need anything, call. He must have been very close to Jack. He's really shaken." Her voice caught and she hurried on. "Ned MacRae called and he'll be in touch."

The doorbell interrupted. Donald handed Louise the coffee he'd prepared and went to answer it. Louise sipped the laced coffee. It was strong and hot. In the hall masculine voices conferred in tones modified to suit a place where there was tragedy. Louise felt no interest. She only wanted to be warm.

Donald returned, followed by Henry Ellingson, the sexton of St. John's, who seemed not at all sure he should be there. Henry held a red and black check wool cap in his right hand, slapping it nervously against the side of his trousers. He nodded first to Louise, then Betsy.

Donald was saying, "Henry can tell us more about the accident, Lou. Sit down, Henry." He gestured toward the wing chair near the fireplace. "A cup of coffee?"

"No. No, thanks, Don." Ellingson sat on the edge of the seat feeling intrusive and uncomfortable. "I can't stay but a minute. The wife and I are going to my son's for dinner—Eldon, I guess you know him—anyway, I have to get home and get changed." He moved his feet, looked down at them keenly and then went on. "To tell the truth, I didn't know if I should bother Mrs. Andrews." He glanced at Donald and Betsy to see that they understood. "But my wife said it would be wrong not to tell her and the Reverend did too. He said it would hurt to hear about the accident again, but you'd want to know what happened. I hope that was right." He looked at Louise.

"That's right," she assured him. "I've tried to figure out in my mind what could have happened. Jack wasn't a careless driver."

Henry had left the church the previous day right after the late choir practice. "The Reverend said I might as well go on home. There wasn't anything more to do. He was going to lock up." Henry left by the Chestnut Street door and walked up Chestnut toward Baker. "A dog ran out from somewhere. A little dog. Maybe a Pekingese. Something on that order. Anyway, the Doc swerved, you see, so as not to hit it. Well, with the rain I guess the street was slick there and the next thing I knew, the car just sorta bounced up the church steps hell bent and hit against the iron rail. Maybe his foot slipped and he hit the accelerator instead of the brake. You know how sometimes your shoes are wet when it's raining and they slip on the pedals?" He wiped his forehead on the back of his sleeve. "I tried to get the door open on the driver's side but it was bent in where it hit the rail, you know, the hand rail."

So it was Henry who was there when Louise arrived.

"Mrs. Andrews, I'm terrible sorry. I wish there was something I coulda done. Your husband being a veterinarian, it was just a natural instinct for him not to hurt that dog, I guess."

Inwardly, Louise smiled at the old man's romantic notion. "I'm glad you saw what happened, Henry. I would always have wondered."

Henry pushed himself up. "I'm real sorry. I didn't know the Doc well but he was a good man. We got a dog, part Great Dane he is, big as a pony. Well, he got the worst of it with a cat one time. The cat near tore his eye out. I wasn't home and the wife had to get a neighbor to drive her and the dog out to the Doc's place. She never forgot how he took care of Duke; that's the dog's name, Duke. He's a big mother to hold onto when he don't want to be held. But she said the Doc was so strong he didn't even ask her to help. Also I guess he could see she was pretty wrought up. Well, he held Duke, just kind of hypnotized him, the wife said, and patched him up. The wife broke down and cried. She couldn't get over how gentle he was with the dog." Henry realized he'd gone on more than he'd intended. He put out his hand and shook Louise's, careful not to step on Fido who had walked into the room earlier and arranged himself on the carpet in front of Louise. "That's a beautiful setter, Mrs. Andrews. Real gentle, real protective."

So that was it. A dog. The irony of it was galling. Still, Louise thought, catching tears with the back of her hands before they reached her cheeks, ironic or not, Jack's death was a *mistake*—an error in the pattern of things. If there were sense in the universe, such an error would be corrected.

Once more Louise stood in the pale green room. Chairs had been brought in. Floral arrangements, expensive and strangely festive, their combined odors nauseating, lined the walls of the little room. Friends and neighbors filed in, signed the registry, washed everything and everyone with commiserative glances, offered sympathy and memories, and left, trying not to appear to be hurrying.

We're all here, Jack. The children, Donald, Betsy, Frank. We're none of us quite sure what we're doing or to what purpose.

Amy says you are like a grown-up doll. Not real. It makes it easier for her to give you up.

Peter sees now that you *are* dead. At first, I think, he expected you to wake up. Christ, Jack, how can you do this to us?

Sorry. Where was I? You've frightened Donald. If *you*, who were more alive than anyone, could die—then *he* can die. He's grieving for you and for himself. Maybe we all are. No one is safe.

Frank looks tired and vulnerable. He's straightening his shoulders and trying to look strong. He should never have been a minister. He's like Tom Benjamin. He takes it all personally.

Betsy is beside me, clutching her handbag to her breast. She says nothing. If she tries, she'll come apart. She was in love with you. I see that now. I feel very close to her.

We were all a little afraid of you. You were so strong. Now what?

Chapter
8

Monday, the day of the funeral, arrived brilliantly clear, the weather unusually warm for late May. If Friday had been like this, Louise thought when she woke, Jack would be alive. She and the children clung together for half an hour after waking. As time grew late, they encouraged each other out of bed.

Time went callously by. It appalled Louise to put a body in the ground when she wasn't accustomed to its being dead. She wanted to call out, "Stop. Wait for me to understand." But of course none of it waited. Though it seemed to her she must be the central figure, Queen of the Death, none of it took orders from her.

She was mocked: cloudless sky; light and warmth; trees with branches newly green. The dog, however, did not mock her. He followed her with solemn sympathy from room to room. He waited patiently in the hall while she showered, then followed her back to the bedroom and lay on the blue braided rug to observe her dressing. Occasionally he sat up on his haunches and cocked his head as though to question some detail.

When, at length, she was dressed, she tied a black grosgrain band around her hair and tried to focus her attention on the person reflected in the mirror. The two-piece black dress of linen-like fabric was all right. The waist was too big but that didn't matter. What shocked her was the face. Except for slightly swollen eyelids, she looked as she always had. How could that be? What had she expected, something hollow and haunted, an Edvard Munch face? She somehow dishonored Jack by appearing normal.

From the top of the bureau she took a small porcelain box painted with violets and lily-of-the-valley. In it she kept potpourri. Sitting in the rocker by the window, she opened the box and held it to her face. It comforted her.

The dog got up and padded over to her. Lowering his front legs, he stretched and whined.

"Yes, you're a good lad," she said. "You'd like some attention." He put his head on her lap suppliantly. "Soon. Be patient."

Clasping her hands tightly together in her lap, Louise tried to rally her attention. If her mind persisted in floating away, she'd have no recollection of the funeral or what Frank said.

Jack, you good-looking bastard, you've gone sailing off without me. Left me here on the dock, which feels suspiciously like a church pew. And you've pushed off in a cushy canoe that resembles a fucking starlet's nightie. Come back. I haven't gotten a bellyful of you yet. Here we all are on the dock waving good-bye and blowing kisses and where are you? I'll do anything you ask, only come back.

Louise looked around Frank's church. It wasn't a comforting place.

"I believe in Christianity, I guess," she'd told Jack a few weeks before, for the one hundred and fourteenth time, "but I don't believe in church. Do I *have* to drag over there every Sunday? Frank would understand. Couldn't I just stay home and try hard to be a good girl?"

"I have to go and I want you with me."

"Why?" She was sick to death of this argument. "You said yourself, if you asked most of those people to live like Christians, they'd call you a goddamned Commie."

"Jesus, Louise, how many times do I have to explain?"

"Until one of us understands the other. That many times."

It was a late Saturday night. They'd driven home from a party at Catherine and Earl Jensen's, Jack had taken the sitter home and now they were sitting in the den because Jack wanted to see at least part of *Horse Feathers* on the "Late, Late Show."

"Look," he said, "if it's going to be hard for you to get up in the morning, go to bed. I'll come up later."

"It isn't that!"

She'd made herself a drink. "Do you want one?"

"Not right now. I'll fall asleep."

"Do I *have* to go to church?"

"Yes."

Just "yes." She wanted more than an unequivocal "yes." Mercifully there were so many commercials at this hour, she could talk without interrupting the movie. If she'd done that, interrupted the movie, he'd really have been furious.

"Why? Tell me again."

He turned to face her, slowly, deliberately, as though controlling himself, holding back the response he felt like giving her. "Because my need to have you there is greater than your need to stay away." He continued to look at her, daring her to go on.

"Listen, Prom Queen" (he used the epithet now to put her in her place), "you can afford to throw things away. You've always had more than enough of everything: relatives, religion, clothes, whatever the hell people want or need. You can afford to throw something away if it doesn't please you. You're spoiled. Something gets to be a pain in the ass, you ditch it." He forgot that he wasn't going to have a drink and went into the living room to make one. He was tense, getting angry, and he wanted something in his hand.

Louise said nothing. She hoped if he went on long enough, he'd begin to see the foolishness of it for himself.

"I'm not blaming you for who you are, Louise," he continued, returning from the other room. "You can't help that, and it's not exactly a crime being who you are." He sat down again, took a long drink, and went on. "I'm different. I don't have all those riches to choose from. I can't afford to throw anything away. I might throw the wrong thing, don't you see? Maybe someday. Not now."

"I understand that," she'd said wearily, and she did, "but why must *I* hang onto something *I* don't want or need? I'm not asking *you* to give up going to church—only let me stay home."

In between all this the Marx Brothers dashed around saying and doing uproarious things. The whole scene was a ludicrous game in which the Marx Brothers took a serve, Jack and Louise watched. A commercial came on, Jack and Louise took a serve. Christ.

It was late. Jack was tired, angry, and impatient. He thought she was stubborn and spoiled. How could he think of her that way after all these years? Did that mean she *was*?

"I've told you, Louise, that part of the experience for me— the church—is your being there. It isn't the same experience if you aren't there. I'd be throwing part of it out, don't you see, if I let you stay home?"

No, she didn't see. He didn't want people at church to think she was independent of him. That's what she believed, but would never say. Before she'd been able to stop them, there were tears of frustration in her eyes. She'd felt childish and went up to bed, defeated.

Half an hour later he came to bed. He was gentle. "Do it for *me*, Prom Queen. Not because you want the damned church or need it, but because I ask you to do it."

What could she say? She'd known from the start, from New

Year's Day all those years ago, that it would be like this. Was it such a big sacrifice? What she had in return, she didn't want to give up. She pulled her nightgown above her hips and moved over against him. He was excited, too, and entered her quickly.

"You have so much, Louise, and I need it all," he told her fiercely.

I'll do anything you ask, you bastard, only come back.

If dead people can look on at what's happening, do they want to meddle? Louise was certain she would. Was Jack around somewhere tearing his hair over that damned Pekingese, telling her to buy municipal bonds, and make sure the kids got plenty of exercise?

What kind of widow will I be? This caught me unprepared. I hadn't thought about it, since it never entered my mind there'd be a fuck-up. Some women think ahead. They spend their lives getting ready to be widows. Great Aunt Cora was a prize-winning widow. She lost two husbands. After laying each of them to rest, she straightened her hat, hopped the next Northwest Orient flight to San Francisco, checked into a lovely room at the Mark Hopkins and spent a lot of time eating seafood down at the wharf and drinking Black Russians at the Top of the Mark. She married a third time. She really took to widowhood and after all, if you're good at a thing, you owe it to yourself. Her third husband outlived her. Cora choked on a cashew nut at a bridge party. He, poor old bat, died of senility brought on by loneliness after her demise. He didn't know the first thing about being a widower. Hadn't the knack.

Frank's voice permeated. "In a world of defeatism, where second-rate is good enough, Jack stood out and will remain an example to those he leaves behind. He was a man of awesome determination, for whom the word 'impossible' had no meaning." A survivor. So, where was he?

Frank sat down. From the choir loft above and behind the

voice of a teenage boy came ringing down on top of them, someone from the junior choir, playing a guitar and singing John Denver's "Welcome to My Morning."

The first thing to learn about being a widow is how to survive the funeral.

Chapter
9

The cortege to the Willows Cemetery was long and slow, over a graveled country road. As it wound past first the Riverside Country Club, then the John Deere dealership, dust rose behind each car until there was a snake of dust curling all the way back to town.

The gravel crested the hill where the cemetery stood and before them were open iron gates flanked by weeping willows swaying in a docile breeze. The hearse crawled along leading the way over the circling road. Sunlight bounced off polished headstones.

From the tall grass beyond the cemetery fence came the calls of meadowlark and mourning dove. The hearse stopped. The limousine carrying Louise, Donald and the children stopped. Back along the line other cars halted and from them issued mourners making their way to the graveside in slow procession.

Louise glanced back in the direction of the gates. The cortege stretched the entire distance. This was one of the largest funerals in his career, Paul Berwick had confided to her as if it were the single solace certain to carry her past her grief. She could hardly wait to tell Jack about it when he got home that night... She gripped the children's hands more tightly, and stared at the horizon.

In the middle distance was a dog. A hundred yards away and partly obscured by a marble bench, its red color stood out against the bright spring green. It wasn't Fido. He was at home in the basement. Dogs of that color were not uncommon, after all. The breeze ruffled the dog's burnished coat but he was otherwise respectfully remote as he watched them bury Jack.

The women of St. Anne's Guild were at the house when the limousine glided to the curb. Their faces were pink with pride and preparations as they bustled from room to room, wearing organdy aprons and addressing each other in hushed voices. The smell of strong coffee filled the house and in the dining room a buffet was laid out.

What a pity Jack couldn't be there. The flow of people in and out of the house, all bearing gifts of praise, would have delighted him, even as he scoffed.

Particularly close friends, mostly couples, gathered in the den, drinks in hand, and restored Jack's presence with laughter. How about the time we all started out for Green Bay in a blizzard to see a Vikings–Packers game and... And then there was the time Jack invited the wives to the monthly poker game... Unconciously Louise glanced around, seeking Jack's eyes, to share the joke.

When the others had left, Brian Doyle, Jack's assistant, sat alone in the den, staring down at his hands. Brian had come to Jack three years before, fresh from veterinary college. He looked like someone's younger brother, freckled, almost gangling, with cowlick-ruled sandy hair that fell across his forehead. Had Jack chosen Brian to be his younger brother? Louise wondered. Quiet, thoughtful, an excellent vet, he was serious to the point of being saturnine. He'd been a foil for Jack's charm.

Louise sat next to him on the sofa. "Brian, it's so good to see you. Thank you for keeping things going out at the hospital. I don't know how you're doing it."

He stirred himself, stuffed his fists down between his knees and looked embarrassed. "Jack was good to me. I owe you two a lot."

"Jack thought he was lucky to have you."

He twisted uneasily as though to avoid posthumous compliments. "I don't want to talk business. I know this isn't the time. But I wanted to tell you that I'll stay on as long as you want." He leaned an elbow on the arm of the sofa and pushed hair back from his forehead. "I like it out there. It's been home for me in a way."

Louise leaned forward hugging her knees and nodding sympathetically. "I want you to stay. We'll work things out." She felt protective and, though he was only three or four years her junior, motherly. Human contacts didn't come easily to him.

"I don't want you to think about any of this right now, see? Later on, when your life gets squared away a little, if you decide you want to sell the business, I thought you should know, I'd be interested," he said.

"We'll work it out," she repeated. "In the meantime, you'll need permanent help out there, another vet."

"I can start looking right away, if it's all right with you." Shyness slipped away when he was on his own ground. He knew the needs of the hospital and kennels.

She had once asked Jack about working at the kennel herself. They'd been married only a few weeks.

He'd worked hard and late that day. She'd laid a fire in the grate and made Manhattans. When he was comfortably settled on the sofa with a drink, she had sat down beside him.

"What if I came out to the kennel and did some of the office work?" she asked. "I could put in a couple of hours after school and we could come home together."

"Absolutely not."

"Wouldn't it save expense? I'd like to know more about what you do. I'm proud of you."

"I don't want to save money that way. I don't want you working at the kennel."

"Why?" She was hurt and bewildered. Wasn't marriage a partnership?

"I don't want you to teach school next year and I don't want you to work at the kennel."

"Why? That's so old-fashioned." She wanted to stamp her foot. "Why can't I work?"

"Because I'm asking you not to."

She couldn't believe her ears. No one talked like that anymore. He set his drink down and took her hand as though to pull her on his lap. She stiffened. He looked at her for a minute, still holding her hand. "Please."

She gave in. Sitting on his lap, she saw in the light of the table lamp the circles of fatigue beneath his eyes. She felt rotten to be fighting him. "I want to help because I love you."

"If you love me, don't work."

"When do I get to have *my* way?" she asked.

He laughed but didn't answer her question. "I have two reasons for not wanting you to work. First, if you're not already pregnant, you damned soon will be."

"Sure-Shot Andrews?"

"Have you had your period since I moved in?"

She didn't answer.

"The second reason is more complicated. I'm not sure you'll understand."

"I'm not sure I understand the first reason."

"So far all the owing in this marriage is on my side."

"The owing?"

"Face it, Louise, I've walked into the kind of situation men usually have to work a long time to get. I'm not knocking it. I want every bit of it. And especially the intangibles."

"What intangibles?"

"Living in this house with you makes me . . . part of a pattern, like I'd been adopted. The sooner we get a kid, the more it'll be that way."

"Hell, I thought you just liked to screw," she said softly, kissing the dark circles beneath his eyes.

"Very funny, Prom Queen." He went on, his voice more tender. "Anyway, I want to be responsible for the business. I want it to be successful and I want to do it by myself. That will be something I can give *you*. Do you understand?"

"I don't understand anything about you. You're a bastard. Bossy, selfish, stubborn. But I'd be miserable if you didn't come home. What can I do?"

"Give in." He wasn't joking.

"I'd like to leave things up to you," Louise heard herself saying to Brian. "Would that be asking too much? I don't know the first thing about the business . . ."

"I'd appreciate your letting me handle it," he interrupted. "I'll keep you informed of whatever I do, of course. I won't make any big decisions without talking to you."

It was a relief to Louise, knowing Brian would be staying on. "I meant to ask you about the dog." She had suddenly remembered.

He was nonplused.

"The Irish setter?" she prompted.

He slapped his hands down on his knees. "My God, I forgot about the dog! What happened to him?" He seemed ready to organize a search party.

She put a hand on his arm. "We've got him. He's all right. He's in the basement. I wanted to ask you about him."

"He wasn't hurt in the . . . accident?"

"Nothing worse than being dazed. Do you know where Jack got him?"

He leaned back and closed his eyes for a moment. "No. No, I don't. I had to go out one day early last week to look at a

guy's pet goat. Somebody came in that afternoon and dumped
the dog in the waiting room. Apparently no one was paying
much attention. The dog didn't have any identification. 'Look
at the orphan I've been left,' Doc said when I got back. Nobody came to claim him so Jack decided to adopt him.''

"Did he really name him *Fido*?"

"Yeah. I told him it sounded like something out of the *Bob-
bsey Twins*. Friday, uh, Friday afternoon, I heard a drug salesman razz him about it. Jack had the dog in his office. The
salesman said the dog should have an Irish name. Jack said,
'Ol' Fido?' You could tell he didn't plan to change it.''

"It's a little silly sounding. But he'll probably be the only
Fido in town.''

They said nothing for a minute, then Brian resumed. "He's
a beautiful animal, isn't he?"

"Yes."

"Unusually large for a setter. He doesn't have his full
growth yet but he's already bigger than a fully grown dog.''

Louise sat back, relaxing for the first time that day. "Donald and I had a dog when we were kids." It was good to forget
why they were there. "Her name was Penny, because she had
a copper-colored spot over one eye. God, she was ugly.
Looked like a big rat, but she was smart and we taught her a
lot of tricks." Then, returning to Fido, "This dog is smarter.
Much smarter than Penny.''

The room was growing dim in the late afternoon light.
Louise rose to turn on a lamp.

Brian stood up. "Lou, I hate to leave, but I've got to get
back out to the hospital.''

"Sure."

"I was wondering. What if I took the kids fishing next
weekend. Would they resent it?''

"I can't imagine why.''

"Well, I'm not their dad.''

"They'd like to go fishing with you. I'm opening the cottage next weekend. Come out there and go fishing." Louise began walking him to the front hall.

"I'll probably be out early Saturday morning if I can get away. I'll call you."

As they stood at the open door, Fido ambled toward them. Brian bent to run a freckled hand along the dog's silky back. "You're some swell dog. Take care of things." He straightened. "If you need anything, call." He shook Louise's hand, then hurried out and down to the street.

Fido pushed open the screen door, and stood on the porch watching as Brian got into the car and pulled quickly out of sight down Baker Avenue. He remained several minutes gazing after the black Mustang, sidelong rays of the setting sun catching highlights in his coat. His tail moved in a slow, contemplative sweep.

After nightfall, when everyone but Donald and Betsy had left and all the rituals had been fulfilled, the possibility of Jack seemed no longer to be in the house. Without expectation there was nothing to do but wait. How dependent upon Jack the forward movement of life had been. The house was like an unpeopled railway station, a place one might visit in a dream. Louise sat on a straight chair and waited for instructions.

"The kids are ready for bed," Betsy told her.

She sprang up. "I'll say good-night to them." She crossed to the hall.

They'd been crying and Louise felt instantly guilty for not having been with them. They were both in Amy's bed.

"Is it okay for a few nights?" Amy asked. "Betsy said you wouldn't mind."

"Also, can Fido sleep in here if he sleeps on the floor?" Peter added.

Louise heard their prayers. They talked a little about the funeral. "We didn't cry at the funeral, Mommy. Did you see

Amy and me not crying?" Peter asked.

"But tonight it was harder," Amy explained. "Do you think Daddy would mind?"

"Daddy didn't like if we cried in front of people," Peter reminded Louise.

"That was when it was something unimportant or you were just angry," Louise pointed out. "When you're very sad, you feel worse if you can't cry. It's normal."

Peter wasn't sure. He couldn't remember his father making exceptions about crying in front of people, and he didn't want to shame himself.

"I promise you it's all right." Louise kissed him and then his sister. "I'll sit here till you fall asleep." She turned off the lamp and sat on Amy's dainty slipper chair. The room was dim, a muted glow from the hall outlining forms. In their privacy, the children wept and fell asleep.

Downstairs the front door stood open and, as she passed, Louise heard Donald on the porch talking with someone. She looked inquiringly at Betsy who sat curled up on the sofa.

"Brian stopped on his way home. He'll call tomorrow to see if there's anything you need." She smiled sadly. "He feels orphaned."

Several minutes passed. Louise wondered if this were how her mother had felt after *her* husband's death. Had she waited for life to happen, unconvinced that it would? Not caring if it did? Had her mother's indifference to life become disdain for it?

"I've been thinking," Betsy began, dragging Louise from her morbid reverie. "Would you like to help out at the shop? You could work mornings while Peter's in kindergarten. It would get you out of the house and give you something to do while you make plans."

"Make plans?"

"Well, you may go back to teaching or back to school or something. You're not going to sit around the house the rest of your life."

The rest of her life. What a long time. She would have to find things to do with it, she supposed. "It's been so long since I decided anything more important than what to cook for dinner. Before I was married, I was a little like you—independent." Before she was married. Before she'd quit her job. She remembered—what was it called?—The Every Other Thursdays.

For two years Louise and three other women who taught at Falls Village High School had met to play bridge every other Thursday. Two of the women, Myrna Hermann and Jeanette Reed, were married. Louise and Phylis Bender were single. None of them was serious about bridge. The group was founded on trust, not cards.

They talked. They advised, harangued, confessed, explained and enthused. They also snacked and drank. Intermittently they played cards. The cards grew greasy, salty and damp. It didn't matter. It was the unvarnished and unblushing female perspective and the nurturing that drew each of the women to the Every Other Thursdays. For Louise, it was like having three sisters.

Then she'd married Jack. After the first meeting subsequent to their marriage, he'd asked, "What do you do at this Every Other Thursday thing?"

Louise had washed her face and put on her nightgown. She sat in the bedroom rocking chair, searching for an article in the *Falls Village Republican Leader* about local teacher salaries. "We play bridge and talk. We have a few drinks. Why?"

"I was just curious." He pulled back the covers and got into bed. "What do you talk about?"

"Everything. Anything. They're intelligent and . . . honorable. I could tell them almost anything and I wouldn't have to worry. Do you know what I mean?"

Would you talk to them about us?"

"About us? Depends on what you mean. I wouldn't go into a lot of juicy details. I can be trusted, too."

He was pensive. "You talk over your problems, though."

Idly he drew patterns on the spread with his index finger. "They'd give you advice about us if they thought you needed it?"

"I don't know what to say. In a general sort of way we discuss our problems. But it isn't group therapy. We like each other. We have fun—woman-fun." She folded the newspaper and dropped it on the floor. Rocking back in the chair, she grinned.

"What's so funny?" he wanted to know.

Giggling, she explained, "One time we got to laughing so hard, we all threw our cards up in the air like confetti. We couldn't stop laughing. Jeanette Reed fell off her chair—actually fell right off on the floor. I got the hiccoughs and had them the rest of the night. Myrna Hermann who was pregnant, wet her pants. It was wonderful. I never had a better time."

"Never?" He smiled lasciviously and leaned across the bed, turning back the covers on her side.

Later he asked if she would "take a leave of absence" from the Every Other Thursdays. To soften her sense of loss, he called it a leave of absence. "I'll make it worth your while," he promised ardently.

Louise never returned to the Every Other Thursdays. She became addicted to not having her way. She erased everything she had been that didn't suit Jack.

Maybe now there wasn't enough of her left to start over with. She blurted suddenly, "I'm afraid!" and looked with confusion from Betsy to Donald who'd come in from the porch.

Donald rushed to her side. "Don't be afraid, Lulu. I'll take care of you." He put an arm around her. "Leave things to me."

Chapter 10

After Monday, life was quiet again on Baker Avenue. At Louise's insistence, Donald went back to his own house, and Betsy returned to Olson Avenue. Donald came for dinner on Tuesday, and Betsy called to take Louise out for a quiet lunch on Thursday, but the stream of calls and visits by the sympathetic or merely curious dwindled to a trickle. By the end of the week, that phase of the postlude seemed concluded.

Amy and Peter went back to school. They were anxious to tie themselves to a familiar mooring and school was it. Home from school, they spent most of their hours with the dog. Fido's patience was limitless and Louise was thankful for their absorption in him.

Tuesday night when the children were asleep, Louise put on her nightgown and lay down on top of the spread. There was no point in sitting downstairs. She wasn't waiting for Jack anymore.

She wept soundlessly for several hours, finding no relief, but unable to stop. About midnight she went down to the kitchen to make cocoa. Carrying it into the dining room, and not bothering to turn the light on, she sat on the window seat, staring into the dark. Here she had sat that first night with

Jack. He had liked window seats. She bent to wipe her eyes on the hem of her gown.

An unearthly sound brought her to her feet. What was it? She was across the room, headed for the stairs in the hall. One of the kids? Please, let them be all right. At the top of the stairs she turned toward Amy and Peter's rooms.

Fido. He stood in the middle of the hall, swaying stiffly on his legs, head lowered. Louise recalled hearing that mad dogs behaved this way. But less than an hour ago he'd been pacing through the house, restless, but well.

He lurched sideways, braced himself and threw his head back, producing again the sound that had sent Louise flying up the stairs. Christ. She'd never heard anything like it. It filled the hall. It must fill the entire house. There was a nearly human quality in it.

"Please make him stop," she whimpered. She sank to the floor, sobbing. "Jack, Jack, please help me." Where was he? "Jack!" she screamed.

Suddenly her voice was the only sound in the hall. Still sobbing, she lifted her head and saw the dog shake himself. He looked at her and began moving his feet in small, apologetic prancing steps, wagging his tail. He took a tentative step toward her.

"No!" she whispered hoarsely. On hands and knees she began backing toward the bedroom, face streaming, hair wild. "No."

He looked at her quizzically, made a small plaintive noise, and lifted one paw. She closed the bedroom door without getting to her feet. Not until she'd reached the bed did she pull herself up.

Lying on the bed, she clung to Jack's pillow and raggedly tried to deal with what had occurred. The dog had seemed so normal as he stood wagging his tail and begging, puppy-like, to follow. But before . . .

She worried the edge of the pillow with her teeth. "What's

happening?" Minutes passed and the incident began to seem unreal. The sense of unreality finally made it bearable.

In the morning, she was wakened by Amy and Peter at her bed, Fido between them, tame and untroubled. By afternoon she knew it had been a dream. That was the reason the children hadn't awakened. It had all been in her unhappy mind.

Louise poured the scummed-over cocoa down the sink and washed the cup.

The days were simple and exhausting. She washed windows, scrubbed and waxed floors, cleaned the kitchen and pantry cupboards, and, finally, sorted through and straightened out the closets, all except Jack's. It would be some time before she would do that.

Stealing herself Thursday morning, Louise walked the ten blocks to Slocum's Garage. A month ago Louise's own car had died a sudden and dignified death.

"There's no point in having it fixed," Jack explained. "It'd cost more than it's worth. Anyway, I want to get you something classy."

"Classy?" Louise rose from the dinner table to get the coffee. The kids had already excused themselves and gone into the den.

"Yeah. Maybe a sporty little Mercedes or Porsche."

She refilled his cup. "What do I need with an expensive car? It's silly." She hadn't meant to hurt him but saw that she had. "I'm sorry," she told him, setting the coffeepot on a trivet. "I only meant that I do so little driving, it doesn't seem necessary to have an expensive car." She didn't know how much a "sporty little Mercedes or Porsche" cost but it would be thousands more than the kind of car she had in mind.

"I want you to drive a *good* car, not the same damned thing everybody else's wife drives," he told her with irritation. "We can afford it and it'll give me a kick having people see you around town in a great little car."

Her father had always said flashy things were for people who had something to prove. Well, that was Jack.

"Would it have an automatic transmission? I've never driven anything but an automatic transmission."

"We'll see. I can teach you to drive a stick shift. It's no big deal."

She was put off by the idea of having to drive a stick shift but already she sensed that a stick shift fitted into the picture Jack had of what and how *his* wife would drive.

Louise noted the anticipation in his eyes as he envisioned her spinning around town in his gift. Foiled again, my proud beauty. She shrugged. Being made to drive an expensive and beautiful car was not quite the same as being flogged and thrown into irons. Was it?

Through the big showroom window Olaf Borg, the manager of Slocum's, saw Louise approach and when she reached the door, he was there to hold it for her. "Morning, Mrs. Andrews. Come in. Very sorry about the Doc." His round, soft-looking face and gray eyes knew few expressions. What he felt was in the gently modulated voice, the expressive lilt of a lingering Swedish accent.

"Thank you, Ole." Louise looked around at the models in the showroom.

"The mechanics have gone over the van and I've got an estimate in the office for you. Runs pretty high, I'm afraid," he explained, leading the way to his office.

"I want a new car. I don't want the van repaired. What about a compact wagon? Something smaller than the van."

"Well, then, let me pick up some literature over here at the desk and we can go out on the lot."

Louise followed him into the bright sun where cars of different colors sat like dyed eggs in an Easter basket.

"Now this little number over here may be what you had in mind. It's smaller. Not everybody likes yellow but I've got this same car without the extras, in green." He held the door while Louise slid into the driver's seat. "The keys are in the ignition. Why don't you take it out for a spin? It's automatic. If you wanted stick shift, we could get you that." He gave the car an affectionate pat on the behind as Louise drove it off the lot.

She knew this was the one. The sunshine color was part of it. The size was right. And it had an automatic transmission.

Thursday night Louise lay down early. She cried briefly, then drifted into sleep. At twenty past eleven she started awake. A scream? She put her feet over the side of the bed and felt for her slippers.

Padding down the hall, left lit so Amy and Peter could see their way to the bathroom, she checked on each of the children. They slept peacefully, bodies flung carelessly across the beds, covers thrust aside in the warm spring night. No sign of the dog.

Down to the kitchen. Fido lay on the floor asleep. He continued to sleep even when she turned on the light. As she watched, he began to twitch. He whined. His body was gripped by small spasms. Louise's pulse quickened. The dog stiffened out to his utmost length and the noise in his throat was a moan. Louise went to him, knelt and ran a hand along his head and back.

"Fido," she whispered. "Wake up. You're dreaming."

He was awake and on his feet in one startling movement.

"It's all right. You were dreaming." She was frightened but at the same time, his pain distressed her and she felt kinship with him.

"Come upstairs," she said and rose to her feet. He followed her. They sat on the bed, Louise feeling heavy with loneliness. A little after three A.M. she slumped over, dragged off by overpowering sleep.

"Louise." She dreamed that someone spoke her name, but she couldn't answer.

"Got enough grub for a couple of bums?"

Louise looked up from the dock where she lay sunbathing. She hadn't heard the car. Sitting up slowly, she squinted and held her hand above her eyes to see who was with Donald.

"What time is it? Did you get away from rehearsal early?" She was on her feet, slipping into a pair of scuffs. "Who's with . . . oh, Ned, it's *you*." She wrapped herself in her towel. "It's good to see you. It must be a year." There were lawn chairs near the cottage. "Have a seat. I'll get dressed. It'll be chilly soon."

"We're going swimming before supper," Donald told her, unbuttoning his shirt. "We'll change in my room. You didn't say if you had enough food."

"It's just hot dogs and salad and potato chips. There's plenty," she called after them as Donald led the way up the path to the cottage.

"Fine. I'll throw some charcoal on. Come on, MacRae, I've got trunks that'll fit you."

Upstairs Louise pulled off the bikini and got into a pair of old jeans and a warm sweat shirt. Why was MacRae here? Legal talk? Hadn't Donald mentioned something about that?

Despite the sweat shirt, she hugged herself. She heard Betsy's white Triumph turn into the drive and brake beside the men's cars. The Triumph's door slammed and seconds later the porch door.

"Anybody home?"

"Up here."

Betsy was hurrying up the stairs. "Hi, kid. Jesus, that Ned is a turn-on, isn't he?" She collapsed breathlessly on the nearest bed. "What a day. I'm dead. Can I move in tonight?"

Louise went down to the kitchen to start dinner. No estate talk, please. Not yet. Her composure wouldn't endure a lot of stomping around by an attorney armed with joint ownerships and cold statistics.

She began tearing lettuce for salad. Betsy handed her a martini. "You'll have to put in ice if you want it really cold. I had the booze in the refrigerator at the shop, but it warmed up on the drive out. Where are the kids?"

"They took the dog for a run on the beach." As she spoke, the children bounded up the back porch steps.

"Okay if we give Fido his supper now?" Amy asked.

"The Ken-L-Ration's under the sink. Don't give him too much. He's going to be a hippo."

"Okay." Amy came into the kitchen. "Hi, Betsy. Can you stay tonight?"

"Yup. How's the pooch?"

"He loves running on the beach. He likes the lake. Mom says he swims like Johnny Weismuller, whoever that is." Amy carefully stirred warm water into the dry dog food. "Open the door, Peter, I'm coming with his food."

"Dammit, Lou, you could at least warn a person." Donald shook his Jack Daniel's and soda at her and the ice cubes clattered in the glass. "Have you been *in* that water?" He gestured toward the lake.

Louise arranged food on the redwood table while Donald

grilled hot dogs. "I went in this afternoon. It was—bracing."

" 'Bracing,' hell. It's ball-breaking. Hand me your plate, MacRae. These dogs are ready."

When they were seated around the table, Donald filled them in on the afternoon rehearsal of *The East Side Girl.* "Jackie Johnson's good. Got a lot of style."

"You're in the show, Ned?" Louise asked.

"It's one way to get every skirt in town to buy a ticket," Donald told her.

"Oh, Donald, shut up. You're such a sexist," Louise retorted and turned back to Ned. "Ignore him. Have you been in shows at Lac des Cygnes before?"

"*Guys and Dolls* last summer."

"That's right. I forgot. Betsy played Adelaide."

Ned leaned over to say something to Betsy, something Louise couldn't hear. MacRae's magnetism was obvious, though difficult to pinpoint. Good-looking, yes. But there was something more compelling there than looks. Behind the easy self-assurance, Louise speculated, there were shrewdness and a secret and skeptical humor. A proceed-at-your-own-risk warning in the eyes, if a woman wanted to read it. He looked lethal. Well, Betsy was a big girl. If she was going to get mixed up with MacRae, Louise doubted there was anything *she* could say to stop her.

As they finished dinner, Amy ran to fetch marshmallows. "The coals are still hot. We can toast them for dessert."

Minutes later Ned stood beside the grill slowly turning a skewered row of marshmallows. Louise sat on a chaise looking at the water, spread now with purple and silver.

"She's a beautiful kid," Ned was saying.

"Yes."

"Your boy was talking about fishing. Does he like to fish?"

"Loves it. Brian Doyle took him and Amy out this morning. They caught quite a few."

"I could take him when I go."

She studied him. "That's kind of you."

"I'm not one of your really serious fishermen. It'd be fun. My place is just down the shore a piece, on the next bay." He lifted the marshmallows and examined them. "I didn't have a chance at the funeral to tell you how sorry I was about Jack. I was due back in court right after the service."

Now he's going to get down to business.

"I didn't know Jack very well. I did his legal work. I understand from people who know, that he was one of the best vets in the state. He was a damned good businessman." He looked at Louise. "I have to talk to you about Jack's estate. I'm sorry."

"I understand."

"What about next week? When will you be back in town?"

"Monday's Memorial Day. We'll be back in town Monday night. If we can't put it off any longer, next week sometime will do."

"I'll try to make things as easy as possible." He walked over, sat down on a lawn chair near her, and slid two crusty marshmallows along the skewer. "Here. You take these."

"Thank you."

"Anytime."

They ate the marshmallows and licked their fingers. Louise was grateful he didn't try to keep small talk going. Silence was her shelter these days.

He wandered back to the barbecue and began kibitzing the others. Twenty minutes later Louise heard him say, "Don, I'm going. I'll see you back at the theater."

She rose to meet him as he started down the lawn toward her, indistinct in the growing darkness.

"Louise, thanks for letting me crash the party," he told her. "Will you be out here again next weekend?"

She nodded. "The kids' vacation begins Friday," she explained, walking him toward the drive where his Buick was parked.

"I'll be at my cottage now that the weather's warm. We can put this estate thing off till next weekend. I'll bring the papers over here. Forget it for a week."

"Thank you."

"You're welcome. Take care of yourself." He pressed her hand and turned toward the car.

From the near-darkness came a rustling sound. A growl, low and threatening. Louise and Ned froze. It was Fido, head raised, teeth bared. For a moment the three of them were a tableau.

"Stop that!" Louise snapped.

She took a step toward the dog, then another, not taking her eyes from his. She wasn't afraid of him, not for herself. Over her shoulder she said, "Get in the car, Ned. I don't know what's got into him."

She was between them now, still moving, slowly but resolutely. Soon she would be close enough so that the dog couldn't leap at the lawyer without knocking her down. She gambled that he wouldn't.

"I'll be all right," she called impatiently when she didn't hear the car door. "He's not going to hurt me. Get in the car." One more step. The dog continued to growl. His bared teeth looked cruel.

There. She reached for the heavy collar, grabbed it and gave a sharp yank, pulling it against his throat and shutting off the angry rumble.

MacRae opened the car door then and got in. "I'll see you next weekend."

Shaken and angry, Louise watched the Buick back, turn, and head out the drive.

Chapter 12

Louise peered at the clock. Five A.M. Chilly. Today was Saturday and MacRae was coming. She turned over and tried to sneak back into sleep. She was irrevocably awake, however, and at five-thirty, inched to a sitting position, sheet, blanket, and spread wrapped around her. Bravely throwing off the warm mantle, she scuttled to the chair for her robe. "Oh, God, that's better," she whispered, teeth chattering.

The casement windows on all three sides of the room were open. She stood at those facing the lake and looked at the morning-gray water. The cry of a loon broke the semi-hush. The air was still. Louise felt better than at any time since the accident. The gray-lavender sky in the west began to turn pale blue.

Tiptoeing downstairs (Donald's rehearsal had run late), she closed the door to the porch where the kids slept, and began laying a fire in the grate.

When that caught hold, she put coffee on the stove to percolate. Fido, who slept with the children, wanted in. Behaving like a lamb since the incident with MacRae, the dog had won his way back into Louise's good graces. What, after all, Louise asked herself, did they really know about him? Maybe he'd been mistreated by someone. Possibly he pined for a life he'd left behind. They'd have to be patient with him for a while.

He sat quietly by as Louise fussed with the logs. He waited with her for the coffee to finish bubbling. When she finally poured a cup, it was only six-fifteen. "Come on, fella, let's go outside and sit." They went out the back and around the side of the cottage. A rabbit or squirrel, startled by their approach, scrambled away through the underbrush. "You're a strange dog. How come you're not interested in rabbits and such?" He followed her out to the dock where she sat and watched the morning move across the water. The cottage was on the shady side of the lake in the morning but caught the long, warm slanting gold at the end of the day.

In the shallow water around the pilings Louise saw silvery minnows and small fish dart in and out, looking for breakfast. "We should have brought them some bread."

Fido lay down beside Louise and rested his head on her thigh. Absently she played with the soft red fur of his neck.

The second week of widowhood had passed. She had spent long hours inside that sheltering silence, mourning and comforting herself. It was a very selfish time, she thought.

The children had hurried toward the summer while she'd sat sifting through nine years, snatching from oblivion half-forgotten conversations, moments of lovemaking, bits of arguments. She was an archeologist to whom a mere shard of the past was dear.

She bent and nuzzled the dog's neck. He turned his head and licked her cheek where it was damp.

"Mommy, there's a fire in the fireplace. Is that all right?" Peter, his hair standing in tufts, called to her from the front porch.

"Yes. I made it. Are you hungry?"

"I think so."

She drained the last drops of coffee and started up the path. "Do you know where those wire-mesh things are that we use for toasting bread in the fireplace?"

"I know," Amy who was now awake told her. "What do you want them for?"

"You and Peter can make toast over the fire this morning."

Amy threw off the covers. "That's a great idea. Peter, you get the bread and I'll get the toaster things."

Fido bounded into the cottage and sat down in front of the fire.

"Mommy, did you *see* that?" Peter exclaimed. "Fido came right to the fireplace. He knows what we're talking about!"

Louise laughed. "Either that or he's cold."

"Amy, I'm putting the dog in Uncle Donald's bedroom until Mr. MacRae has left. Don't let him out." She called the dog into the downstairs bedroom and closed the door.

"Poor Fido," Peter lamented.

"Don't worry about 'poor Fido.' He'll be okay. After Mr. MacRae leaves, you can take him for a run on the beach."

At ten past nine Louise heard Ned's Buick turn into the drive. She went out to meet him.

"Hi," he called, pulling a brown briefcase from the backseat. "Am I late?" He came across the drive. "How's the killer dog?"

"You're early and he's in Donald's bedroom. Want to sit out here?" she asked, "or would you rather go inside?"

"This is fine." He pulled a chair up to the umbrella-covered table. "I can lay my things out here."

"I'll get coffee. How do you like yours?"

"Black. No sugar. Thanks."

"Have you had breakfast?"

"I grabbed a glass of milk."

"I'll make toast."

Returning minutes later, she carried a tray of buttered toast, raspberry preserves and coffee.

"Looks good. Sit down now." He took the tray and set it on the table. "I've forgotten what civilized living is. I've been batching for . . . seven, eight years. What a mess."

"You must have a housekeeper or cleaning woman. Some-one who does for you."

"Oh, yes. I've got a cleaning woman who gives me one day a week." He handed her a cup from the tray and sat down. "Cleaning women are funny. They only want to clean. They're not keen on organizing your life or buying your underwear." He took the second cup from the tray. "After Estelle . . ." Looking discomposed, he took a quick bite of toast, wiped his hands on a napkin, and dug into the briefcase for papers.

His appearance was "crisp." That was the first word that came to mind. Medium height, maybe five ten or eleven, lean, athletic. Louise looked him over while he shuffled through documents. She feared for Betsy if this were to be her next attachment.

He wore tan twill shorts and a short sleeved oatmeal colored knit shirt. His arms and legs were hard and muscular. Obviously the parts that didn't show must be also. He was compact, military-looking, whatever that meant. The coarse, black hair was speckled with gray and he wore it fairly short. His eyes were very dark blue, his mouth sensual without being full.

Louise began flipping through mental files to see what she had stashed under MacRae, N., Attorney at Law. He'd been divorced from someone named Estelle whom Louise had never met. Jack had inherited him as an attorney from old Doc Bieber which meant that MacRae must be at least forty, maybe forty-five or so. She had a vague feeling that Jack hadn't liked him, though she couldn't remember anything specific. It was true that MacRae had the kind of reputation that's bandied about at the hairdresser's and the bridge table. Well, whatever he was, he got invited to a lot of dinner parties. Presentable single men weren't glutting the local market and sleeping around didn't represent moral leprosy in Falls Village. Not for a man.

When he had Jack's will and several other documents spread out in front of them, MacRae looked at her for a long minute as though trying to assess her state of mind.

"Did Jack ever talk to you about his will?"

"No. I assumed that it was pretty much like my own. Why do you ask?"

He gave a small grunt of displeasure. "I was under the impression he'd discussed it with you."

"What was there to discuss? You're not going to tell me he left everything to the ASPCA," she said with a laugh.

"No." He wasn't smiling. "I have to tell you, Louise, that I didn't approve of this will when I drew it up. I told Jack I didn't like it. He said he'd go to someone else if I wouldn't handle it for him."

Louise was puzzled by the lawyer's tone. What in hell was this all about?

"Frankly, I didn't want him going to anyone else. Under the circumstances, I wanted to retain as much power as possible in the situation."

"Under *what* circumstances? What situation?"

"Before we get into the details of the will, I want to assure you that the money and investments that came to you from your parents' estate are intact. Those are still yours and you are free to do with them what you will."

"But?"

"Jack's estate will be in trust, with the money coming to you as you need it for yourself and the children . . ."

"In trust?"

". . . and, if you marry, the estate reverts entirely to the children. In other words, the money's yours just so long as you're single."

Louise stared at him.

"This must be a helluva shock to you. Jack assured me he'd discussed it with you."

Louise was shaking. She felt as though she'd been slapped.

She knew there were tears in her eyes and she accepted the handkerchief MacRae handed her.

"I'm very sorry, Louise. If I'd had any idea Jack hadn't explained this to you, I could have been more tactful."

"Oh, for God's sake, it's not your fault! I feel insulted and . . . naked." She stood up. "But it's not your fault." She stumbled down the path to the dock.

He watched her go but remained where he was. She didn't want anyone near her at this minute. She didn't want anyone to see her humiliation.

Louise stood on the dock, still shaking. She couldn't seem to get her breath. Her cheeks burned from heat she felt inside: anger, sadness, betrayal. Why had Jack done it?

She didn't give a damn about the money. She had enough of her own. It was his lack of trust in her. And what else? What else had been behind this?

Finally she turned. MacRae was still sitting at the table. He smiled a wry, lopsided smile and waved. She waved back. The moment unearthed a memory that had lain buried beneath several years of life's clutter. She couldn't move until she'd played it out.

The bedside clock said ten past two. It took her several seconds to realize that Jack wasn't in bed. Pulling herself up on one elbow, she looked around the darkened room. He was at the window, back to her, staring out at the lake.

She waited a minute thinking he would be coming back to bed. When he didn't, she spoke. "Jack?"

"Yes?" He didn't turn around.

"Are you okay?"

"Yes."

She slipped out of bed. The night was warm. He had on a pair of jockey shorts and seemed suddenly, surprisingly vulnerable standing alone at the window.

"Hey," she said, putting her hand on his arm. "What's

wrong?" The moon cast a dim light through the open window and she saw that he'd been crying.

She was shocked. "What's the matter?"

"It was a dream."

"About what?"

"A weird dream." He didn't look at her. "A guy came here, to the cottage. He was driving some really expensive Italian car. The kind they make individually for the buyer. You seemed to know him from somewhere. I'd never seen him before. He sat and talked for a while out under the trees. About things I didn't understand. The only books he mentioned were ones I hadn't read."

He paused, remembering. "He was from the East and he was rich. Everything he was, he was *because* he was rich. Confident, polished. It was old money."

He was trembling.

"After a while," he continued, "you got up and took his hand. I kept saying 'no.' " But I couldn't move. The two of you walked over to his car. You turned around and waved and smiled and got in."

Jack seemed to be held in the dream. She squeezed his arm gently. "It was only a dream, Jack."

He turned and grabbed her wrist, holding so tightly she moaned. His voice was cold. "Don't ever try to leave."

"Don't be silly. You know I'd never leave."

"I'd kill him," he said quietly, still holding her wrist and pushing her backward toward the bed.

Chapter 13

Putting away the few dishes from the children's lunch, Louise wandered aimlessly through the cottage, sighing abruptly, clasping and unclasping her hands. She couldn't sit still and she couldn't concentrate. The morning's session with the attorney had been like opening a closetful of snakes.

Why had Jack written such a will? Did he think she'd run off with a lion tamer, leaving the children to Christian charity? Was it paternalistic? Or was there another motive?

MacRae had asked her frankly before he left, "Was Jack a particularly jealous man?" Well, yes. But certainly a man wouldn't let his jealousy and possessiveness outlive him.

As she fluttered from room to room like something driven by a capricious breeze, the dog followed her. Now and then he emitted a soft whine or brushed against her leg or sniffed at her hand, attempting to capture her attention. She paid no heed, hardly noticed that he was there. At length he seemed to grow tired of this treatment and he swung around in front of her and barked sharply.

Distracted, Louise looked down at him. "Poor boy, what is

it? Do you want out?" He threw his head sideways and snorted impatiently, but he didn't run to the door. In any event, the screen was unhooked and he could have let himself out.

"Well, if you don't want out, I don't know what it is," Louise told him, brushing past. Drifting out to the porch, she watched Amy and Peter who were playing in the beach sand with plastic buckets and shovels.

"Hey, you guys, want to go for a walk?" She was not going to stay in the cottage, pacing up and down and driving herself crazy with questions.

"Yes!"

"Can we go into the woods across the road and pick up pinecones?" Amy asked. "Please?"

"And arrowheads?" Peter added importantly.

"Well, put on jeans and sneakers then."

As they left the cottage, Louise closed the heavy inner door against a complaining Fido. She didn't want the kids chasing the dog through the woods.

Up the drive and across Swan Lake Road through dusty gravel, the three tramped, Amy carrying a shopping bag for pinecones. The woods were another country, dim and cool and rustling. They were dense and uncivilized, an adventure.

Amy and Peter would run ahead, find something which demanded their closer attention and while they scrutinized and poked around, Louise would catch up.

The woods were not easy going. Low branches, vines, and animal burrows required one's attention. As she'd hoped, Louise had little time to puzzle over the will.

Except for the occasional noisy complaint from a bird, the wood sounds were delicate: the soughing of soft branches, the scurrying of small animals in retreat, the quiet giving-way of hundreds of years of leaf and needle mulch beneath one's feet. The children matched themselves to the surrounding hush, speaking low and only when necessary. They were intent upon their quests and a little enchanted by the quiet. It wasn't long before Amy's shopping bag was half-full. Peter seemed to have forgotten arrowheads since pinecones were more abundant.

On they hiked, down gullies and over ridges left behind by glaciers. Louise grew warm and drowsy. As she climbed down a broad and tangled ditch, her foot caught in an exposed root and she fell awkwardly, twisting her ankle. The children were already clambering up the other side.

"Wait there," Louise called.

They turned. "Are you okay?"

"Yes. I just twisted my ankle. Give me a minute and I'll be fine."

"We'll count our pinecones," Peter called back to her, and she saw them sit down and empty the bag.

Louise sat massaging her ankle and catching her breath. She thought it was about time to head home. The woods had soothed her and she was ready for a nap. If the ankle were going to swell, she wanted to get off of it soon.

About to rise, she glimpsed something on the ground eight or ten feet away, half-buried under a low spreading bush. If she hadn't fallen, it would have remained unnoticed.

Curious, she crawled on hands and knees, stretched her arm beneath the bush and pulled out not one, but two items. The second, a much-gnawed bone, had lain beneath the other. She tossed it aside. Examining the soft, soiled article in her hand, she was at first perplexed, and then increasingly uneasy. It was hers.

She glanced quickly across the ditch. Amy and Peter were there. Any minute, though, they might grow concerned and come running back to her. Keeping an eye on them, Louise hastily shoved what she'd found into the pocket of her jeans. Trembling, she struggled to her feet.

"I want to go home," she said, almost to herself. The shade felt encroaching; the quiet, smothering. Again and louder, "I want to go home."

It was late. Donald, Betsy and the children were asleep. Louise was exhausted but restless. She roamed through the cottage, made tea and forgot to drink it, threw Donald's sweater around her shoulders and walked out to the dock.

She shivered although the night wasn't cool, and put her arms into the sleeves of the sweater. The smell of her brother's aftershave lotion warmed her and she pulled the sweater against her face.

She wished that life could back up and go around this day as if it were something dangerous in the road. Until this morning she'd thought she knew Jack.

Exhaling in a painful sigh, she thrust her hands into the pockets of her jeans. Slowly she pulled them out and in one she held the delicate piece of clothing she'd found in the woods.

Lavishly trimmed with imported lace and designed to leave little unrevealed, the black panties had been a gift from Jack. The matching brassiere was upstairs in a drawer.

Why had they been out there in the woods, half-buried beneath a bush? Who had taken them? Louise lay on her back and, concentrating on the night sky, tried to control her rising nausea.

Clad in a white bikini, Betsy lay stretched out on the dock. Book in hand, Louise had drawn a chaise into the shade.

"Do you think Frank was embarrassed by the bikini?" Betsy asked.

"Why should he be?"

"I never know what ministers are thinking." A moment

later, "It's hard carrying on a conversation when you're way up there on the grass. Why don't you bring your book out here so I won't have to shout?

Louise got up, snatched a towel from another chair, and strolled slowly out to the dock.

"Here I lie," Betsy went on, "accelerating the aging process, when I could be sitting in the shade like you were, reading a dirty book." She sat up and reached for the tanning lotion. "When I don't have a man around, I'm trivial as hell. All I can think about is my hair and fingernails. How can I ever become a liberated person?"

"Sounds hopeless."

"I was a philosophy major. I really enjoyed it. You know why?"

"Why?"

"Because there were so many men around. When I don't have to worry about where sex is coming from next, I become a deep person." Betsy was doing her best, but Louise had no light repartee. It was an uphill struggle. "When I'm not getting any, I just look at the pictures in *Vogue* and do my nails. I hate myself when I'm like this."

"Why don't you pick somebody up if you're that desperate?"

"I'm too deep for *that*."

Louise lay on her stomach to avoid the glare from the water. "I thought you and Ned might have something going."

Fido who had been lying on his side in the shade, eyes closed, got to his feet and trotted out to join the two women.

"I don't think I'm his type."

"Have you told him how deep you are?"

The dog arranged himself proprietarily alongside Louise's thigh.

"Last summer during *Guys and Dolls*, I sort of indicated that I was fathomless."

"And?"

"I guess he didn't want to drop his anchor in anything that deep."

Sunday afternoon Frank drove into the yard with swim trunks, fishing rods, tackle box, bait and even a small outboard motor for the dinghy. In the black Mustang directly behind him came Brian Doyle.

"Ran into him over at the live bait shack," Frank explained. "Okay if we borrow your boat and kids?"

Peter fetched the Mae Wests. Off they had roared, shouting promises to be back by five, cheered on their way by a barking dog and two women waving straw hats.

Once in a while Jack had taken the kids fishing, but he wasn't keen on the sport. It was too tame. He'd rather swim.

"I'm going to swim across the lake this morning," he'd inform her matter-of-factly. "Drive the car around and pick me up by Bennett's Station."

Fear bore down on her but he hated if she allowed it to show. It was a reflection on his prowess, his manhood. "Why don't I follow you with the boat?"

"That's cheating," he'd reprimand with genuine sternness. "Meet me with the car."

She recalled her fear as she'd driven around the lake, full of horrible imaginings, and then stood on the shore, afraid something might happen while he was still too far away for her to reach. But she recalled, too, his body, glistening, powerful, parting the water with grace and precision. His body. Jesus.

With towels and a terry robe, she'd wait, half holding her breath during the last couple of hundred yards. As he struggled out of the water, stumbling and panting, grinning triumphantly, she'd wrap the robe around him, rub his red curls with the towels and slowly her fear would subside, to be replaced by desire. She could not get enough of him, of looking at him and touching him. On one such day Peter had been conceived.

Louise's belly and thighs ached with the memories. Sometimes at night her need for him felt like a kind of madness.

Louise looked across at her friend. "Are you interested in Frank?"

"He's a brick."

"His mother says the same thing."

Louise lay back, hands clasped behind her head. Fido lay close beside her and rested his head across her thighs. Long, warm minutes floated by.

"Louise?"

"Mmmm?"

"Do you have any Victorian-looking things I could borrow for the show? Brooches, bags, lacy handkerchiefs, that sort of thing?"

Lacy things. Flimsy, lacy panties. Soiled, half-buried in the dirt. Oh, God. Louise turned on her side as if to turn away from the image.

"Lou?"

"I'm . . . I'm sorry. I, I'll look. Maybe I have something." She sat up. "Donald said Ned's the leading man. Can he sing?" Louise was too preoccupied to notice the dog flinch as though he'd been stung.

"He's not bad. To hear the girls in the chorus, you'd think he was going to be snatched up by the Met. It's obscene. Everything in a skirt wants to run lines with him. He was the first person in the cast to have his lines cold."

"Have you had any costume fittings?"

"Costume fittings are my *duty*. You don't imagine I'd measure a man's inseam simply for the pleasure."

The dog stirred, wanting to be petted.

"I sold over nine hundred dollars' worth of resort rags to Ned's ex yesterday." Betsy lit a cigarette. "Have you ever met her?"

"I don't think so."

"She's good-looking. Tall. Black hair, olive skin. Comes from money. Papa owns a brewery in Wisconsin."

"I wonder why they split up."

"Ned caught her playing house in the wrong house," Betsy told her.

"Who was she playing with?"

"You would never guess in a million years." Betsy looked at Louise over her cigarette. "I suppose he's handsome in a re-pulsive sort of way, but why anyone would want to fool around with *him* when they could be fooling around with Ned, I can't figure." She flicked ashes into the water. "She must be some kind of pervert."

"Tell me."

"You ready for this?" Long pause. "Paul Berwick." She noted the expression on Louise's face. "That's right. Berwick and Sons Mortuary. Isn't that the goddamnedest thing you ever heard?"

"Yes."

The afternoon grew warm and around three Betsy suggested a swim. The dog joined them. He was a powerful swimmer. Louise was floating on her back. "I think I'll try to find some-one to build a raft we can anchor out from the shore for swimming and sunbathing. What do you think?"

"Sounds fine."

"Jack was going to do it last summer and then he got so busy at the kennel we had to put it off." Louise swam back to-ward shore. "We were going to use it . . . at night." She pulled herself out of the water, suddenly cold and weary.

Frank and Brian cleaned the six small fish they'd caught. "You and the kids have these for breakfast."

With no Sunday night rehearsal, Donald was home. They sat around the front yard before dinner, backs to the sun, drinking lemonade and gin, and discussing the show.

Donald turned to Frank, "Could I interest you in trying out for the second show?"

"What *is* the second show?" Louise asked. "I've seen the title—*Perfect Union*, isn't it?—but I've never heard of it."

"The plot is pure melodrama but the piece is more a satire of American history. There are a few songs and some simple dance routines but you couldn't call it a musical." He looked at Frank. "There's a snake oil man that Frank would be perfect for. It needs someone with a big voice and a big build."

Betsy put a hand on Donald's shoulder. "Are there any parts for me and Lou?"

"Eight or ten homesteaders' wives, about the same number of dance hall girls, and maybe half a dozen Indian women."

"That's a lot of female parts to fill."

"I'm not anticipating any problems once word gets around that Frank's coming out. And MacRae's trying out again."

"You may be trampled to death."

Donald sat forward. "Lou, speaking of MacRae, I almost forgot to tell you. He said the dog was at his place last night."

"He said *what*?"

"He was working at the cottage. A couple of times he thought he heard noises in the yard. He looked out and didn't see anything. Then, kind of late, he went out to get some papers he'd left in the car, and the dog was there. He was sitting in the drive. Just sitting. When MacRae went inside, he checked to see if Fido had left. He hadn't moved."

"Does MacRae think the dog's planning a break-in?" Brian joked. There was an unamused note in his voice and Louise wondered why.

At bedtime Amy and Peter were fretful.

"We locked the screen door, Mommy," Amy said.

Peter pleaded, "Don't let him out."

Louise sat on the edge of Peter's bed. "What on earth are you talking about?"

"What if Fido doesn't come back?" Peter whimpered, wiping away tears with the back of his hand. "He went all the way to Mr. MacRae's last night. What if he got lost?"

"I have to let him out. You wouldn't want to have to clean up a mess in the morning. But I'll take him on the leash." She took the child on her lap and held him.

Amy sat cross-legged, preoccupied, abstractedly smoothing the bedspread around her. At length she fixed Louise with a solemn gaze as she admonished, "Remember, he's from Daddy."

Throughout the day the picture of what she'd discovered in the woods intruded, slipping between Louise's thoughts, and releasing a small dose of poison. Now the cottage was silent and the build-up of depression overwhelmed her. She fastened the leash on the dog and took him out.

He was subdued, as he had been throughout the day. He seemed thoughtful, however, rather than weak or ill. He didn't strain on the leash but stayed close, and a number of times his flank brushed her leg as though he would remind her of his existence as a creature to be heeded, not merely tolerated.

They strolled south along Swan Lake Road for nearly a mile (MacRae's cottage was north), and back again. Opening the door to the sleeping porch, Louise let the dog into the cottage. He went without protest, but when she told him, "Now, stay here," he whined softly and scratched the screen with his paw as he watched her move away.

Louise dragged the canoe from the boathouse and pulled it into the water. Slipping out of her sandals and leaving them on the dock, she climbed into the canoe and pushed away.

The craft skimmed almost silently, the paddle making a sibilant slip-slap in and out of the water. Louise guided it north toward Pedersen's Bay. When she reached the spit of land that separated the south channel from the bay, she continued around it.

There were no cottages along the spit because the land disappeared during wet years. Louise and Donald had picnics here when they were children and pretended to be pioneers in the wilderness. Donald staged their adventures meticulously, fleshing them out with dramatic detail. Because she was younger, Louise sometimes had difficulty remembering her speeches, especially if she were a Sioux. Donald insisted she use an accent that would sound plausibly Indian.

Louise smiled to remember, "You take red man's land, red man bring much slings and arrows to your people."

A thin westerly breeze lifted the hair at the back of her neck. Grudgingly, some of the depression she'd felt began to ease and when she let the canoe drift, she, too, drifted, breathing deeply, yielding. The canoe floated toward shore. It was late and she ought to get home. She wasn't sure the peace she felt would follow her there.

In the swaying blackness of bushes and stunted trees a few yards away, Louise heard a sharp snap, distinct from the natural soughing of leaves and branches, distinct also from the headlong rustlings of small animals startled and fleeing.

She sat up. Leaning toward shore, she strained to hear. "Who's there?" In the quiet, her own voice frightened her. Again, "Who's there?"

Hair rising along the back of her arms, she sat, frozen, eyes glued to the dark shadows of the spit. "Who is it?" She was being watched.

The dull crunch of the canoe coming aground jarred her. Grabbing the paddle, she thrust it into the sand and heaved. The craft slid off the ground and away from shore. Immediately she began paddling with full, swift strokes, toward home, eyes riveted to the beach, probing the vegetation.

The canoe slid swiftly along. Once Louise thought she saw a shadow slipping through the darkness. When she reached the shallows in front of the cottage, she bounded from the canoe, running through the water, mooring rope in hand. Dashing toward the front door, she dropped the rope on the grass and leapt into the sleeping porch.

The slumbering bodies of her children registered in her mind as she raced through the cottage and up the stairs. As though it were a place of refuge, Louise threw herself into bed, still in jeans and shirt, and wrapped herself closely in the covers. In the bed opposite, Betsy slept undisturbed.

It wasn't yet light when Louise woke, sitting up in bed. Her pulse was beating in her temples as though her skull would splinter. Beside the bed Fido sat, studying her. She lay down, closed her eyes tightly and drew the covers high.

Chapter 14

With checkbook and current bills in one hand and a cup of coffee in the other, Louise backed through the screen door a little before seven, carrying her work outside.

July eleventh had dawned opalescent and motionless. It would be stifling before noon. She would take care of the household accounts while there was still a hint of breeze off the lake.

Paying bills was new to her and she hadn't developed a system yet. For the past nine years Jack had paid the bills—or the bookkeeper had. "For tax purposes" it was more convenient he'd told her if one person who understood what he was doing, did it all. Well, all right, if that was the way he wanted it, what did she care?

But now it was like being dumped into a foreign-language course halfway through the semester. Still, mess that she was probably making of it, she felt good about trying and, with a little help from someone, she thought she'd eventually be efficient.

Licking a window envelope after first making certain the address showed (a couple of times she'd put the statement in backwards and had to steam the envelope open), she noted that Fido wasn't around fussing at her for attention. He hadn't been in the cottage either. She must remind herself to get a proper chain for him. They'd been tying him on a rope when they didn't want him to run free. It wasn't satisfactory. Several times he'd managed to slip the rope. Fortunately Amy and Peter no longer went into a tearful panic during his brief disappearances. On a scrap of paper she scribbled "dog chain."

Louise found the May and June bank statements on top of the refrigerator. Returning to her makeshift desk in the yard, she sorted through cancelled checks, ticking them off against entries in the book. She was only now getting around to the May statement.

Frowning, she studied the check in her hand. Like most of the others it was in Jack's handwriting. Emerson Florist. Forty dollars.

Emerson Florist. Louise couldn't recall receiving or sending flowers during May. She was quite certain. She'd only just now written a check to Emerson's for flowers at the time of Jack's death. This check was earlier and written by Jack. She set the check aside. When she was in town she'd stop at Emerson's and inquire. Beneath "dog chain" she added "Emerson's."

The children woke. Amy made breakfast. Passing Louise on their way down to the dock, they saw that she was working and didn't stop to chatter.

Louise stiffened. Her hands were shaking and she laid the pen and papers on the table. She was being watched. It had happened again and again since that night in early June in the canoe.

The raft she'd had built and anchored out beyond the dock at first seemed a perfect escape. But it wasn't far enough from shore. As she lay sunbathing or splashing with the children, she was watched.

After she'd been cast in a small part in *Perfect Union*, she sometimes felt the hair rise at the back of her neck, even as she hurtled madly through rehearsals in the midst of a noisy, whirling chorus.

Now several days had passed and she hadn't felt the covert gaze. Whoever had been watching her—it might have been a vagrant camping out in the woods—had stopped, gone away, she'd told herself.

She felt his eyes graze her hair, her shoulders, and move down her back. His stare was like a physical touch. It made her squirm and sicken. But she couldn't tell anyone. She had no proof.

Later she called out the screen door, "Let's go to town."

Amy and Peter came running from the grove, the dog bounding gracefully along behind them. He'd returned. Louise opened the car door and they all tumbled into the backseat. Fido thrashed innocently with the kids as each sought his favorite spot.

"How come we're going to town?" Peter wanted to know.

"People are coming over after the show and I have to buy food." It had been Donald's idea to have an opening night party. To pick up her spirits, she suspected. If it wouldn't have worried him, she'd have tried to get out of it.

"Oh, goody," Amy piped. "Who's coming?"

"Cast, crew, and some of our other friends."

"Can Amy and I come?" Peter asked.

"Only for a little while. It's going to be late by the time the show's over."

Donald had cast Peter and Amy as two of half a dozen children he was using in crowd scenes. They'd abandoned themselves to the ambiance, absorbing, like blotters, terminology, technology, and craft. It wasn't a substitute for Jack, but it helped.

Louise was one of a "gaggle of homesteaders' wives." Frank had been cast as Major Disaster, divinely devilish snake oil man. Betsy was tarnished but true-blue Miss Bella Donna, owner of the Road to Hell Saloon. Also in the cast but in a smaller role because of his commitment to the previous show, was Ned MacRae as Ernest Pursuit, editor and publisher of *Vox Populi*, Sin City's crusading newspaper. Louise wished she'd been caught up as the others had in the color and excitement and anticipation. Maybe next summer.

There wasn't a cloud in the endless sky as Louise pulled into town. The downtown streets were blinding with heat as they went about their errands.

Louise remembered the cancelled check in her handbag. When they left Harry's Value Market, she gave Amy a dollar. "I have to stop at Emerson's. You take Peter to Royce's Drugstore and have root beer. I'll meet you there in a few minutes."

"Gee, Mrs. Andrews, I'll check that," the tall teenage girl chirped. "That was May eighth? Just a minute." She dug into a file of invoices for May.

"Oh, yeah, here it is. Forty dollars. Mmmm. Let's see. That was a memorial bouquet."

"A memorial bouquet? What's that?"

"It's a bouquet we deliver out to the cemetery. To somebody's grave. You know?"

"I see. But whose grave?"

"Let's see. The addition on the northwest side, it says." She read on. "Oh, here it is. Nell Pierson? The grave was Nell Pierson's, whoever that is . . . was." She looked up. "Was that what you wanted to know?"

Louise slid into the booth at the back of Royce's Drugstore.

"We didn't order anything for you, Mommy. Did you want anything?"

"No. I'm not thirsty."

Nell. What a thoughtful gesture on Jack's part. Odd that he hadn't mentioned it. Nell had shot herself over two years ago, using Jack's .38. None of them knew when she'd got hold of it although she would have had countless opportunities. It was no secret that Jack owned one. Nor was it a secret that the key to the gun case was on a hook above the case where the children couldn't reach it.

Although he was in no way to blame, it had bothered Jack a good deal. Maybe that was why he'd ordered flowers for her grave. Had he decorated it other times as well? As close as they had been, much of her husband remained a mystery to Louise. He'd let her know what he wanted her to know.

Before they left the drugstore, Louise made a call from the pay phone.

"MacRae and Silverman."

"Is Mr. MacRae in?"

"Who's calling, please?"

"Mrs. Andrews."

"Mrs. *John* Andrews?"

"Yes, that is, Mrs. . . . yes, Mrs. John Andrews." It was rare that anyone called him John. He'd always been Jack. She supposed that was how his name appeared on the folder in MacRae and Silverman's files. It placed him one step further away from her.

"Louise?"

"Yes. I was in town. Downtown, in fact. I wondered if you had the papers you wanted me to sign. You mentioned something about papers . . ."

"Gee, I'm sorry. I have to pick them up at the kennel. Brian has them. Did you make a trip in especially for that?"

"No. Oh, no. I had to do marketing. For tonight. Did you see the notice on the bulletin board about the party?"

"Yes, ma'am. Hold on a minute." There was a click and she waited. Click again. "Can I take you to lunch?"

"No. Thanks. I have the kids along and I have to get back. Things to be done for tonight."

"Been hit by opening night jitters yet?"

"I don't think so. That'll probably come later."

"Look, it's so damned hot in town, I'm ducking out of here early. I'll run by the kennel, pick up the papers, and stop at your place on my way out."

"That's a lot of trouble. It can wait."

"No trouble. Have a cold beer waiting. I'll see you about four."

The kids were napping and the dog lay on the cool boards of the porch floor. Pouring a glass of Riesling from an open bottle she'd found behind the milk cartons, Louise proceeded listlessly, laying out the buffet table for the party.

A car turned off the road. The dog sprang from where he lay, ran to the living room and put his paws up at the window. The grumbling in his throat seemed as much a warning to her as a threat to MacRae.

"Damm you," she pronounced slowly and, taking hold of his heavy collar, pulled him roughly out to the back porch. Whining, he resisted and threw her an imploring glance.

"No," she said sharply. "You're in the way." She slammed the door impatiently behind her. He yowled once and threw himself against the door, then was quiet. Louise stood for a moment, retrieving her calm.

"Do you think we can remove a shelf from your refrigerator?" MacRae began as she opened the screen door. Noticing the kids asleep on the beds, he lowered his voice, "And stick this in?" He shifted the keg of Michelob.

"What on earth is that for?"

"Your party."

Louise drew two redwood chairs under the birch tree and opened a can of Bud for him. He declined a glass.

"Thanks for the keg. I hope you know how to tap it."

"No problem," he assured her unbuttoning his collar, removing his tie and hanging it over the arm of the chair. Tiny beads of perspiration stood out on his brow and across his nose. Taking a folded handkerchief from his back pocket, he wiped it away and returned the handkerchief to the pocket. "I tried to call you one day. You don't have a phone here."

"I decided not to . . . this summer."

"Sure."

"If it's an emergency, you can call the Dockers, next door."

"How's it going?"

"The party? It's coming together. It's nothing elaborate."

"I mean how's it going with *you*. How's the summer going?"

"All right, I guess." All the little lies were like pinpricks. She glanced sidelong toward the grove separating her yard from the next. Would they be watched? She shifted uneasily, turning toward MacRae.

He regarded her over the top of the can, eyes narrowed slightly. "You sure you're okay? You look a little peaked. 'Peaked'—that's one of my mother's words. People are always looking 'peaked' to her. It covers everything from minor depression to ptomaine poisoning."

"I'm fine."

"You've probably been going all day, getting ready for the party. Relax. Is there anything I can do?"

"I don't think so. I could have used you this morning, though."

"What were you doing this morning?"

Louise grimaced. "Household accounts. I don't know the first thing about them. When tax time rolls around, I'll probably have thrown out everything vital and kept everything that's of no consequence."

"You haven't done this before?"

"Not really. When I was young and single, there wasn't anything to do. My dad even did my income tax. Jack took over from there."

"Would you like someone to teach you?"

"Yes."

"I'll give you a hand."

"I don't want you to do them *for* me. I want to know how to do them for myself."

"I understand."

She put a hand on his arm. "You can't know how much that would mean. Will you really teach me?"

He laughed. "Of course."

"I'll be happy to pay you, Ned. Just add it on whatever legal fees I owe." She beamed. "This is the best thing that's happened all week."

"You must have had a pretty grim week. It'll be my pleasure. No fee."

"Don't tell Donald, okay?"

"Okay," he said conspiratorially, "but why not?"

"Donald has this idea that he's obliged to do things for me because I'm his little sister. Also, I think he likes to feel smarter than me. If he found out, he'd be embarrassed. He'd say, 'Louise, *I'd* have done that for you.' " Unconsciously she mimicked her brother's voice.

He laughed. Louise cocked her head at him. Was he making fun of her?

"I'm not laughing *at* you, Louise, I'm . . . well, actually I *am* laughing at you. You're fun." He was suddenly serious. "If there's anything I can teach you—accounts, taxes, whatever, tell me."

"You're very different than I had thought."

"What had you thought?" he asked puckishly.

Louise flushed. "I, well, I don't know. It doesn't matter."

"A Don Juan image is a damned nuisance," he lamented, grinning at her. "Like being a 'dumb blonde.' Difficult to sustain."

"If it will make you feel more comfortable," Louise told him, "I'll think of you as Old Uncle Ned, kindly family counselor."

"Don't get carried away." He finished the remainder of the beer, crushed the can and sat forward as though he would rise. "I should be going," he said. "You'll be having dinner soon." He bent to pick up the tie which had fallen to the grass. The pale blue dress shirt stretched tight across the muscles of his back.

"Stay."

He turned slowly, openly exploring her face.

"Please stay."

"He's gone again, Mommy," Peter told her as they were leaving for the theater.

"Fido?" She'd forgotten to buy the chain.

"When was the last time you saw him?" Amy asked her.

"After the two of you lay down for your nap, I guess. Mr. MacRae came so I put him on the back porch." Louise snatched up her handbag from the end table and fumbled in it for the car keys. "What did I do with the car keys?"

"Are these the ones?" MacRae asked, handing her a set lying on the mantel.

"Okay. Now what was it? The dog." She closed her bag. "We don't have time to worry about the dog. We've got to get the show on the road."

MacRae held the door while Louise shepherded Amy and Peter out.

Bedizened faces were slathered with cold cream and their gaudiness tissued away. The gingham and calico gowns in the women's dressing room bore large dark patches of perspiration. Someone opened the window but there was no breeze.

"The audience loved it," Betsy announced. "We'll be sold out."

A chorus of agreement.

Riding the high of a successful opening, everyone threw himself into the party afterward with silliness born of exhaustion and relief. It was two A.M. before all but Frank and Ned had departed, noisy and replete. In the rocking chair Donald lectured on the history of satire. Frank and Betsy listened, politely bored. Ned, the party's lifeguard, wandered in.

"With my hawk-like eye and mighty prowess, I saved every last one of the booze hounds from a watery grave."

Donald turned around. "Any of them require mouth-to-mouth resuscitation?"

"Funny you should ask. I've never seen so many women at death's door. A veritable epidemic of near-drowning," he explained, à la W. C. Fields. He looked from Louise to Betsy. "Either of you ladies going swimming? I figure I've got a couple of saves left in me."

"No, thanks," Louise told him.

"How about a picnic?" he asked. "Anybody hungry? I haven't eaten yet."

"What do you mean, picnic?"

"You know, Louise, it's where you pack a lunch and go someplace and eat it."

"Hmmm," she murmured skeptically. "Where do you picnic at this hour?"

"The raft?"

"Sorry, I'm bone-tired," Donald told him. "You young people run along."

"Betsy and I have packed it in like trenchermen," Frank informed him. "You'll have to picnic alone, I'm afraid."

"Well, I haven't eaten," Louise said. "You get the rowboat out of the boathouse, Ned, while I make sandwiches." She turned toward the stairs. "First I'll check the kids."

The children had been put to bed upstairs. The reading lamp was still burning. The windows stood open. From below, came the cocky urbanity of Sinatra. *Mary Poppins* and *The Cat in the Hat* had fallen to the floor. Louise put them on the lamp table and pulled the sheet up to cover each child. Their faces were pastel and cloudless.

She brushed the hair back from Peter's moist forehead, exposing the naked, perfect brow. Extinguishing the light, she stood beside them for a long moment.

"They're beautiful, Jack," she breathed, closing her lids against tears.

The night was suddenly still as the tone arm on the phonograph lifted and paused before the next record. Within the stillness, a hint of sound. The faintest jingle of ID tags? Louise froze, listening. The dog. She'd forgotten about the dog. She whirled and ran to the windows overlooking the lake.

The front yard below was lit, though dimly, by a pair of yard lights at either end of the cottage. There was Fido, hackles raised, moving across the yard with the stealth of a hunter.

For a moment Louise couldn't imagine what he was doing but the way he moved frightened her. In his measured, calculated advance there was cunning.

The boathouse. She pressed her body against the screen. Her nails dug into the wood of the sill.

"Ned!" The sound was lost in the dog's furious cry as he sprang.

She spun away from the window and raced down the stairs. There was no one in the living room as she ran to the front porch. "New York, New York" played on the stereo.

She threw open the screen door. MacRae sprinted toward the cottage, burst past her through the door. It slammed behind him and Louise secured the hook, collapsing against the jamb.

Behind her she heard Ned panting, trying to catch his breath. She couldn't turn around and face him. She whispered finally, "Are you all right?"

"That damned dog attacked me," he gasped.

She turned. "Are you all right?" she demanded.

"Yes, I'm all right," he said roughly. "But I'm mad as hell."

"I don't blame you," she said lamely. "Come in and sit down."

He threw himself down on a couch.

Betsy and Frank appeared in the kitchen doorway. "Anything wrong?"

"The dog," Louise told them, "he tried to—bite Ned."

"Bite, hell. He'd have killed me if he could."

Frank and Betsy sat down opposite Ned. Trembling, Louise poured scotch and handed it to him.

"You went out to get the boat," Frank said.

MacRae nodded. "It was in the boathouse. I thought I heard something outside but I figured it was maybe a deer. All of a sudden the dog was standing there in the door acting crazy."

Louise, hovering nervously, recalled the dog's stealth.

"He came at me twice. The first time I grazed him with an empty gas can. The second time I got him across the shoulder with a canoe paddle. I wish I'd killed him. Next time I will." He drank off some of the liquor.

"The dog," Louise asked hesitantly, "is he ... hurt?"

A second of disbelief ticked by."I didn't stay to find out. Would you like me to go check, Louise?"

"I just meant, that is, maybe we should do something?"

"He ran off, probably into the grove." He downed the rest of the liquor. "My goddamned knees are still shaking," he laughed hollowly.

"It's insane," Betsy told him. "That dog is as gentle as a nun."

"That was no nun in the boathouse."

"You're sure it was the setter?" Frank wanted to know. "It couldn't have been another dog? It must have been pretty dark out there."

"It was the setter. The yard light's on and I could see that red coat."

"You know what I think?" Louise put in unsurely, "I think he didn't recognize you. He probably thought you were a prowler." She didn't believe that. The dog had meant to kill him.

Ned said nothing.

"Sure as hell takes the fun out of a picnic, doesn't it?" Frank laughed.

"You have the food ready?" Ned shot at Louise.

"I'll get something." She stood up, eyes guarded.

"Then find a pitcher for beer and let's get the hell out of here." He turned to Frank. "Damned if I'll let that bastard spoil my picnic."

Obediently Louise got a pitcher down from the kitchen cupboard. Under the circumstances the picnic seemed preposterous. But, if Ned wanted to whistle in the dark, she owed him that. Feeling absurd, she hastily assembled sandwiches. Starting outside with the pitcher and the picnic basket, she turned back, "You're welcome to use the couch tonight, Frank."

"I have to get back to town."

"See you tomorrow."

He followed her outside. "I'll have a look around for the dog, Lou."

"Thank you. If you find him, put him on the back porch." She carried the food out to the dock where Ned had the dinghy tied.

He grabbed the basket and set it on a seat, skillfully handed her into the boat, and then took the pitcher to fill. Returning with beer and paper cups, he told her, "I don't see the Hound of the Baskervilles around." He passed her the pitcher. "If he knows what's good for him, he won't be back till after I leave."

Louise was silent as they pulled away from the dock. There was nothing she could say except how sorry she was.

They reached the raft and tied up. The kerosene lantern that Donald had temporarily bolted to one corner was still aglow, casting flickering light over them as they sat back on their knees laying out the unlikely meal.

Ned promised, "I won't say any more about the dog."

"You don't owe me any favors."

"That's a moot point, but I am damned well going to enjoy this picnic if it kills me."

When she'd divided the food between them, Louise said, "I don't believe it—I'm hungry."

Finishing the sandwiches, they lay back, exhausted, and listened to the water lapping against the raft. Infrequently a car could be heard rushing along a country road, miles away, carrying someone home from a late Saturday night.

"I like this raft," he said in a voice so low Louise could barely hear.

"Yes. It's removed from things." An illusion.

"Did you ever notice," he asked, "how kids understand escape? They have tree houses and forts and secret hiding places. It never occurs to them that they're neurotic when they want to get away."

He fell silent and the silence stretched out until Louise guessed he had fallen asleep. She lay on her stomach, face toward him. He was close enough that she could see in the lamplight the rise and fall of his chest. She scrutinized him as closely as the simple light permitted. She used to enjoy studying men in this way, speculating about them. A sweet, idle pastime.

He lay with his hands behind his head and one knee drawn up, a languorous pose. Black curly hair, speckled with gray, grew on his chest. A fine, almost invisible down of black hair grew in a line down his belly. And on his legs and forearms was a light covering of the same.

His skin was tanned dark. Beneath the tan on his cheeks there were, she knew, a few freckles scattered below his eyes. Louise thought he must have been pretty when he was young. He'd escaped that, and now looked toughened, and maybe a trifle self-indulgent.

She didn't try to prevent herself imagining him without clothes. That, after all, was much of the pleasure in these speculations. But her mind switched reels. There was the dog, ready to tear the skin and muscle she lay admiring. She moaned.

Immediately his hand was on her shoulder. "Are you all right?"

"Yes. I . . . my arm fell asleep."

"That's good. I mean, I'm glad you're all right. More beer?"

"I'm full. Well . . . maybe half a cup."

Childhood hiding places. They took up the subject again.

Louise's retreat had been the hayloft in the barn which was now a garage.

"It was dusty and musty up there, and very dim and close because there were no windows. But when I wanted to get away, I'd sneak up and open the loft door to let in fresh air. It was always hell getting it closed again without falling out. For some dumb reason, it swung out instead of in, so you had to reach way out over nothing to pull it closed."

"That was where they loaded the hay in."

"Right. If you stepped out, you stepped into space. It still makes my heart race to think of it. Whenever I felt abused, I'd climb up in the loft and imagine myself falling out and breaking my leg. I never had a broken bone and I thought it would be lovely and exciting—only a little painful. Everyone would cry a lot over poor Louise and say how sorry they were that they'd been mean and they'd never do it again."

Ned's father had built him a tree house in an old cotton-wood. "It was a giant of a tree out in the meadow."

"You lived on a farm?"

"Not really. We had a little piece of land on the edge of town."

"What town?"

"Red Wing. Anyway, we had a meadow out behind the house and my dad kept a horse and a cow and a few chickens. I had a pony named Sunny and usually two or three mutts."

"Do you like animals?"

"I guess, though I'm not too sold on Irish setters. I have a couple of crazy squirrels over at the cottage. Frick and Frack. You'll have to come see them. Bring a present. They prefer edibles. They're completely tame and spoiled rotten. I put food out for them before I leave in the morning. Sometimes I'm late for work because I get engrossed watching them. They make the damnedest fuss, chattering at me like they're doing me a favor to cart the stuff away. The best squirrel food money can buy, mind you."

She caught him glancing at her to see if she were finding any of it amusing. He was kind.

"A grateful squirrel would probably be a terrific bore," he said.

Louise smiled. He looked at her closely, then got to his feet.

"Now, before the sun comes up, I'm going to row you back to the mainland." He pulled her to her feet. "Let's fold up our tent."

Louise gathered the picnic gear into the basket, and they loaded themselves into the boat. Ned cast off, pulled the boat about and started toward shore.

"Would you like me to put it back in the boathouse?"

Louise felt a pinch of fear. "It isn't necessary. If you beach it up where the grass begins, it'll be all right."

He let her out at the dock, got out himself and pulled the dinghy up toward the cottage where it wouldn't slip back out during the night. What there was left of it.

Inside the cottage, he changed hurriedly into street clothes. "I'll pick up the keg tomorrow. Just leave it out there. It'll be okay."

Louise walked him to his car, peering apprehensively into the shadows. The dog was not visible. Ned threw his swimsuit into the backseat and turned to say good-night. Expecting a comradely grasp of her hand, Louise was unprepared when he took her hand, but pulled her against him.

She had been up nearly twenty-four hours and her brain was gummy. Digging about for proper protests was exhausting. It was easier and more pleasant to be kissed.

"Everything's going to be all right," he murmured against her cheek. The next minute he was gone.

Louise stood rooted to the spot, the skin along her thighs and arms icy. How long? How long had he been watching?

Chapter
15

The night's dream began pleasantly, almost in slow motion. She and Ned were in the hayloft. It was empty except for them. The loft door was open and afternoon sun cast rays of Venetian yellow across the room, catching dust motes and laying down a rectangle of light on the floor. On this rectangle Ned and Louise lay side by side as though it were a carpet.

"Aren't you glad we escaped?" he asked.

"Yes." She'd forgotten what it was they had escaped. Whatever it was, she was glad.

Her body was not tired but, rather, languid, relaxed. She hoped they could stay a long while.

"Let's sail away in the tree house."

"Could we?" If they sailed away, they'd be gone at least until sundown.

"Why not?"

"Aren't we running away?"

"Sure. That's the point," he told her. It seemed to make profound and obvious sense.

She was delighted to have her own desires validated. She smiled at him.

He leaned over her and kissed her. She put her arms

around his body and pulled him on top of her. They were both clothed but she wanted to feel his weight on her.

"Yes, MacRae," she breathed, and ran her hands along the muscles of his back and inside the waist of his trousers, pressing him tightly against her.

From the opposite end of the room, the voice, so soft, "Louise."

"Oh, God," she moaned, "Oh, God, Jack, I thought you were dead. You're supposed to be dead."

His footsteps advanced across the bare boards of the loft. His voice sounded deadly and smooth as the barrel of a revolver. "I told you I would kill him, Louise."

"There was a small tragedy at my place," MacRae told Louise when he stopped by in the late morning to pick up the beer keg.

"What was that?"

"Remember Frick and Frack?" he asked, carrying the empty keg across the yard to his car.

"Your tame squirrels." Louise followed.

He opened the trunk, deposited his burden, slammed the lid and stood, leaning against the car, preoccupied. "Yes."

Louise waited. He was subdued, thoughtful. She wondered what had provoked the mood.

"I found one of them on my doorstep this morning," he said with great wistfulness. His jaw muscles tightened. Finally, "He'd been torn apart."

She drew a sharp, audible breath. "The other one?" she demanded. "Is he all right?"

He sighed. "I haven't seen him."

After lunch Louise gathered up bed linens and soiled clothing from everyone. "If you and Donald will keep an eye on things," she told Betsy, "I'll be back before dinner."

As she loaded the pillowcases full of laundry into the back of the wagon, Fido jumped in and settled himself peremptorily in the front passenger's seat. Where had he been all morning? Or night, for that matter? Louise slammed the car door. "At least I'll know where you are this afternoon."

The car bumped along over Swan Lake Road. Louise's empty stomach twisted as she thought of the squirrel that had been "torn apart." She didn't want to think about it but she couldn't dismiss it. She glanced over at the dog, but shook her head. No. No, he wouldn't do that.

When the first load was in the dryer and the second sloshing in the washer, Louise rolled the lawn mower from the garage and started on the yard. She looked up at the loft door. It was closed.

Physical labor and cold showers, the gentlewoman's nostrum for sweaty palms and lewd thoughts. She grunted, pushing the mower ahead of her. Finishing the yard on the north side of the house, she paused to empty washer and dryer. She found a can of frozen lemonade in the freezer.

Lowering herself into an old wicker armchair on the eating porch, glass in hand, she put her feet up.

She'd been sitting like this another July day. Jack was mowing the lawn. Whistling, he came into the side porch wearing a pair of denim shorts. His chest and shoulders glistened with perspiration. "Want a beer?" he asked on his way to the kitchen.

"I'm drinking lemonade."

She heard him in the kitchen pulling the tab from the can, drinking, and saying "ahhhh" like a commercial.

"We deserve a weekend away from this place," he told her, standing in the doorway, idly rubbing his chest. "Fly to Chicago next weekend? Stay at the Palmer House, have dinner in the Pump Room? Would you like that?"

Peering seductively over the top of her glass, she asked, "How about drive across the county line and stay in the Hump Room at Howard Johnson's?"

"You're a woman of easy virtue, Louise." He winked at her.

"But you're a cheap date." He took the beer with him out to the yard, whistling as he went.

Easy virtue. A curious expression. Was she a woman of easy virtue? Jack, of course, had been teasing. But she'd been aroused last night. Even remembering, she felt excited. And the dream. That sure as hell hadn't helped anything.

What was wrong with her? Two months. Two months since Jack had been killed and she was excited by another man. How could that be? She'd been insane about Jack, never looked at anyone else when he was alive. What kind of woman was she?

Above the sound of the washer and dryer, she heard the dog's nails click across the kitchen floor. He appeared in the doorway, perusing her, then crossed the porch and laid his head on her thigh.

"What am I going to do with you?" Louise asked. "If you attack anyone again, we'll have to get rid of you."

The dog raised his head and looked at her with an expression of infinite sadness. He whined a long, tortured whine, thrusting his head this way and that as though he could lose some thought, like a painful bur, that stabbed him. He lifted a paw to her. Louise held it, caressed it. It would be terrible to get rid of him.

"I'm going to finish my lemonade and tackle the front yard," she told him briskly, releasing his paw. "You can come out with me if you like." But when she rose to go, he preferred to remain in out of the hot sun. The last load of laundry and the last lap of the front yard were completed about the same time.

"That's all," Louise announced. The south yard and back would have to wait for another day. She pulled the mower back into the garage. Before her was the loft ladder. The temptation to climb it was irresistible.

Up she went. The rungs were filthy with disuse. At the top she paused, glanced around the dusky space, half-filled with broken furniture which ought to be carted away. Satisfied, she descended. Closing the sliding doors, she returned the padlock to its hasp.

At the kitchen table she folded laundry, packed it into a plastic basket, emptied the dryer filter, turned off the laundry room light and called the dog. No sound of clicking nails or jingling ID tags. She called again. He hadn't left the house while she mowed, she was sure. Setting the laundry basket beside the front door, she called once more, received no response, and decided to look upstairs. He might have gone up to Amy or Peter's room and fallen asleep.

He wasn't in either. The house was quiet. Even if he were asleep, he would wake when he heard her call. As she started back toward the stairs, something caught her eye. She changed course and turned into her own room. There, on Jack's side of the bed, his head on the pillow, was the dog. He was awake and waiting for her. He didn't move as she entered the room, but his eyes followed her. He looked at her with meaning, and waited.

"Go away!" She flew at him, striking his shoulder with her fist. "Who do you think you are?" She raised her fist and struck him again.

Chapter 16

With any luck, I'll be flat on my can faster than a pig on skates. Louise drained the double Manhattan and made herself another. Her hands shook and liquor spilled onto her dress. Absently wiping at the stain, she stepped out of her shoes and returned to the couch.

If I were clever and imaginative like Donald, I'd know what's happening, I'd make some sense of it, she thought, laying her head against the back of the couch and letting tears slip from beneath closed lids.

Oh, hell, I'm crying in my Manhattan. She pulled a handful of Kleenex from the box on the lamp table. I've cried so damned much the past two months, I'm going to wear out my eyes. But sobs shook her and she held the tissues over her face, trying to muffle the sound.

Maybe she would go on accepting things at face value, not looking behind them or trying to make connections. Sleeping dogs and all of that. "Sleeping dogs," she muttered mockingly.

Abstractedly she worried a ragged fingernail and looked around the room as though hoping something might divert her. *Anna Karenina* lay on the coffee table, but she'd had too much liquor.

She got unsteadily to her feet, drink in hand, glided (It seemed to her that she glided. It always seemed, when she'd had too much to drink, that she glided) through the cottage, and stood at the back door, peering out through the screen, and sipping from the glass.

The dog, fastened to a length of rope, which was in turn secured to a strong young pine tree, heard her. He pulled himself up, gently shaking himself. He didn't move toward the door.

Louise didn't move toward him, but stayed behind the screen, regarding him. She didn't want to touch him. She didn't want him to touch her. They faced each other mutely for some time, then Louise turned away, after hooking the door.

Later, one hand on the wall, the other with a glass again full, she started up the stairs. I certainly don't want to sleep. It can't be avoided. But I don't want to. Sleep was no longer a place to hide. Sleep was a detective you didn't hire who nonetheless went through all your rooms, even as you stood by saying pointedly, "I don't think you ought to *do* that," and made sense, however nasty, of what you hadn't the courage to make sense of yourself. That's right, Louise. That's right.

It was two-thirty when she slipped over the border of sleep and found herself walking, arm linked through Jack's, across soft, manicured lawns, toward the brightly-lit entrance to the country club.

She was excited and happy, dressed in a long pale gray chiffon dress. She squeezed her husband's arm affectionately. He was terribly attractive and elegant in the navy blue blazer and white slacks of summer wool.

He smiled and winked. He never winked at anyone but her. The wink said, "We have a lot of secrets, don't we?" It always made her feel a little short of breath and aroused.

Tall windows and French doors stood open and through them floated music from a six-piece combo. Beside the open entrance was a man-sized cardboard cutout of a brown and white spotted dog, standing on its hind legs and holding a placard reading, "ASPCA Benefit."

They entered a large foyer and were greeted by someone wearing a dog mask who handed each of them similar though not identical masks to put on.

Grinning sheepishly at her, Jack donned his. Louise supposed it was necessary to go along with the nonsense and she, too, put hers on, thinking as she did, "They won't get me to do this again."

Strolling into the main room of the club, they mingled with other members, all of whom wore dog masks. Around the periphery of the room were more gigantic cardboard dogs like the one outside. Louise thought the club had overstepped the bounds of good taste or good sense in carrying out the motif.

The masks they all wore were not actually uncomfortable despite the warmth of the night, but they made Louise uneasy. She liked to see someone's face when she spoke to him. Without a face to interpret, you didn't always know what the speaker meant. What he really meant. And the mask blurred the voice slightly so you couldn't always tell who was behind it, even if he were someone you knew. Louise found herself struggling to see through eye slits, straining to catch intonations of voice.

For long periods of time she lost track of Jack's whereabouts and that unnerved her. In this obscurely frightening sea of canine faces, she wanted to know where he was.

In the powder room Louise struck up a conversation with a tall woman wearing a poodle mask. The woman's body was sheathed in a lovely red silk dress. The jewelry she wore was heavy, gold, and antique-looking.

"My husband is a dog, with or without a mask," the woman told her, laughing a deep, voluptuous laugh.

Louise didn't know what to respond to this.

"I'm Estelle MacRae," the woman continued, extending a hand for Louise to shake.

"How do you do." A tiny spark of indignation exploded in

Louise. "I think your husband is kind. At least he's very kind to me." She was at a loss for further comment. The other woman laughed again, an overriding laugh that belittled Louise's opinion.

Full of unaccountable pique, Louise snapped, "I understand Paul Berwick is here. As a jackal." She turned quickly and pushed through the heavy door into the foyer, Estelle MacRae's laughter following her. Why did I do that, she wondered as she made her way into the bar.

She ordered a double Manhattan and carried it back to the main lounge where the combo filled the room with the cloying music of "How Much Is That Doggie In The Window?"

Where was Jack? She wanted to be with him. Slowly she circled the room sipping her drink and searching for his beautifully shaped head and red curls. Once she bumped into a cardboard cutout and excused herself.

When she found Jack, he was seated at a table with a woman in a flowing white dress who held a bouquet of flowers. There was a flower in Jack's lapel. From the woman's bouquet?

"I don't think I like this party, Jack. Can we leave?" She sat down beside him.

"I can't leave, Louise."

"Why?"

"Number one, I don't want to leave and Number two, because of my position, I think it would be wrong."

"Your position?"

"Yes. I've done a lot of work with the ASPCA. I'm probably the best known vet in the county, or in several counties, for that matter, and I think I should stick around."

The woman with the flowers said nothing.

"I suppose you're right," Louise admitted. "I hadn't thought about that. I'm scared, though."

"Scared?"

Why had she said that? She didn't know what she meant by it. Boy, she just kept saying stupid things tonight.

"Could we dance?" she pleaded, wanting him to hold her, protect her from her fears.

"Excuse us," Jack told the woman and Louise nodded.

As they danced, she clung to him, pressed her breasts and thighs against him. She wanted him to make love to her. Her fears would go away then.

"Can we sneak out to the car for a few minutes?" she whispered.

"Maybe later," he said.

When the music stopped, he returned her to the table, saying he would be right back. Louise watched him pick his way through the throng, heading toward the door that led to the foyer, bar, and restrooms.

The woman in the flowing dress excused herself and drifted across the dance floor. Louise waited for Jack to return. He didn't. She went looking but couldn't find him. She felt panicky. The dog masks everywhere she turned began to unsettle her. Weren't they rather cruel? Wasn't the whole idea rather cruel? Someone took her elbow and spoke as he led her to the dance floor.

"Louise. How are you?"

It was Ned MacRae's voice.

"I'm . . . I'm frightened. I don't like the masks. I can't find Jack." She allowed herself to be led.

With an adroit flourish, he removed his mask. She felt inordinate relief.

"Thank you. That was kind."

They danced without talking. She felt a little better. He was an island of surety in an ocean of charade and disguised threat.

Suddenly Jack was there, taking her hand abruptly, pulling her away from MacRae. He led her roughly across the room and out the French doors to the back terrace. Outside, he grabbed her shoulders and yanked her around to face him.

"What's the matter?" she asked.

"What the hell is going on here?" he demanded.

"What do you mean?"

"You know what I mean. Why did MacRae take off his mask? What are you two up to?"

"I was frightened. He was kind. That's all, Jack."

"Kind!" he hissed. "Kind! Is that what you call it?"

"Jack, really, there was nothing . . . wrong," she exclaimed, fear in her voice.

There was something strange here. His voice was somehow altered.

"Jack?" Was this even Jack?

His hands were cruel, biting into her bare shoulders.

"Don't you ever try to leave," he snarled. "You know what would happen."

"Yes," she whispered.

Chapter 17

Monday Louise drove to town for groceries and a chain. Monday night as they prepared to leave for the theater, she searched for the chain.

"Who took the chain I bought this morning?"

No one answered.

"Well, it was on the back porch, right by the door."

Everyone joined in a cursory search but it didn't turn up. It was late. They couldn't spend any more time looking.

After the show Fido was outside the theater, waiting for her like a stage-door Johnny. The cast praised him for a clever fellow as he fawned and pranced and threw simpering glances at Louise that made her ill. Each night that week he was there. Saturday she would buy another chain.

But, waking feverish and fragile Saturday, Louise nursed herself through the day with aspirin and iced tea. Amy and Peter tiptoed and ministered, making her feel guilty and grateful.

Despite hot weather, the show that night bounced along effortlessly, a bright ball tossed from actor to actor. After the final curtain Frank and Betsy whisked the kids back to the cottage while Louise stole away to join Tom Benjamin at the Yacht Club.

Fido would be waiting in the parking lot, sitting on his haunches beside the station wagon. But tonight there would be no head-tossing, no tail-wagging, dancing-around-himself scene as he caught sight of her leaving the theater. No muffled, welcoming yips as he nosed her toward the car door. No self-congratulatory snorting from the backseat on the ride home as he reminded himself again and again what a canny charmer he was.

Louise escaped through a backstage fire door and made her way along the beach, behind Ginger Charlie's Drive-In, and into the Yacht Club through the kitchen door, apologizing to the startled help as she pressed between them and out into the public rooms.

The keen satisfaction, amounting to glee, that she felt in eluding and thwarting the dog, caused a giggling euphoria to well up in her. She still felt weak, a bit shaky but all she required was a little escape. She smiled as she spotted Benjamin.

Tom, a spindle-shanked Falstaff, was waiting, holding down a huge semi-circular red leatherette booth. He ordered drinks, toasted the show, and plunged into a rambling, bawdy account of his exploits many years earlier in a college production of *Aaron Slick From Punkin Crick,* ending with "and that's what befalls innocent med students who mess with concupiscent philosophy majors. Sure changed *my* philosophy, I can tell you."

Wiping away tears of laughter, Louise leaned back, absorbing the moment and the surroundings. They were a balm.

"Would you like to dance?" she asked the doctor.

"I sure as hell would, but at my age I have to save myself for more important things."

"Which are?"

"Sex and finding my glasses." He signaled the waitress and ordered them a bowl of popcorn. "You know, Eve and I had a cottage out here. Cotter's Bay. I sold it after she died."

"Are you sorry?"

"Yes. I got too much into the work thing. A mistake. I should have looked for another woman." He took a swig of scotch and soda and smacked his lips. "If you run into any likely candidates, send 'em around."

"I thought you and Mame Goodin might make a match. People said she'd set her cap for you."

He looked horrified. "God, no. All she wanted was somebody to escort her to church. That woman's juices dried up years ago, if she ever had any. I'm looking for someone who doesn't go to bed just for the rest." He paid for the popcorn and ordered another round. "Meet any men in this show you're in?"

"Men?"

"The other sex, Louise."

"There are plenty of men in the show. Half the cast."

"You know what I figured? I figured you and Frank for something. He's one helluva nice man."

"And so convenient. Right next door."

"It couldn't hurt."

Louise patted his bony hand. "I love you. You make me laugh."

"That's not a good enough reason. Try loving me for my body."

Art Christopher slid into the booth for a brief conversation. He was worried. He'd managed the Yacht Club for Bill Hermann for twelve years, but Hermann was getting up in years and wanted to sell. Art didn't have enough money, doubted he could raise it, to buy the business. He was afraid of what would happen if it were sold to outsiders.

"I'd hate to see this place wall-to-wall Formica and fast food," he said, shaking his head and looking around the room. "If you hear of anybody local who's interested in investing, let me know." Preoccupied, he finished his beer and left to check the kitchen. "Next round's on me," he told them.

The Yacht Club possessed a seemingly changeless, intimate tackiness. Louise felt invited by it: lighted beer signs; plain wood floors shining with run-together, spilled-oil colors from the ancient and majestic Wurlitzer; red leatherette booths, scarred wood tables and chairs worn to a dusky patina by years of merciless use. The bar stood near the entrance. What a noble work of man was a good bar, Louise thought. Long, polished, richly dark, and sinuous.

Like Art Christopher, Louise dreaded the idea of the club being sold to outsiders who might try to make it more than it ought to be. When she and Donald were children, during the summers while they lived at the lake, their parents took them to the Yacht Club for Sunday lunch. Many of the lake families gathered there after church, or instead of church.

Louise thought there should be a deck—sufficiently seedy to blend in—along the water where customers could drowse in the sun and drink summer coolers. If she owned the Yacht Club, that would be the only significant alteration she'd make.

"I hope this place doesn't change," Louise said aloud.

"If they spruce it up, they'll ruin it," the doctor agreed.

Watching a couple dancing to an early Stones hit, Louise saw the door open and Donald push his way through, followed by Ned MacRae, an eventuality she hadn't planned on. Except on stage, Louise had been avoiding MacRae. Ned was trouble of one sort or other. The days would pass smoothly and safely if she steered a wide path, sat with her hands folded, and went alone and early to bed. She bit her lower lip and glanced about. There was no way to escape. Donald spotted them, said something to Ned, and they headed toward the big booth.

After exchanging greetings, the two men sat down, Ned next to Louise. "You look nice," he told her.

"Thank you." She felt shy.

"I thought the show went well, didn't you?"

"Yes. I'm glad Tom saw it tonight." Louise sipped her drink. Minutes earlier she'd been relaxed.

They picked desultorily at several topics of conventional conversation. Duke Ellington's "Mood Indigo" slipped under the needle. Ned touched her elbow. "Dance?"

Louise stood up and he followed her onto the dance floor.

The hand on her back was firm. "Have you been avoiding me?"

His directness, the absence of conscious game-playing always startled her. She didn't answer at once.

"That's what I thought," he said.

"Whatever you think, it's wrong."

He laughed and she felt relieved. He pulled back to look at her when he spoke. He was casual and kind, determined not to put her on a spot. "I thought last Saturday night might have scared you off. Was I right?"

"Yes and no." The kiss had scared her off but not for the reasons he thought.

"You get a failing mark in Polite Conversation."

"I'm sorry. I had a nice time last Saturday."

"That's good."

"But . . ."

He pulled back again, smiling but with his brow puckered. "But? But what? Our astrological signs are incompatible?"

His voice was rich. As a lawyer-sometime-actor, he used it with practice, conveying a range of subtleties, often with only a word or two. It was taunting now, teasing and light. He was trying to draw her out, she knew. She wished she could run off at the mouth for about an hour, spilling all the beans of fear she carried around.

"I can't really explain. I'm a little afraid, I guess."

"Of me?" Boyish innocence.

"No, no, no. Not that kind of afraid."

"Well, what other kind is there?" His eyes wouldn't allow her to look away. "I wish you'd tell me. Maybe I can help. You know me—the Perry Mason of Falls Village. No problem too small, no fee too large. What are you afraid of?"

She felt like a fool, but she couldn't tell him. She hated lying to him, though. "I'm not being coy. It's sort of a pre-monition."

"You mean like if you were to see more of me, it would be bad? That kind of premonition?"

"Not quite that simple. Don't worry. I'll be all right. It's something I have to work out on my own."

He drew her closer in a protective gesture. She felt the hard flatness of his belly, the flexing of his thighs. What she wanted was to end the night with him on top and her underneath or some similar arrangement. Oh, Christ, Louise.

He said nothing more until the record concluded, then led her by the hand to the jukebox. "Help me pick out some more music." He fed change into the coin slot and they punch-ed a couple of numbers. Like children, mesmerized by the mechanics of the box, they stood gazing into it as the first record moved purposefully out, separating itself from the stack and descending to the turntable in an ordained way.

Louise appraised the man beside her. She wanted him. Ig-noring the cold voice that whispered, "I told you I would kill him," she moved close to him and placed her hand on his shoulder.

His right hand went around her waist and he began to dance her out of the light of the jukebox.

His bed was unmade and rumpled. How many women had slept here lately, she wondered, and was immediately contrite. That's none of your damned business, Louise. You're not here gathering evidence. There was a table and lamp on either side of the bed. The one on the far side held a low wattage bulb. That's not the one he reads by, she told herself.

She watched him undress and discovered that all was pretty much as she had imagined, maybe better. She stepped out of her half-slip and panties first, leaving the halter on the dress for him to untie. That had been a wise decision. He sat on the edge of the bed, untied the halter, pulled the dress slowly down, kissing her body as it was bared.

MacRae was the gentlest lover Louise had ever known. The unhurried grace and delicacy in his lovemaking lured her along with patience and indulgence. She had been prepared for his skill. She was surprised by his tenderness.

Later, quietly curled against his body, she knew that what she'd done was dangerous. A woman could, she saw, fall in love with a man, based on what she came to know of him in sex. Louise wasn't sure she would forget what she'd learned about MacRae. Breathing a contented moan, she put her arms around his waist and gently eased her thigh between his so that she could lie closer to him.

About two A.M. he suggested a swim.

She sighed and paid no attention.

"Come on, a swim will refresh you."

"I don't have a suit."

He laughed and kissed her inner thigh. "Louise, I promise not to look."

So they swam for ten minutes. It *was* refreshing. He'd spread a soft, thick towel on the dock and after the swim, they lay down whispering.

"MacRae?"

"Mmmm?"

"Do you think you could feed something other than my passion?"

"Hungry?"

"You're a master of understatement. I'm delirious. I thought at first it was sex. Now I realize I'm starving to death."

"You really know how to hurt a person."

"A peanut butter sandwich will put you right back in the picture."

A few minutes later he returned with two peanut butter sandwiches and two glasses of milk on a tray. They ate with quiet concentration. Louise set her empty glass on the tray next to Ned's, pushed the tray away and kissed his forehead. From there she worked her way gratefully south.

Stealing home at four A.M., she killed the engine at the driveway and coasted into the yard with the lights off. Certain she was the last one in, she hooked the screen door, kissed each of the kids, pulling the sheets up to their chins. She stepped gingerly lest she trip over the dog, then realized he wasn't there.

The stairs were mercifully quiet and when she reached the top she peeled her things off for the second time that night and crawled in under her own sheet. Slipping beneath a wave of sleep, she wondered where the dog was.

Chapter
18

It was ten-thirty as Betsy and Louise began to wash breakfast dishes. "What're you wearing to the Murphys'?" Betsy inquired.

They were all invited to brunch at a neighbor's, halfway between Louise's cottage and Ned's.

"I don't know." She pushed hair back from her face with a forearm. "It's so hot, maybe shorts."

"Is Ned going?"

Louise stopped scrubbing the plate she held. "You know about last night?"

"Donald came in as Frank was leaving. He told us you'd left the Yacht Club with Ned. Anything wrong with that?"

"I guess not."

"You weren't planning to keep it a secret, were you?" She was perplexed.

Louise smiled unsurely. "No." She dried her hands and went to the back door. The dog's dishes, food and water, were there on the floor, looking untouched.

"Have you seen the dog?" Behind her breastbone, apprehension fluttered.

Betsy considered for a moment. "Not recently. He was wait-

ing for you in the parking lot last night. I didn't think anymore about him after that. You worried?"

"A little." She went back to the sink.

"Don't worry. He always comes back."

"Yes."

Twelve-thirty arrived and so did Frank. Since Betsy was in
the bathroom applying makeup, Louise met him at the door.

"You going to the Murphys'?"

"Yes. As soon as Ned gets here." She looked at her watch.
"He should have been here fifteen minutes ago."

Betsy rushed breathlessly in. "Sorry to hold you up."

The screen door slammed. "Mommy, Mrs. Docker says
you're wanted on the phone," Amy panted.

"That's probably Ned," Betsy told her. "We'll take Amy
and Peter with us and you can catch up later." She stuffed a
pack of cigarettes into her bag and looked up at Louise.

"You don't mind?" Louise asked.

"Don't be silly. We'll see you in a little while." Betsy
grabbed the children's hands, shooing them ahead of her.
"See you there."

Louise ran all the way to the Dockers'. Suzie held the door
open. "He didn't say who it was, only that it was important.
I'm glad he caught us before we left for the Murphys'. We
were just walking out the door when the phone rang."

"Thanks, Suzie. Sorry to bother you."

"No bother." She handed Louise the phone.

Louise's hand shook. Pulling off an earring, she put the receiver to her ear. "Hello?"

"Louise?" It was Ned but his voice sounded distant and
whispery.

"Ned? What's the matter? Where are you?"

After what seemed a full minute, "My place."

"The cottage? You sound so far away."

There was a sharp noise at the other end of the wire and

then nothing. Without stopping to relieve Suzie of her anxious expression, Louise ran, calling behind her, "Emergency."

Reaching out last night on the dance floor to touch him, she'd known there'd be a price to pay. Whatever lay ahead in his cottage was her fault.

It was only a mile to the cottage, but Louise drove very fast, nearly colliding with a car that was turning in at the Murphys'. When she pulled into Ned's driveway and slammed on the brakes behind his Buick, everything seemed ridiculously calm. She jumped out and ran across the yard.

"Ned!" She saw him in the dim light, sprawled across the couch, naked, his left arm flopped over the end of the couch. The telephone lay on the floor, the open receiver buzzing. His face, what she could see of it, and his torso and limbs were covered with long red welts. Spots of blood flecked the beige slipcover.

"My God, what happened?" She was on the floor beside the couch, turning his head. "Ned, can you talk?" His eyes opened slowly, closed again.

Louise got to her feet and looked around the room. She grabbed a bottle of brandy and a glass from the bar. Pouring out half a glass, she got down on her knees. "Ned, can you move? We'll have to get you turned around." Setting the glass aside, she grasped him under the arms and began hauling him onto his side, hoping he had no internal injuries. When he was turned far enough, she put the glass to his lips. Most of the brandy stayed in his mouth. She picked up the phone and dialed the Murphys' number.

Bea Murphy answered. "Louise, are you all right? Suzie and Ralph just got here. They said there was an emergency. Can we do anything?"

"Thanks, Bea. Is Tom Benjamin there?"

Hours went by as Louise waited. Tom was on the line, his voice dry and concerned. "Louise, where are you? What's wrong? Are you all right?"

"I'm at Ned's. Can you come right away? Bea can tell you how to get here. Ned's hurt."

"I'll be right there."

Ned was moaning. Louise hurried into the bedroom, plucked the bedspread up, carried it into the living room, and wrapped it around him. He was shaking.

"It's all right," she promised. "Tom Benjamin's coming. Just lie still."

Back to the bedroom to hunt for a blanket. There was one folded on the closet shelf. She took that down and put it over him. Pouring out another half glass of brandy, she lifted his head and began once more helping him drink.

She strained to hear Tom's car. The brandy was having some effect. Ned's eyelids fluttered open and he mumbled several words. The canoe. An accident with the canoe? She heard the VW turn into the yard.

"What's happened?" Tom bounced up the steps, bag in hand.

Louise led him into the living room. "I don't know. Something about the lake. An accident with the canoe, maybe. It's hard to understand him." But she knew. She just didn't know *how* Jack had done it.

The doctor looked up from examining MacRae. "There doesn't seem to be anything serious. Mostly exhaustion and exposure." he told her, "But, Jesus, these welts. What the hell do you make of these? Give me a hand, we'll get him on his feet and into the bedroom."

When they had him in bed, Tom handed her cotton and a bottle. "I want you to swab those scratches. All of them. I'll give him a tetanus shot." He went to fetch his bag. Returning, he told her, "When you're done there, see if you can find a can of broth or something to heat up for him and put some coffee on. Oh, and see if you can find another blanket."

Louise did as she was told, glad to mend some of the damage her husband had done. As she poured hot soup into a mug, Donald came in. "Bea caught me at the theater, working on books. What's going on?"

"I'm not sure. Ned can barely talk. Give me a hand, will you? I'm supposed to get this into him."

While her brother held MacRae, Louise spooned soup into him. "Jesus," Donald said, seeing the welts. "What the hell happened here?"

Later, Donald called his assistant director. They discussed covering for Ned in that night's performance. The house was dark on Monday, and by Tuesday the doctor felt Ned would be back in the show. Donald would step into the role for the one performance since he was familiar with the lines and blocking.

"You go on, Donald," Louise urged. "You have work to do. We'll be all right."

Tom Benjamin stayed for another hour, listening with horrified fascination to bits and pieces of Ned's tale. He dragged a straight-back chair into the tiny bedroom and sat beside the bed, arms crossed, legs propped on the bed. His eyes were screwed up, imagining the scene as it must have unfolded on Pedersen's Bay. When? Around ten-thirty. Until?

Ned had got up about ten, full of energy. Pulling the small canoe out, he decided to row across the bay and back before the brunch. Halfway across, he let the canoe drift, lay back and closed his eyes. It was a warm, still morning with no one around.

Then the canoe capsized and he was clinging to it, fighting off the animal. He didn't know how long he'd struggled or when he'd given up trying to stay with the craft. He swam toward shore, certain he wouldn't make it.

"From about halfway in, I don't remember a thing until Louise started pouring something down my throat." He hesitated. "No, wait, that's not quite true. When I got to the beach, I fell." He was remembering. "He'd have killed me then. I couldn't have stopped him." He shuddered. "But . . .

someone came roaring down the bay with a motorboat... I remember a motorboat. The guy made a couple of turns up and down the bay. The dog wouldn't touch me while the boat was there. It gave me enough time to get off the beach." He looked at Louise. "I was lucky." Another wave of chills gripped him. He closed his eyes and his body shook.

Eventually Tom rose, "Get some rest, MacRae." In the living room he confronted Louise. "Tomorrow check out what he told us. Whose dog is this? Something has to be done about it." He picked up his bag, gave her a peck on the cheek. "I think he'll sleep almost straight through the night. Stop in here after your show and have a look. Call me if you need me." Pushing out through the door, he waved and disappeared up the drive.

When his car was shifting gears along Swan Lake Road, Louise locked the screen door and looked out into the bay, trying to comprehend how the dog had swum so far, tipped the canoe.... She collapsed on the couch, hugging herself, and crying soundlessly. Please, Jack, please don't. I'll be good.

"Peter and Amy are worried about you," she told him, unwrapping thick roast beef sandwiches and setting a plate beside him on the bed. "Start on these. I'll get you something to wash them down."

"There's beer in the bottom of the refrigerator."

"I know." She got up. "I didn't tell them everything." She pulled a bottle of Michelob from the bottom shelf of the refrigerator, removed the cap, and carried it into the bedroom. "Here. I told them you'd be all right. You will be all right, won't you? I mean, other than those damned scratches?"

"I'm all right now. Tired but all right." Half of the first sandwich had disappeared.

"The cast sends love."

"These are good sandwiches. Where'd you get them?"

"The Yacht Club. Art made them himself." She sat on his

side of the bed, nudging him over. "Will you be able to work tomorrow?"

"I think so. Part of the day anyway. I can't take off right now."

She waited quietly while he finished the first sandwich.

"Ned?"

"Mmm?"

"I don't know what to say. 'Sorry' doesn't . . ."

"No, it sure as hell doesn't," he broke in bitterly. "Something has to be done. You know that, don't you?"

"Yes."

"Do you have any ideas?"

No answer.

"Today was just lucky, Louise. I don't want to sound melodramatic, but next time he'll kill me."

"Don't say that!" He won't hurt you, she thought, because I won't sleep with you again.

He set the plate and beer aside. "You're afraid of him, too, aren't you?"

Louise couldn't look at him.

He took her hand. "Last night you said you were afraid of something. Did it have anything to do with the dog?"

There was no way to explain.

"I don't understand you. It sounds like a goddamned French farce, but you've got to chose between me and the dog." He paused. "That *is* what it comes down to, isn't it?"

She shivered. The dog was listening.

"Louise, if I were a stranger, I'd go to the police in a minute to have that dog destroyed. I'm not a stranger. Can't you do it, because you know it's right?"

"I won't let him hurt you again," she said. "I swear."

"That won't do."

"I can't kill him, Ned."

"Wasn't I good enough?" he gibed, dropping her hand. "What does he do that I can't, Louise?"

Chapter 19

Somehow she got home. She woke the next morning, so she must have slept. An endless stretch of day lay before her. She filled it with routine.

Housework all morning. Lunch for the kids. The dog still wasn't back. After lunch Louise and the children drove to town, making brief stops at Dahl's Hardware for a new chain and brighter bulbs for the yard lights, and Royce's Drugstore for a couple of trashy paperbacks and a tube of lipstick.

While the kids waited in the car, Louise went into the Cavern to buy bourbon and gin.

"Louise, you look terrible," Stella Gordon told her. "You've lost weight, haven't you?"

"A little, I guess." Stella and Louise's mother had grown up together in Falls Village. Stella was like an aunt and she spoke with family candor. "What's wrong? Frankly, you looked better at the funeral."

"I think I've lost the weight doing the show at Lac des Cygnes. It's a lot of work."

Stella looked openly skeptical. "Your mother was my best friend. I'll never forget how she died and how senseless it seemed to me, Louise."

Louise rapped her fingertips nervously on the countertop. She wanted to escape this lecture.

Stella continued. "I want to talk to you as a friend. I'm not just an old meddler."

"I know that."

The older woman glanced about to make sure there were no other customers, then leaned over the counter and looked directly into Louise's eyes. "Don't jump into Jack's grave the way your mother did into your father's. That's what it amounted to. Falling down stairs," she said with scorn. "Your mother was a strong, athletic woman. She wasn't someone who fell down stairs—in her own house! She wasn't herself. She couldn't think and she didn't want to live. That's why she fell down those stairs. The last time I saw her before she died was a Sunday at church. She looked like you do—thin and defeated. I asked her to come over that afternoon for a game of bridge and a drink. 'Oh, no, I *couldn't*,' she said as though your dad wouldn't want it. She didn't think she was a person without him. It made me mad, at her and at him, too. She didn't owe your dad her life."

She took a tissue from a box on the counter and blew her nose. Gazing around her she explained, "I'm so glad I had to take over running this place when Sam got cancer. I knew I was *somebody*. I was somebody separate and capable, somebody who could enjoy life by herself if it were necessary. I didn't operate off someone else's electricity."

She bagged the bottles and wrote up a sales slip. "I'll put this on your bill." Then she walked to the door with Louise. "You've got to generate your own power," she said as Louise left.

From the Cavern they drove up the river bluffs to East Park. Amy and Peter piled noisily out of the wagon, legging it to the play equipment.

Louise sat under an old maple tree and opened the trashier looking of the two novels, something about forbidden love in the ruins of a lost Mayan village. At the end of half an hour she hadn't turned the first page. She lay back on the grass, hands clasped behind her head, and surveyed the leafy patterns overhead. Lovely, graceful, betokening rhyme and reason in the universe.

Again she saw Ned's cottage with the blood-flecked slipcovers. Back beyond that, Saturday night, lovemaking in soft light on a rumpled bed, and more lovemaking on the dock in warm, voluptuous darkness. He had watched them and listened to them. She moaned, turning over to bury her face in the fragrant grass. Her cheeks burned with humiliation and anger.

And guilt. As though she'd committed adultery. Not when they'd been making love, but now. With the punishment it had come, making her sick of herself. I might as *well* throw myself in Jack's grave, she thought. It couldn't be any worse than this. To be rid of fear and guilt would be nearly as good as being happy.

The kids bounded back from the play equipment to lie down on the grass beside Louise.

"What time is it, Mommy?"

"About four."

"Can we go pretty soon?"

"What's the rush?"

"We want to practice diving when we get home," Amy told her.

Peter added, "Fido helps us."

Oh, Jesus. "Oh? How does he do that?"

"He watches."

Although she had steeled herself during the drive out from town, the sight of the dog sitting sentinel beside the front door was like a physical blow. Refusing to look at him, she marched stiffly into the cottage telling the children to feed him.

She made a double Manhattan. Her face twisted sardonically. It was still *their* drink. She drank it quickly, then told

the children, "We can't go swimming. I have a headache and
I want to lie down."

"Can't Amy and I go anyway?" Peter wanted to know.

"Of course not. You know better than that. You have to
have a grownup with you."

"But Fido can look out for us."

"For God's sake, it won't hurt you to miss swimming this
once! He's just an animal. He can't look out for you!"

Peter was stunned and angry. "He can, too," he yelled at
her. "Better than you." He turned and stormed out, chanting
"Can too Can too Better than you."

Louise made another drink and carried it upstairs with her.
Kicking off her sandals, she sat, knees pulled up to her chin,
and leaned against the dormer wall. I am going, have gone,
mad. No, not mad. Mad was what dark, dramatic women in
nineteenth century novels were. I'm too Midwestern to be
mad. A little unbalanced? Unbalanced had a nice, passive
sound to it, as though someone had given you a small shove
and you'd simply lost your footing.

She stared at the glass she held. How long could a dog live?
Fifteen years? Fifteen years of—marriage? She gulped the
drink, and nibbled the maraschino cherry, like a child, trying
to make it last. Unbalanced.

Wednesday afternoon Louise was surprised to hear Tom's
VW jolt around the turn and down the drive, screeching to a
halt. She remained on the chaise, embattled. The car door
slammed. Fido's new chain rattled as he got to his feet, but
the doctor ignored him.

"Well, Louise," he said briskly, not waiting for an invitation
to sit.

"Tom."

Pulling his chair next to hers—why did people have to be
close when they were going to be unpleasant?—he removed
the golf cap he wore and wiped his forehead.

"Playing golf on your day off?"

"No. I wear this to keep the sun out of my eyes." He put the cap back on his head. "I had lunch with Ned MacRae."

"Oh?"

"Remember him?"

"Yes, I remember him."

"It was *your* dog that attacked him, wasn't it? And this wasn't the first time."

"Did he tell you that?"

"Sure he did. I cross-examined him pretty damned thoroughly. Is it true?"

"The other time the dog only *tried*. It didn't actually touch him."

"Christ, Louise. That dog should be destroyed."

"I can't."

"Why?" He was angry with her. "Because Jack gave him to you?"

"No." But wouldn't that be easier? "Yes. Because Jack gave him to me."

"You know," he began, "Saturday night I got the impression you were . . . interested in MacRae."

"All right."

"But not as interested as you are in the *dog*?" He waited for an answer he didn't get. "Is this some devious way of unloading MacRae?"

Louise wanted to scream. She looked away.

"Louise, I feel sorry for you. You took Jack's death harder than you think." He put a hand on her knee. "You going to punish all men because one of them up and died on you?"

Dashing from the theater that night, Louise hustled Amy and Peter into the station wagon.

"Why are we in such a hurry, Mommy?"

"I'm tired. I want to get home to bed."

But, once in bed, sleep was always five minutes away. She

lay listening to the empty house. Donald had a date. Betsy was with Frank. She didn't feel like reading.

Slipping downstairs, she poured brandy in a glass and threw in an ice cube. Then she wandered to the back door to check on the dog. More and more she found herself "checking" him, assuring herself he was securely chained. Tonight she sat down on the steps, drank the brandy, and conferred.

"What is going to happen?" It would be easier if she could hate the animal. He probably deserved to be hated. But she pitied him, and she remembered what life had once been like.

Fido stood up, walked, stretching the chain out, to where she sat. The chain clinked as he moved. A prison sound. He rested his head on her knees.

"Fido. 'I am faithful'."

He whined softly.

"I don't see a way out." She stroked his head with her free hand.

He licked her knees, rearranged his head on them.

"Pretty boy," she crooned. "You ask too much." She rose and went into the cottage, took the glass to the kitchen, rinsed it and set it on the drain.

Below the stairs was a closet. On the top shelf, in a case, was a .22-caliber pistol. Louise got a chair and, climbing onto it, reached the case and, beside it, a box of bullets.

Carrying it into the living room, she removed the gun from the case and checked its condition. Opening the box of bullets, she loaded it.

For fifteen minutes she sat, the gun lying on the sofa beside her. Killing him this way was the only solution. He couldn't be happy surely. He couldn't want to go on for years, both of them prisoners. Finally, she rose, carrying the weapon with her as she went to the back door.

Again he got to his feet and walked to the steps. She could see his face in the spilled light from inside the cottage. She pushed the door open and went out.

She couldn't speak. She raised the gun and sighted along the barrel. He was motionless as a marble dog, but in his eyes was accusation. The look told her he wanted to live. She remained for a moment, lowered the gun, opened the screen and went back into the cottage.

Unloading the pistol, Louise put it in the case, and the bullets in their box. Taking them with her, she went slowly up the stairs. She opened the drawer of her bedside table and laid the empty gun and the box of ammunition beside a gold chain—the sort a woman would wear around her neck—from which hung a gold padlock and a gold key.

An awful peace went with knowing she wouldn't shoot him. Undressing, she crawled into bed, and fell into a dreamless sleep.

In the deep end of the night, Louise stirred. Something had brushed along her thigh. Not enough to waken her, the touch was woven into sleep, becoming a snatch of erotic dream. Her back arched.

"Ned." Speaking aloud, she woke herself. And then she screamed.

The dog was on the bed. A light came on. Betsy was standing by her. She herself was standing though she couldn't remember getting out of bed.

"Get him out of here!" she screamed. "Get him out!"

Donald took the stairs three at a time. "What's the matter? Lou, what's the matter?"

"Get him out of here! What's he doing here?"

"I don't know," he told her quietly, alarmed. Taking the dog by the collar, he spoke to her soothingly. "Maybe one of the kids let him off the chain."

"No one let him off the chain," Louise sobbed. She hadn't let him off, had she? No, she would remember. She sat on the edge of the bed. Oh, Jack, I never would have done this to you.

Chapter 20

She had only a half-slice of toast at breakfast and a cup of coffee. Afterward she vomited. She spent most of the morning in the bathroom.

Donald stayed to look after Amy and Peter. They were with him at the Dockers' while he called to arrange for Louise's lines to be taken by another actress. Fortunately, she had only half a dozen.

Returning, he told Louise, "Suzie wants to keep the kids this afternoon. I said fine. She said something about teaching them five-card stud. Okay with you?"

"Perfect." She sat on the couch, feeling limp and clammy. "Donald?"

"Yes?"

"Did I wake them up last night?"

"Ralph and Suzie?"

"Yes." She waited. "Tell me."

"Suzie didn't say so. I told her you had a helluva nightmare and were coming down with the flu. That was all that was said. By the way, Marie Oster's taking your lines. See you at dinner."

When at last Donald and the kids left for the afternoon,

Louise sighed, "Oh, God," and made her way to the bathroom. She ran the tub full of hot water. It was indecent enough being sick, it was degrading to be sick under everyone's watchful eye.

A couple of hours of sitting on the cold edge of a tub, leaning over the cold edge of a toilet was enough to send you pretty far down the road to lunacy. When I'm completely down the road, she thought, the world will be a small, white, windowless, doorless ceramic room, marked "vitreous."

The others left for the theater at seven-thirty, Betsy first checking the dog's chain as Louise requested. They were all very solicitous and Louise could hardly wait for them to go. She lay on the couch, screwing her eyes to the pages of forbidden love. Occasionally she dozed, waking fretfully, afraid she might find the dog beside her.

At nine-thirty, setting the book on the coffee table, she got up, locked the screen doors, and closed the inside doors. There. Unless some harpy flies down the chimney, you're temporarily safe, she assured herself. She sat down on the couch and murmured soothing words of encouragement. Then, laying her head on the arm of the couch, she fell asleep.

When Louise woke, it was to a loud pounding. She started up, heart racing. The dog, what was he doing? Sheepishly recalling the locked screen doors, she stumbled into her slippers and scurried to the front door. Donald and Betsy were home. And the kids. "I'm sorry. I fell asleep. How long have you been pounding?"

"Only a minute. We were afraid you might be in the bathroom, sick."

"No. I feel better." She pulled her robe more securely around her, noticing for the first time that Ned was with them, hesitant, hanging back.

When the others had gone to bed, he sat down opposite her. "Louise, do you mind if I stick around for a few minutes?"

"For a few minutes."

"It beats catching smallpox?" he asked, grinning.

She wanted to reach for him. Sex was only part of it. Fear for him, and other emotions not easily labeled, were confounding her.

"I don't know where to begin," he said. "Are you okay? You look terrible."

"That's always a good place to begin."

"Betsy told me about last night. About the nightmare and the dog."

"I don't want to talk about the dog," she told him firmly. She was trying to find a sticking place for her courage. "You can't come here any more. If you do, it'll all start again. It's too difficult for me to control him. I'll do anything to keep him from hurting you."

"Except kill him."

"Right."

"He's destroying you."

"He doesn't mean to."

"Some consolation." He was on his feet, full of frustration. "Tom Benjamin called me after he was here yesterday."

"And?"

"He's worried about your . . . mental state."

"What do *you* think of my mental state?"

He sat down. "I don't think you're crazy. I think you soon *will* be if you let that dog get control of your life."

"He already has control of it."

He came around the table and sat beside her. "I do think there's a solution to this. There has to be."

She put her head back and closed her eyes. Where was her resolve? She had been determined to keep him away. Without opening her eyes, she asked, "This isn't just a ploy?"

"It's no ploy."

"Could we talk someplace else?" The idea that she could get away from the dog seemed to her a small but necessary delusion.

"I'll take you to my place."

"You don't think I'm crazy?"

"No."

"You're not just saying that to humor me?"

He laughed and it was the best thing Louise had heard in days. So sane.

When she'd changed into jeans and a shirt, they drove to Ned's. Louise stopped inside the door. The previous Sunday came back, Ned sprawled on the couch, blood-spattered. She was insane to come back. She was putting him in jeopardy again.

"It's okay. I took the slipcovers to the dry cleaners," he said, misreading her lagging in the doorway. He led her to the couch. "You're shivering."

"I'm all right." She sat down with her feet under her. Immediately she was up again, closing the front door securely, shutting the windows, and pulling the shades.

"Cold?"

"Partly. Partly paranoid," she said, sitting down once more.

"I think I know why you won't kill the dog," he announced without preamble.

She started to rise.

"Don't worry. I'm not going to get into it. I *should.* I may be making a mistake by not getting it all in the open. But I don't want you to run away."

Louise relaxed a degree.

"Once I had figured out some of your feelings," he continued, "it was even more important to find a solution."

"I've been over it a hundred times," she said wearily. "I even thought of keeping him out at the kennel. But penning him up isn't enough. He's too clever. At least where he is, I can watch him. There's no solution," she finished lamely.

He brushed her cheek with the back of his hand. "There's a possibility. What if you took him away?"

"Away?"

"Do you have anyone—friends, relatives—who might like to have the dog? Remember, it's only me he's taken a dislike to." He waited a moment, then continued. "You mentioned cousins in Red Wing, for instance."

She shook her head. "They're out. They live in a little apartment."

"Well, there may be someone else. A place where he wouldn't be likely to find his way back."

Louise sat silent, examining the idea for flaws. Would he go? If he thought it was that or death? Was there anybody who would take him? If he were with a relative, at least she would always know where he was. Paul and Barbara, maybe?

"I don't know," she said.

"Isn't it worth a try?"

"I don't want to get my hopes up. If it didn't work, I don't know what I'd do."

"Don't hope if you don't want to, but think about it."

"You're very different."

"Different from what? From Jack?"

"Don't."

"Louise, I'm not going to tell you to forget someone you loved and lived with for years, but let him rest."

"I wish he would."

He put a hand on one of hers. "You're still cold. I'll build a fire."

She watched him work. The fire crackled, flared and caught hold, its light outlining his face. Louise thought she saw character there, but was she sane enough to judge? Maybe she credited him with qualities he didn't possess, because he was her ally. She caught herself up. That was the kind of unsureness Jack would like her to feel. She understood MacRae better than that.

He'd given her the key to his cottage, saying, "Use the phone here to find a place for the dog. And don't stop until you've got something."

Amy and Peter put out fresh food and water for the dog, rolled up their swimming gear and helped Louise pack dinner ingredients into the wagon.

While they changed into swimsuits, Louise began making calls. Later Peter found her working in the kitchen. Leaning against a cupboard, he smiled at her cunningly. "Isn't it awful hot to do so much work?" he wheedled. "Come swimming."

"Give me half an hour and I'll be out."

"All right, but I'm going to tell Amy. She can tell time, you know." He gave her a wave and skipped out.

Not for the first time, it struck Louise how much Amy and Peter reflected her state of mind. It was a strong argument for sending the dog away. What good was she to the kids, half-crazy?

She ran the vacuum and picked up. That was enough. She didn't want him to think she was getting in practice for something. And, as Peter pointed out, it was a hot day.

Ned's canoe was beached on the grass. How had he recovered it? No. No more about Sunday. It was almost over. Still, standing ankle-deep in scruffy, unmowed grass, the hot July sun warming her, she was shot through, for the briefest moment, by a subterranean chill. Someone padding softly over her grave?

She had a pitcher of cocktails ready when Ned, briefcase in hand, opened the squeaky screen door at quarter to six.

"I think I'm in the wrong place. Can I stay?"

Louise took the briefcase, putting it down on a chair, helped him off with his tie and out of his jacket; then poured two martinis, handing one to him.

He raised his glass. "Here's to neatness," he said looking around. "It *does* count."

"Come in the kitchen while I put the steaks on." She turned and led the way.

"All this and steaks, too? You'll spoil me."

"Would that be so bad?"

"Where are the kids?" he asked, setting their drinks on the cupboard and pulling her gently to him.

"Out gathering wildflowers, if they can find any."

"And we're in here gathering rosebuds while we may." He cupped her buttocks in his hands, holding her tightly against him.

She gave him a long, teasing kiss and enjoyed feeling him grow hard against her. "As many rosebuds as you can gather in five minutes. That's how long it'll be before they're back."

He groaned and released her. "How about the calls? How did they go?"

She laid the steaks on the broiler pan and slid it under the flame. "We have a place."

"You're kidding. Why didn't you call me?"

"I wanted to surprise you."

"Where?"

"A farm outside of Worthington."

"That's about a hundred miles, isn't it? Christ, we really have something to celebrate now." He handed her glass to her and raised his own. "To rosebuds."

Louise suggested that it would be wiser if Ned didn't see her and the kids home after the performance.

"It's only for a few days," she said, not sure that could be true, "and then it won't matter. He'll be gone."

Standing in the busy hallway between the men's and women's dressing rooms, cast members milling around them, they argued briefly.

"Please?"

"You're the one who said he was going to kill you," she reminded him, keeping her voice low.

"I know, I know, but I can't stand being dictated to by the bastard, having to slink off, scared and beaten."

"You only want to come to prove that you can," Louise told him with asperity. "It's sick. Are all you men the same?"

He leaned close. "No."

"It's sick," she repeated. "It's macho nonsense. I hoped you were different."

"I want to be with you and the kids tonight. Let me be your protector," he said, smiling boyishly.

"Oh, Christ, why can't *I* be the protector? My way is simpler and surer: you stay away until he's gone. It's not me he's going to hurt."

"What about the other night when you woke up screaming?"

"That was . . . a nightmare."

"I want to be there tonight," he declared flatly.

"Oh, God, you're just like *him*. It's all a great competition, isn't it?" She closed her eyes. She wanted to weep but instead bit her lip. She was betrayed.

When the children were in bed, no longer present to fill in the gaps in conversation, MacRae and Louise were tense and unsure as they lay on the raft. She was angry. Her independence had been fragile. Here she was, being bullied again.

"Louise?"

"Yes?"

"I'm not like Jack."

She didn't answer.

"I don't want to defeat that poor dumb beast just to prove I can." He paused to find words. "But I don't want him deciding what we can and can't do. If you don't want to be with me because you're sick of me, that's one thing. I won't strong-arm you. But if you don't want to be with me because you're afraid, that's wrong."

Maybe he was right. She was confused about many things. She didn't want to destroy what was good between them. He'd tried to see things from her side. That had touched her. It was something Jack would not have done.

"When will you take the dog?" he asked.

"Next Monday when we don't have a show. In case I can't get back early."

"I wish I could go with you."

"No. It's important that I do it alone."

He turned to look at her in the darkness. "I'm surprised your kids don't resent me, or that they don't show it."

"Why?"

"They're bound to resent the first man after Jack, don't you think?"

"They're very loyal to Jack, but they like men." She sat up. "Jack was domineering. He seemed very strong. They look to men for strength. Men make them feel—safe." She thought for a moment. "I resent that lately. *I* want to make them feel safe."

Talking about Jack was difficult. From feelings of grief and longing to lurking fear was a sickening trip. The marriage had been her life's work. She couldn't bear to think of it now.

She shivered and turned to MacRae. Bending over him, she let her hair fall forward and brush his belly. He wriggled, laughing, and grabbed her.

His laughter skipped over the calm water, tumbled against the pebbles along the shore and floated on the night to the dog, who lay listening.

Chapter 21

While Betsy poked among soiled tissues and boxes of makeup, hunting a folder of advertising copy she'd left in the women's dressing room, Louise raised the brittle, cracked window shade to provide daylight for the search.

The channel was dotted with the boats of Sunday morning fishers, seeking relaxation more than fish. They were hearty and gay, waving and calling to each other.

Behind Louise, Betsy mumbled, "It has to be here," as she pulled open dressing table drawers.

Louise had tagged along when Betsy'd taken off in the Triumph to retrieve the folder. They saw so little of each other lately.

"Ah. Success," Betsy rejoiced, holding up the folder.

She crossed the room and stood beside Louise, gazing out at the boats. "A gorgeous day," she commented. "I wish I didn't have to work on these." She slapped the file of ad copy against her thigh.

"It's beautiful." Louise turned from the window. "I should check my costume while I'm here. I think I spilled coffee on it last night." She rummaged amongst a rack of costumes until she found her own gingham gown.

"Can you come into town tomorrow and have lunch?

They've got a new salad bar at the River House."

"I wish I could," Louise told her, holding the dress up to the light. "I'm taking Fido to Worthington tomorrow."

"What for?"

"I'm giving him to a cousin and his family. They live on a farm."

"Because of last Sunday?"

"Mainly that. Isn't that enough?"

"I guess. What do the kids think?"

"They don't know."

"You're going to tell them?" Betsy asked, reaching in her bag for cigarettes.

"Mmmm."

Betsy lit a cigarette, inhaled deeply and threw the match in an ashtray on the dressing table behind her. "That's going to be hard. They're crazy about him."

"Yes." Louise pulled the ironing board out into the room and turned on the steam iron.

"I don't understand what it is with Ned and the dog," Betsy said. "That dog is an angel with everyone else. Does Ned provoke him?"

"Of course not. I don't know what it is." She removed the costume from its hanger; she'd found no stain. "I can't have a dog around that attacks people. Whether it's Ned or somebody else. You don't think I should keep him, do you?"

"I guess not. It's just that it seems a shame. He's only that way with Ned." There was a barely noticeable frown between her eyes. She spoke casually. "Do you think you'll be seeing a lot of Ned after the show closes?"

Louise tried to read her. "I don't understand. Don't you like Ned? I thought you liked him. Do you think I should stop seeing him on account of the dog?" Louise was mystified.

"I like him well enough. He's fun to be around."

"But?" She yanked the dress roughly over the end of the ironing board.

"He doesn't seem like your type."

Louise felt as though she were standing on a sandbar that was shifting out from under her. She had counted on Betsy to understand.

Betsy went on, "He's somebody I might have fallen for a couple of months ago. Do you know what I mean? I'd like to see you with somebody . . . better, is all I'm saying. I want the best for you."

She gestured with the hand that held the cigarette and the smoke from it rose in confusing little eddies. Louise watched it, fascinated, feeling suddenly nauseated. The smells of makeup and cold cream, usually pleasant, were cloying.

"Please don't be angry," Betsy said.

Louise couldn't be angry. She would like to believe Betsy said these things out of jealousy but she knew that wasn't true. She said them because she loved Louise, wanted to help her, didn't want her to make a mistake.

"I'm not saying he's a monster," Betsy continued. "When his marriage broke up, he decided to do a Don Juan number, and it stuck. It's a little sad, really. I don't hold it against him." She sat down on a rickety wooden kitchen chair and blew smoke at the ceiling. "I shouldn't have said anything. I'm sorry."

"Don't be sorry." But she felt sick and alone. "Don't worry about me. If one of us is using the other, it's more likely me than MacRae."

"I hope so." Betsy regarded Louise intently. "The last couple of weeks have been hard, haven't they? Why is that, do you know?"

Louise shook her head. "Damn. I've scorched this." She wasn't going to get into *that* with Betsy. If her friend thought her judgment shaky with regard to Ned, what would she think if Louise laid out her feelings about the dog? The easy confidence they'd always had would have to remain out of joint for a while.

"And how are things in *your* life?" she asked, returning the gown to the hanger and turning off the iron.

"Well," Betsy grabbed the ashtray from the table and set it on her knee. "You'd think I was in the porno prayer book business the way tongues are wagging here in Carson's Corners."

"Oh, come on."

"Cross my heart." She picked her cigarette up and inhaled, gulping smoke into her lungs. "You're looking at the Mary Magdalen of Middle America."

Louise laughed. "Are you sure?"

"Sure as hell." The tone of her voice had changed.

Louise saw that she was genuinely upset. Returning the costume to the rack, she drew up a chair near the other woman. "Hey, kid, these things work out. They'll get used to you and Frank. What does he say about the situation?"

"He says he doesn't give a damn. He's been thinking of getting out of the sin business since Nell killed herself. He *says*. I don't know."

"I wouldn't be surprised if that were true," Louise said.

Betsy ground out the cigarette and set the ashtry aside. Getting to her feet, she moved restlessly to the window and stood, back to Louise, staring at the lake. After a minute she asked, "Why did Nell kill herself? Do you know?"

"I'm not sure."

"She left a note. What did it say?"

"If I remember correctly, it was ambiguous. She said she was sorry for what she'd done, but it was difficult to know whether she meant she was sorry for something she'd done before the suicide—something that had prompted it—or if she was sorry about the suicide itself."

"I hardly knew her at all. That's odd when you think about it." Betsy spoke quietly. "We were both friends of yours. Why didn't I know her better?"

"Well, you'd only been here, what, two years when she died? The last year or so of her life she kind of withdrew. I hardly ever saw her myself unless I made a point of going over to the house. I think she was always unstable but she seemed to get unhappier each year. She hated Frank's work and the work she had to do with the women in the congregation. She was certain none of the women liked her."

"Did they like her?" Betsy was doubtless thinking of her own problems.

"Some did, some didn't. The ones who didn't never discussed it with me because Nell was my friend. I've heard there was gossip the last year before the suicide."

Betsy turned from the window. "What kind of gossip?"

"Some of the women thought Nell was having an affair."

"What do you think?" Betsy's eyes narrowed.

"I haven't a clue. Somehow it didn't strike me as impossible but she surely didn't confide in me. As I say, the last year she almost avoided me. Maybe she was afraid I'd ask her about it. I don't know."

"She was beautiful."

"Yes. Frank was crazy about her. But she just wasn't strong."

Betsy seemed to shrug off a nettling thought. She crossed to the table where the file of ad copy lay. Her voice was calm. "I'll tell you the truth, Louise, I wouldn't marry a minister."

"Have you told Frank?"

"No. I don't want to influence him that way. If he leaves, it's got to be for reasons that have nothing to do with me."

"I understand." She hesitated. "If Frank doesn't leave, then what?"

"I think it'd be easier if I pulled up stakes."

"You're kidding! You have a home here. A business. You can't do that. It's insane."

"I'll see. I have to play it by ear." She gathered up her things. "Ready?"

"Can we stop at the Yacht Club? I have to talk to Art Christopher. I'll only be a minute."

"Can we walk as far as the bridge?" Amy asked.

"If we don't get too hot and tired," Louise told her, pushing a stray strand of curl back from Amy's forehead.

Betsy was occupied with her ads. Donald was water skiing with the Dockers. A Sunday afternoon walk down Swan Lake Road appealed to Louise. Amy and Peter were enthusiastic.

As they set out, Peter begged, "Mommy, let's take Fido. He hasn't been for a walk in a long time."

Louise hadn't wanted him along. She'd been going to tell the kids about the trip to Worthington. That could wait, she supposed. It was true they hadn't walked the dog for some time.

"Get his leash, Peter."

The sun was hot, the road dusty, and they sang kindergarten songs as they meandered, dragging their heels to keep the dog from setting the pace. He'd have pulled them willy-nilly at a run. Snooping into roadside vegetation, poking his nose down gopher holes, flushing startled pheasants from their nests, he was the innocent pup, guileless and beautiful, trotting in the sun, catching every scent in the still afternoon air.

To Louise, it seemed that he was saying, "See how it could be? The four of us, happy together, like old times." A last effort to make her change her plans.

They reached the bridge, panting and laughing. Louise tied the dog to a piling. They lay down to rest in the tall yellow grass. Amy lay on her stomach near Louise, pulling little blades of grass and eating the sweet, white roots.

"Mommy?"

"Yes?"

"Can Daddy see us?"

It was a natural question.

"Mommy, can he?"

"I don't know. Maybe." Louise took a deep breath. "We don't know what it's like after we die. Maybe he can see us. Would you like him to?"

"I think so."

"I'd like to see *him*," Peter said.

Amy continued with her train of thought. "Maybe heaven is too far away for Daddy to see us. Maybe he left Fido to watch us."

"Maybe. It's hard to know, isn't it? But I doubt he gave us the dog for that reason. I think he just wanted another friendly face around the house." Wasn't this the time to tell them she was taking the dog away? She glanced at him, lying in the shade of the bridge, his glorious head held high. He looked like a redheaded sovereign.

"Mommy?" Amy again.

"Yes?"

"Are you lonesome for Daddy?"

"I have been very lonesome."

Peter held her hand. "Me, too."

"Is that why you like to be with Mr. MacRae?" Amy asked. "Because you're lonesome for Daddy?"

"That's part of it, I'm sure."

On the return home, the dog was tractable, calm. Louise held the leash but he didn't stray from her side. Did he finally understand, perhaps?

"Fasten your seat belt, lady." Ned put his head into the car to make certain it was fastened. "I'll see you in ten minutes. Make us a drink and see if there's cheese or something in the refrigerator."

"Ten minutes?"

Emerging from the theater Sunday night, they found her yellow wagon standing forlornly lopsided, its left front tire flat. She was going to leave it there but remembered immediately that she'd need it in the morning for the trip to Worthington.

"I'll change it now," Ned told her. "It'll only take a few minutes. You take the Buick and go ahead."

"I don't want to leave you here alone."

"I'm a big boy."

She drove the Buick out of the lot and turned it down Swan Lake Road in the direction of Ned's cottage. Amy and Peter had left with Betsy who was doing Sunday night baby-sitting for Louise. "Frank's got church something-or-others staying the night so he has to go right home."

Louise realized she was driving with high beams, unnecessary and dangerous on a narrow, twisting road. She pulled the lever on the steering column. It didn't seem to work quite the same as her own. Rounding the slight curve after Arthur Mack State Park and heading toward the wooden bridge, Louise was still fumbling with it. This is stupid, she told herself, I know it has to go one way or the other. For a second she looked away from the road, searching for the arrows on the lever.

In that moment she was conscious of a form leaping up from the undergrowth beside the bridge, onto the road. Without time to consider, she hit the brakes and pulled the wheel sharply to the left to avoid the dog.

This was how Jack had died. Loose gravel spun away from under the wheels. Louise was certain the car would hit the bridge. She heard a scream and recognized it for her own.

When the world settled into the proper angle on its axis, the car remained tipsy. Spinning around a hundred and eighty degrees, it rested with back wheels slipped down off the road, headlights beamed into the treetops on the opposite side of the road. Louise pulled the hand brake. Shaking, she gripped the wheel for support.

Murder. That's what it would have been. First, last Sunday's attempt and now this. It was Ned who would ordinarily be driving the Buick, who drove too fast and wouldn't be slowed down groping with a low-beam lever when he came upon the bridge. This was a last-ditch effort to hang onto her. Seized by fury, she groaned and pounded the wheel with her fists.

By the time she heard Ned approach in her car, Louise had herself under control, a plausible explanation prepared. She simply told everything as it happened except that the dog was now a young deer.

"I'll look for something to put under the back wheels," he said when he'd examined the situation. "I think I can drive it out." Leading her by the arm to her car, he opened the door and helped her in. "Wait here."

After five minutes she heard the engine of the Buick roar and saw the car pull itself from the sharply sloping shoulder onto the road. Ned turned it around and parked behind her. Leaving the lights on and the engine running, he got out and walked to where she sat.

"How are you feeling?"

"I'm okay."

"Can you drive?"

"Of course."

"I'll lead the way in the Buick."

"What time will you be back tomorrow?" he asked, searching the refrigerator for cheese.

"By dinner, I hope. I'm not going to stick around there very long." She reached for a box of crackers from the cupboard.

"Come here with the kids when you get back," he suggested, unwrapping a package of Brie. "What did you tell them?"

"Nothing." She gave him a look that implored understanding. "The moment never came. I'll tell them in the morning. That's awful, isn't it?"

"Yes. Quite a scene to cope with before you start." He carried the cheese and a knife into the living room.

Louise followed. "You realize they're going to blame *you*."

"I've thought of that."

"Still sure you want me to bring them here when we get back?"

"The sooner we all confront each other, the better."

"It's such a mess," she lamented. She accepted a glass of wine, but set it aside. Getting to her feet she moved to the door and looked through the screen into the darkness. The kids had probably let the dog out for a run before bed. He'd slipped away from them. What if he stayed away now? What if he wasn't there in the morning? She clenched her fists. I wish I'd hit him.

She moved to the window. Tomorrow night would it all be over? Behind her MacRae was spreading Brie on crackers and humming a melody from the show.

"Hungry?" he asked.

"No. Thank you." She said nothing for several minutes. Then, without turning, she said, "MacRae, I want your help."

"What kind of help?"

"I want to invest some money."

"In . . .?"

"The Yacht Club."

"What the hell is this about?"

She turned. "Bill Hermann wants to sell. I want to buy it."

"You don't know the first damned thing about running a place like that."

"Art Christopher will manage it. He'd like to go into partnership eventually."

"What if something happened to Christopher or he got a better offer? What if you were stuck with it alone? You haven't thought this through."

"I have." She returned to the sofa. "I'm going to start learning the business as soon as the kids are back in school. Art says he doesn't really need me to help run it. He's always run it without Bill, but I want to learn, and it's okay with him."

"What's the reason for this? Why would you want to own a run-down roadhouse?"

Louise picked up the wineglass, but she wasn't thirsty. "I grew up with the Yacht Club. I have a personal feeling about it and I want to have a hand in it. I know it's a dump, the paint's always peeling and the neon sign never works. But the food is good and the drinks aren't watered." She added, "I don't want it to change."

"You've been through a lot of upheaval and change recently," he pointed out. "It looks like you're trying to keep another element of life from getting away." He studied her. "You can't keep things from changing. People die, kids grow up, buildings get torn down."

"Oh, Christ, I understand that. But I need to be a part of the machinery of things. I've been an ornament too long. I want to get started. This is the thing I want to do and if you won't help me, I'll get someone who will," she declared, feeling none of the certainty the words implied.

He asked, "Aren't you scared? It's a damned big undertaking."

"Of course I'm scared," she told him. "But if I wait for something that doesn't scare me, I'll never do anything. I'm more scared of *not* doing it. Don't talk me out of it," she said quietly. "You could. But don't." Her voice was thick. "I want to grow up."

He sat for some time, silently considering. "If the dog were going to be here, would you be able to do this?"

"No."

He frowned.

"But he's not going to be here. That makes all the difference, don't you think?" She waited for his answer. "Ned? Please don't depress me. Don't scare me. I need this."

It had been his idea to send the dog away. But she could see that as time drew close, he was edgy. He didn't want to talk too much about after the dog was gone because—what if nothing really changed?

She sipped the wine. She'd thought this hour would be a celebration. Instead, the celebration was held in abeyance and unspoken worries made the wine bitter.

She set the glass on the table. "When the dog is gone, you'll see. I'll be strong. I promise."

Chapter 22

Waking at six, Louise dashed downstairs and out to the back porch, pulling her slippers on as she went.

He was there. Lying beside the steps, he raised his head and regarded her with sad eyes.

She opened the door and he came up the steps and into the cottage, resigned, incurious. Following at her heels, he padded slowly into the living room and lay down to wait.

By seven Louise was dressed and ready. He hadn't moved. He seemed drugged by defeat. She led him to the rocker and sat down to brush his coat. He stood, impassive, allowing himself to be groomed, not caring. She had never seen him like this and she was oddly distressed. She had prepared herself for any number of scenes, but not this.

"It will be all right. You'll see." She ran the brush along his flanks. "If you stayed here, I'd have to kill you."

When she finished, he shone, clean and coppery. She surveyed him. Big, strong and elegant. She was on her knees, burying her face in his fur, kissing him and weeping. He licked her tears and nuzzled her neck.

"It's getting late," she told him. She began loading the car:

leash, bowls, dog food and brush. They all fit in a cardboard carton and seemed a meager collection. She wished there were something she could send along that would signify—what? That he was not Rufus, King, Red or any of those.

She returned to the cottage, made coffee and set the table for Peter and Amy. After pouring juice, Louise called them in, inquiring what kind of cereal they wanted.

"When you're through," she told them, "I'd like you to dress quickly. We're going on a trip and we have to get started."

"Where are we going?" Peter asked eagerly.

"We're driving to Worthington." She got out cereal. "You remember our cousins, Barbara and Paul? They have a farm near Worthington."

Amy and Peter looked doubtful.

"You haven't seen them since the family picnic at Aunt Gert's."

They vaguely recalled the picnic. Everyone played horse-shoes and softball.

"Barbara and Paul have three boys," Louise continued. Some leading up was called for. "You might remember the boys. Eric and Paul, Jr. and, let's see, Ernie, yes, Ernie, that's the other boy's name."

They had so many cousins, they weren't sure. "Why are we going to see them?"

Louise didn't answer at once. She put away the milk carton and cereal boxes. Pouring a cup of coffee, she returned to the table and sat down.

"We've had trouble with the dog. You know how strange he behaves sometimes and how he's always running away."

They said nothing.

"You do know. I've been worried, not so much about the running away but about times when he's been bad."

They listened warily.

"He's done things I haven't told you. They were things people don't like."

"Like who?" Amy pressed.

"Well, like Ned and Dr. Benjamin, for instance."

"What did he do?" the child challenged.

"You know the party we had opening night? After you were asleep, he tried to attack Ned."

"He didn't either," Peter denied.

"But he did," Louise assured him. "And the day of the Murphys' party, he hurt Ned. We had to call Dr. Benjamin."

That held them for a minute. Calling the doctor was serious.

Finally Amy overcame this. "I don't believe it. He's a good dog." Her eyes shone with anger.

"No one would make up something like that."

"He's a good dog. You know that. They don't know him!" Her face trembled and broke, tears pouring down. "*You* know him, Mommy!"

"Stupid Ned!" Peter shouted. "I hate him!"

Louise couldn't stop now. "We can't keep Fido. It isn't safe and somebody would eventually report him to the police."

"What do you mean we can't keep him?" Amy sobbed. "You're not going to give him away, Mommy!" She was out of her chair and around the table.

"We have to," Louise told her gently, reaching for the child's hand.

"No!" Amy screamed, pulling her hand away and running out of the room, out of the cottage, Peter behind her, stomping his feet and crying.

Louise sat very still. What was she doing? Tearing the kids apart so she could sleep with MacRae? No, that wasn't true. That's what Jack would like her to think.

Amy and Peter would accept no comfort from her. They refused at first to get in the car. Louise loaded the dog and his chain in the back and slammed the hatch.

"If you don't come, I'll ask Suzie if you can stay with her."

They were sitting side by side on the dock. Seeing that she

meant to go, they began to fidget, looking for a way out of their unhappy corner.

"I don't want to stay with Suzie," Peter protested. "I don't want to stay with Suzie and I don't want you to take Fido."

"There's no choice about the dog. He has to go. You two can stay or go, as you please. I'm going to get my handbag," she told them, starting up the path. "When I come back, you tell me what you've decided."

Louise put on fresh lipstick, turned off the light in the kitchen and picked up her bag from the coffee table. Leaving the cottage, she saw that Amy and Peter were no longer sitting on the dock but had climbed into the backseat of the car where they sat, one on either side of the dog.

The day was warm, the sky clear as they pulled out of the drive at nine-fifteen. Louise turned on the car radio to a local station. The kids were not in the mood for conversation. The music would fill the silence and rob it of its use as a weapon.

She glanced at the dog in the rearview mirror. The ceremony said, "till *death* do us part."

They'd exchanged gifts on their wedding night. Louise gave Jack an expensive watch, engraved "My time is your time." If he were any other man, she would never have chosen such a corny phrase. But Jack soaked up sentiment like a blotter, the more outrageous, the better. He'd always make a face as though he were embarrassed and say, "For God's sake, Louise, how could you?" But he had difficulty hiding his pleasure.

He put the watch on immediately and reached under his pillow for a small box he had hidden there. In it was a gold padlock hanging from a gold chain. He put it around her neck and fastened the clasp. The padlock, too, was engraved with a single word: "Forever."

At once he began making love to her as though the love-making were the seal to the compact. "You notice, Louise," he murmured against her throat, "*I* have kept the key."

And so he had, as she later discovered. It was on the same ring as the keys to the kennel, the house and the car.

Outside the town of Windom they pulled into a truck stop, walked the dog, and had doughnuts and milk. As they ate and drank, Amy and Peter spoke little and then only to each other. Back in the car, Louise tuned the radio to WCCO in Minneapolis.

Jack's emotional problems were never discussed, except obliquely, during their marriage. That life was one long overcompensation for his beginnings was obvious even to him and occasionally he would refer to this. But he and Louise never explored his insecurities with the purpose of overcoming them. He didn't want to.

When they had moved Jack's things to Louise's that New Year's Day, he had said, "From now on, I don't want to talk about the orphanage or anything that happened before I came to this house. My life started here." How short his life had been.

So Jack had adopted her family. He kept in touch with far-flung relatives whom she might have allowed to escape. He took her background for his own and in doing so, locked Louise into it. She would, by God, continue the traditions, life-style, and aspirations of her family. He became more a Coleman than either she or Donald. The vulnerability behind all this was wrenching to Louise.

Jack demanded absolute fidelity from Louise. She could not flirt, no matter how innocently, with another man. They'd had fights coming home from parties about that. And, as he had made clear, if Louise ever had a lover, he would kill him. And now she had a lover.

What if I came back to the cottage tonight and discovered Jack sitting on the dock drinking beer and waiting for me? What if the past weeks had been a fevered dream in an afternoon nap?

"Jack?" It would be hot and she would be barefoot.

He would look up. "How was the nap?"

"Weird. Awful dreams."

"Want to talk about it?"

"Not really. They're starting to go away. I'd just as soon forget them."

But he would want to know. "Was I in them?"

"Not too much."

"Oh." He wasn't sure if that pleased him or not. "Were they frightening?"

"Yes. Really, Jack, I don't want to remember."

"If I was in them and if they were frightening, why didn't I help you?"

She would sit near him, her feet playing in the water. "It was just a situation where you couldn't."

"But it's my job to look after you, to keep bad things from happening to you."

"Honey, it was only a dream."

"Well, in the dream, why didn't I protect you from whatever it was that frightened you? You can tell me that."

"You were dead."

He didn't know whether to be pissed because she had dreamed he was dead or laugh because the idea was so absurd.

"I didn't want you to be dead."

"I sure as hell hope not."

She bit his bare shoulder playfully. "I missed you. I said if I could have you back, I'd do anything."

"Don't worry, I'll hold you to it."

His skin smelled of the lake and the sun.

"How did I die?" he wanted to know.

"A car accident."

He grunted. "And after you were through crying over Poor Jack, what did you do?"

"What did I do?"

"Did you sell the business, for instance?"

"Brian bought it."

"Yes." That made sense to him. "Did you remarry? You were probably a regular Merry Widow." His tone was light and teasing but Louise wasn't fooled.

"No. I hadn't remarried when I woke up." She smiled, dismissing the subject.

"But everybody wanted you."

"Oh, for God's sake, Jack."

"Tell me the truth." He ran his lips along her cheekbone. "Who was after you, Frank?"

"No. Now, that's enough. This is sick."

"It's only a dream, Louise, you said so yourself. What about Brian?"

"Jack, stop." She hated these games where she had to try to stay a step ahead of him or end up in trouble.

"Not Brian? Hmmm. Let me see. Who else is there?"

"Why does there have to be anybody? There wasn't anybody."

"Now, that doesn't make sense and, besides, you're fibbing. I can always tell."

"What do you want for supper? There's hamburger or pork chops."

"I know you'd never give Earl or Ralph a tumble. They're not your type."

"Please, let's drop this. It was a terrible dream and I don't want to think about it."

"Where are the kids?"

"Still sleeping."

"Let's go upstairs." If he made love to her, he could break her down.

"No. They'll wake up any minute now."

"Then tell me. If it wasn't important, you wouldn't mind telling me." The tone was still light but they were on dangerous ground.

"If I tell you, will you stop this? Promise?"

"Tell me."

"Promise."

"Tell me."

"Ned MacRae."

"Jesus Christ, Louise, you're kidding."

"Well, you wanted to know."

"I can't believe you'd be interested in that prick."

"Why?"

"Why! Because he's a goddamned flashy stud who's into anything in a dress. I thought you had better taste than that."

"I married *you*."

"I'm beginning to wonder why, if MacRae is the kind of stuff you're interested in."

"For God's sake, Jack, it was a dream!" It was going to require ingenuity to get past this one. "The next time you dream about some young thing who brings her poor little pussy to the handsome vet to be fixed, wake me up and tell me about it, Jack."

He wasn't going to go along. "MacRae. Where do you see MacRae? I mean, our paths don't cross all that much."

"I don't see him. I hardly knew him at the beginning of the dream."

"But by the end you knew him a lot better."

"Oh, Jack, please, honey. Please don't."

While the rest of them ate shrimp salad and croissants and drank Chablis, the dog sniffed and turned away from bowls of food and water on the back porch. That was not so strange. He didn't usually eat until later in the day. Everyone had made a great fuss over him. Barbara's boys, especially, were ecstatic. Fido would be a house dog, as opposed to Mrs. Chips, who was a farm dog and didn't command house privileges.

After lunch they took their coffee out to the side yard and sat under a pair of walnut trees watching the five children and two dogs run off through the grove and into a golden meadow dotted with cottonwoods.

"You're going to miss the dog," Barbara commented. "He's lovely and so gentle." She paused. "Isn't it strange that he disliked just the one person? A man, you said?"

"Jack's attorney."

Paul, a taciturn man with a friendly, leathery face, turned to Louise with a chuckle. "I don't suppose you'd remember, Louise, but Dad had a prize Holstein bull, the gentlest damned bull you ever saw except when Dad came around. Then he'd go crazy; you'd have thought he was going after Manolete. Who knows what makes an animal react the way he does? Could be dozens of reasons. Maybe this attorney reminds him of somebody who mistreated him before Jack got him."

Wouldn't that be a joke on me? Louise thought, with unamused irony.

"I wish you didn't have to go right back, Louise," Barbara said. "Why don't you come down and stay for a few days?"

"We can in the fall. Right now we're all in Donald's show."

"That's right. I forgot. Well, after school starts, come for a weekend. Most kids kind of enjoy the farm."

"Amy and Peter would. And they'd have a chance to see the dog again."

"Good," Paul said, getting to his feet, and shaking hands with Louise. He had to get back to a field where there was a sluice problem. He told her they would plan to see her and the kids in the next couple of months.

When he'd gone, Barbara poured Louise and herself another cup of coffee and said, "After losing their dad, it's a pity for the kids—this business with the dog. Are you planning to get another one?"

"On the drive down, I told them I would. When they've had a chance to understand this, they'll want another dog," she said with conviction she didn't feel.

About three-thirty the children came up from the meadow, hot and mussed looking. Barbara poured them each a glass of cold cider.

"It's almost time to leave," Louise told Amy and Peter, "But we're invited back for a weekend."

Although they shot a look of gratitude at Barbara, they showed no softening toward Louise. As four o'clock approached, Louise began preparing for their leave-taking, unsure how to deal with the dog. Barbara took charge, suggesting they put him on the screened porch. He seemed stoical enough as they led him in and Amy and Peter went through a lengthy and tearful farewell. He calmly forebore as they hugged, petted and spoke soft, ragged words.

Louise wondered what he felt. This was as difficult for him as for them. More difficult. He knew precisely what he was losing. They didn't.

She lay her hand on his head, turned and shepherded Amy and Peter toward the door. They were coming apart and she was desperate to get them into the car.

"Please! Please, Mommy!" Amy cried, sobbing as she grasped Louise, trying to pull her back.

"We can't leave him, Mommy!" Peter screamed at her.

Now that the screen door was firmly closed behind them, the dog began to howl and throw himself at it, trying to tear through it.

Amy and Peter wrenched away, starting back, both screaming. It was only with Barbara's help that Louise pulled them into the car. In the meantime the boys snapped the leash on the dog, opened the door before he could destroy it completely, and dragged him, howling and straining, toward the barn.

Quickly Louise got into the car, turned on the engine and called, "I'll phone you." Gravel sprayed wildly as the car leaped down the drive, putting distance between them and the dog.

Please forgive me, Jack.

How far had they gone when she felt Amy's fingers on her shoulder?

"Mommy?"

Louise looked at the speedometer. She was going eighty-five. Braking slowly, she pulled the car over to the shoulder and stopped. She folded her arms across the steering wheel and lay her head on them. Her head pounded savagely. Minutes went by while she gave herself up to the pain, let the blossoms of it break and dissipate. Slowly it began to subside.

Hands were gently patting her back. She sat up.

"Are you okay, Mommy?"

"I'll be all right." She turned the key in the ignition, smiled thinly in the rearview mirror and put the car in gear.

With Amy asleep beside her on the front seat and Peter in the back, Louise swung the wagon into Ned's yard shortly before six-thirty that evening.

Ned was listening for the car and came out to meet them. Seeing the children asleep, he smiled crookedly. "Poor kids." He put his head in and kissed Louise. "How are you?"

"Don't ask."

"Difficult getting away?"

Louise twisted her hands in her lap, fidgeting with her wedding ring. "They had to lock him in the barn till we were gone. It was . . . I couldn't ever do it again."

"Maybe you should call and see if he's all right."

"I called from the pay phone at Bennett's."

"And?"

"He'd quieted down. I left the Dockers' number if they need to reach me." She looked at him ruefully. "They like him."

"Good." He opened the door and took her hand. "It's over."

She stepped out on the gravel. Amy and Peter were beginning to stir. "We're here. Wake up," she told them.

They sat up, noticed Ned and looked away. "Why are we *here?*"

"I know you're mad at me," Ned told them. "I'd feel the same in your place. I'd appreciate it though if you'd come in a minute and let me talk to you."

Grudgingly they got out of the car. Each took one of Louise's hands.

On the porch was a willow basket and from it came whimpering sounds. When they were alongside, Peter and Amy looked in. A Dalmatian pup squirmed and yipped.

"Whose dog is that?" Amy asked coldly.

"He's mine," Ned told her. "But I can't keep him because they don't allow dogs in the apartment where I live."

"He's cute," Amy said, bending to pet him. "People shouldn't get dogs if they're not going to keep them."

"You can hold him, if you want."

"Who's going to take him?" Peter asked.

"I don't know. I have to find someone who knows how to take care of dogs," Ned explained, sitting on the porch railing.

"We know how to take care of dogs, don't we?" Peter looked at Louise.

She nodded.

"Would you give him to us?" He glanced warily from her to Ned.

"We could discuss it."

Peter took the puppy from Amy, held him solemnly and petted him. Ned opened the door and they all filed quietly into the cottage.

"I want us to be friends again someday." He sat on a straight-back chair and leaned forward, elbows on his knees. He studied the three of them, seated side by side on the couch. "I like you," he told Amy and Peter. "I hope before long you'll understand what happened today. Until you do, I don't imagine things are going to be friendly between us. But, I want to go on seeing your mother. If you have anything you want to say—about that or the dog or anything else—I'll be here."

They would have nothing to say now so he went on, "I know you want to get home. Your mother's tired. It's been a long day for all of you.

The children were mute, not soon to be won.

Chapter
23

Beau, the children decided, would be the Dalmatian's name. Ned drew up an agreement full of terms they must fulfill with regard to the animal's care. All parties signed three copies, one retained by Ned, one by each of the children. Amy and Peter were favorably impressed by the businesslike nature of the transaction. It neither obliged them to accept MacRae, nor to be grateful. Beau was a nice dog. He wasn't Fido.

Wednesday, August fifth, Donald drove into town following a quick breakfast. "Why don't you get a sitter and meet me at the River House for lunch?" he asked over toast and coffee.

Louise was surprised but willing. "I was going in this afternoon anyway to do some chores. All right. What time?"

"One o'clock? The crowd starts to thin out around then."

The River House sat high on a bluff above the Minnesota River. It was a rambling frame hotel with a large dining room overlooking the river. During the summer there were tables on the terrace and that was where Louise headed when she arrived. She was early.

She wore a white piqué sun dress trimmed with yellow daisies. She felt as crisp and attractive as the dress. The maître

d' found her a table near the low wall where the land fell
away to the water below. A waiter took her order for a gin
and tonic. She saw no one she knew. That was fine. She
wanted a few minutes to consider how to tell Donald about
the Yacht Club. She'd explained her plans to Betsy but she'd
had little time alone with her brother in recent days.

Louise wasn't really worried. Donald wanted her to be
happy. She knew that. When he realized how much the proj-
ect meant to her, there would be no problem. Why on earth
should there be?

She wondered why he'd suggested lunch. He had something
on his mind. At breakfast he'd been preoccupied and when
he'd asked her to meet him, his manner implied a definite
purpose.

The waiter brought the gin and tonic. Louise gazed at the
river. It was a purposeful-seeming river, neither rampant nor
lazy, but moving deliberately. It reminded her of Donald himself. Gentle, reassuring and pleasant to look at.

The maître d' was leading Donald across the terrace. She
smiled and raised her glass. His answering smile was reserved
and tight-fitting. He sat down opposite her and ordered a
vodka martini, straight up. Normally he drank nothing
stronger than beer or white wine with lunch.

When the waiter had left, Donald spread the linen napkin
across his lap, smoothing the edges abstractedly. At length he
looked up but stared beyond Louise as though the words he
sought were written in the distance.

"Is something wrong?" she asked.

"I don't know what to say. I don't know how to begin." He
looked at her. "Betsy says you're planning to buy the Yacht
Club."

"Yes."

"I can't believe it."

"Why?"

"It's the damnedest thing I ever heard. I can't believe it,"
he repeated.

"I'm sorry you heard it from Betsy. I wanted to tell you but you've been busy. I was going to tell you."

"I'm going to put it to you straight, kid. I'm here to talk you out of it." There was a compression of feeling in his words.

Panic spread through Louise, raising perspiration on her palms and forehead. She could recall no occasion since high school when Donald had been seriously angry with her. She loved and admired him. She liked to please him.

She had enjoyed being the little sister over whom he kept a protective watch. Her panic had far less to do with his present anger than with the inevitable and permanent change this luncheon would bring in their relationship. Shedding old and comfortable patterns was a frightening thing, but she couldn't forever be Donald's surrogate child if she were going to grow up. And Donald was going to suffer even more than she. It made her feel guilt and shame.

"I'm going to buy the club if it can be worked out," she told him. She tried not to fidget. She wanted to seem calm. He might have more confidence in her.

"What does MacRae say about this?" His tone was casual before the waiter who brought the martini and left menus.

"At first he was opposed because . . . well, for a lot of reasons. He said I didn't know anything about the business." She glanced at the menu without seeing it. She would order chef salad. There was surely one listed. There always was. "But gradually he saw that I was serious."

"Serious? What does serious have to do with it? You *don't* know anything about running a business like that. You're playing grownup."

"You may be right. It's the only way I know to learn." She handed the menu to the waiter and ordered another gin and tonic and chef salad with Roquefort dressing. Donald ordered shrimp salad and indicated he would be wanting another martini when the present one was finished.

"I have so many objections to your doing this," he told her, "I don't know which to produce first."

"If it will make you feel any better, Art Christopher is going to stay on as manager. When he has enough money, he wants to make it a partnership. But he's going to teach me the business. I want to know everything about it."

"You know nothing about *any* kind of business. You never even answered the *phone* at the kennels, for God's sake. This is a helluva lot of money to throw away on a 'learning experience'."

"It's my money."

"Shouldn't you be thinking down the line to the kids' future?"

"Their future is provided for in Jack's will," she said, not without bitterness. "Everything of his is in trust. I never told you that."

"Well, he was a damned smart man. I hate to think what you'd do if you had that, too."

"Donald." She had never seen him so angry. "Let's not say a lot of awful things we'll be embarrassed about later."

"I'm sorry, but I have to take hold here, Louise. It's my responsibility to make you see what a mistake this is."

"You can tell me what your opinion is, but you can't—you don't have the right—to stop me."

"Louise, you're just not capable of making this kind of decision. You're too . . . off balance emotionally. You're still reacting to Jack's death." His voice was sympathetic. "If you want to get into a business later, fine. When you've had a chance to adjust. Don't do something foolish while you're in mourning."

Mourning. It seemed a strangely foreign word. Often it was herself she mourned. Donald had stopped talking for the moment. He was giving her time to run back to the person she used to be, to climb inside the safety of that other Louise, the one who was sheltered and cherished.

While they sat in silence, the food and drinks arrived and in continued silence they ate. Louise knew this was only a respite. He was surprised and wounded by her intransigence. But it lay between them and he would attack again.

After some minutes he said, "Let's get back to MacRae and what he thinks about this. You said he was against it . . ."

"In the beginning," she cut in. "His objections were a lot like yours. But he's seen how much it means to me. It's a chance to be productive and to work at something I care about," she said firmly.

"In other words, you've stamped your foot and cried and he's fallen in line."

She stared at him, stunned.

"Don't you see, Louise, that I can't indulge you that way. I have to be the heavy because I'm responsible for you in a way that MacRae isn't."

"Donald, stop talking like that. I'm not your child. If you want a child, go out and get one and stop using me!"

His head jerked as though she'd hit him. "Is that what you think? That I look after you for some selfish reason?"

She had laid him open. Gone was his reserve of calm. Her hands shook. She set down her fork and grasped the edge of the table. "No. It's not that simple. But you've got to let me make my own mistakes."

"You never turned down my help," he said dully. "If you didn't want it, why didn't you say so?"

Louise was near capitulation. She put a hand over one of his. She loved him terribly, maybe more than freedom. He removed his hand, whether consciously or otherwise, she wasn't sure. As she watched, his pain translated to an acrimony rooted in betrayal.

"What would Jack say about this? Have you thought of that?"

"Jack is dead."

"That's not an answer. He'd put his foot down—after he'd had a good laugh. Can you imagine what he'd say about his wife running a roadhouse and tending bar? It's a charming picture, Louise. What will Amy and Peter say when people ask what their mommy does?" He leaned close. "Don't you owe Jack some respect?" He rose, tossed his napkin on the table and left.

Her eyes didn't follow as he stalked across the terrace and through the French doors. She didn't owe him a dramatic exit. She turned her chair toward the river. Only a sprinkling of diners remained on the terrace. They paid no attention as she gazed for half an hour at the gray-green water.

She placed a large tip on the tray and left. Her step was brisk and the white piqué dress, still crisp.

Stepping into the small, sunny waiting room of Valley Kennels and Animal Hospital, Louise was apprehensive. She was an outsider now.

The all-purpose office girl was nowhere around so Louise took a seat on a chrome and leatherette chair. It looked the same, the blue drapes and framed lithographs. So far Brian had changed nothing.

An old man, rather down-at-the-heels, sat nearby with a fat and ancient tabby which he stroked softly and to whom he spoke in subdued and reassuring tones.

These surroundings brought Jack closer. She would never be able to come here without bringing him to life. It would not be wise to come too often, not for quite a while. His face and voice were everywhere and here he had been without flaw. On those rare occasions when she'd watched him work, she'd been awed by him. And each time suffered something like a schoolgirl crush for days afterward.

Glancing about, she felt a painful proprietariness. It was difficult letting go. She still loved him, so why wasn't he still here?

Coming from one of the inner rooms, striking-looking in his white coat, he'd stroll out into the waiting room to have a look around. When he saw her, he'd break into a smile so richly private, she wanted to look at the others waiting, to see if they appreciated that it was *she* at whom he smiled. He was one sweet son-of-a-bitch and he was hers.

"Louise? . . . Louise? Can I help you?" Brian stood in the door, the hall beyond him leading back to examining and surgery rooms. "Come on back to the office." He led her to the office he'd shared with Jack.

Coming out of the room was the new vet. Louise was surprised but not disappointed to find he'd hired a woman. There were brief introductions. "Annie, Louise. Uh . . . sorry, Annie Johnson, Louise Andrews." Annie was small and pleasant-looking. From what Louise could see, Brian seemed quite pleased with her.

He pushed open the door and held it for Louise. She was relieved to see all personal traces of her husband had been removed. Brian gestured her to a chair near his desk. "Sit down and tell me about things. How are you and the kids?" He ambled around behind the desk and sat in his own chair.

There was a difference about him. More assurance? Not so boyish. He was becoming his own person. Maybe the new vet had something to do with it. Or Jack's death.

"We're fine. We miss you but I know you've been busy. How is it going? I like the new vet."

"Annie's terrific. Easy to work with."

He was certainly more relaxed than she'd known him to be in the past.

"We've been busy as hell," he went on, "but we're getting it under control."

"I'm pleased that you hired a woman."

"Yes, well, I guess Jack probably wouldn't have been so keen on it, but she's absolutely top-notch. I couldn't have gotten anyone better."

"Good. I've meant to tell you how much we love the Dalmatian you sold Ned. He's lovely."

"Glad I could help." Some secret thought shadowed his face. "I was surprised when MacRae said you were getting rid of the setter."

"He was dangerous."

"With the kids?" He made no effort to conceal his disbelief.

"No, no. Not the kids or me but, well, others."

Brian said nothing for a moment. "That's too bad. He was a beautiful animal."

"Yes." Louise was anxious to change the subject. "The reason I'm here is to invite you to a party at the lake on the twenty-third. I'll be closing the cottage after Labor Day. The party's on Sunday. In the afternoon. Can you come?"

"Is it okay if I bring Annie?"

"Of course."

"I'd like her to meet people. She hasn't had much time so far."

"Where's she from?"

"Iowa. Waterloo."

"Well, we won't hold that against her. By all means, bring her and your swimming suits."

As Louise prepared to leave, Brian inquired, "Who did the dog go after, Lou?"

"Ned."

"I see."

"You don't like Ned much, do you?"

"It's your life, Louise."

"It is."

From the kennel, Louise drove through the town and up the hills to the house on Baker Avenue. *My* house again, she thought somberly. She pulled up in front and looked at it. It seemed very big, bigger than before. Jack had filled it. Would she and the kids? Or would they feel like end-of-the-summer guests in a resort hotel, staying on when the excitement is gone?

She got out and went in. She'd put off disposing of Jack's things but this was the day. She'd begin at least. Opening his closet, she snatched shirts, jackets, slacks, and ties and threw them on the bed to be packed into Goodwill bags. I ought to go through the pockets, she thought, sitting beside the pile of clothes.

On one of the hangers, under an old sports coat Jack hadn't worn for a year or more, hung a cloth bag, like a small shopping bag. What's this, she wondered.

Removing the jacket from the hanger, she opened the bag. Inside were notes and cards she'd given him, dozens of them, from birthdays, anniversaries, Father's Days. There was even a lacy valentine from Nell. Scrawled on the outside of one particularly large envelope in Jack's handwriting, "Okay, Snoop, now you know all my secrets. See what a sentimental rube you married?"

Throwing herself backward on the bed, she clutched the clothes, pulling them on top of her. She rolled over with them, finally stuffing them into her mouth to muffle her cries.

"What would you like to drink?" MacRae asked, unlocking the door to his cottage when they returned from the theater. He switched on a table lamp.

"Nothing." Louise pointed to the couch and said, "Sit. I'll make *you* a drink." After first lowering the shades, she pulled a Peggy Lee album from the shelves beside the stereo and set it on the turntable. As the first notes came through the speakers, she strolled into the kitchen and emptied a tray of ice cubes.

Today she'd won hard ground in the battle to survive. Tonight she felt confident and playful.

She poured MacRae a scotch and soda. Handing it to him, she stepped out of her sandals and smiled a wry half-smile. Slowly she unbuttoned her blouse and removed it, tossing it over the back of a chair. Next the denim skirt was unzipped and joined the blouse on the chair.

"Uh . . ."

Languorously she moved her head side to side, motioning him to stay where he was. She unhooked her bra and slipped it off, letting it fall to the floor, then eased the pale blue bikini panties to her ankles and kicked them off. It was all accomplished with unhurried smoothness.

Louise took his hand. "Stand up." When he was on his feet, she explained, "Now I'm going to undress you," and she began unbuckling his belt. Though she neither kissed nor fondled him, the slow disrobing became a form of lovemaking, not without glances and inevitable encounters of flesh. When he was naked, she led him into the bedroom.

"Lie down," she told him, turning on the low-wattage lamp.

He said nothing but did as she asked. She sat beside him and with her fingertips gently massaged his temples and brows and his scalp along the hairline. Her nipples brushing across his skin, she leaned toward him and whispered, "You have elegant ears," then ran the tip of her tongue around the outer shell. Still whispering, she said, "Turn over on your stomach."

From a plastic bottle on the bedside table, she poured lotion into her palm and began to knead his neck, shoulders, and back. She lingered with the small of his back where it dimpled just above the buttocks. Softly she pummeled his buttocks with her fists before moving down his legs. After massaging his feet and toes one at a time, she ran the very tips of her nails delicately over the bottom of his feet for several minutes. Finally, she bent and kissed the hollowed arch of each foot. Grazing the crease at the back of his knees with her lips, she murmured, "Okay, MacRae, now the other side."

Moaning softly, he rolled over and she poured more lotion into her hands and started on his shoulders and arms. When she got as far as his chest, she stroked it tenderly and, with only a breath of contact, caressed the skin around his nipples with her lips.

"You are a pleasing man," she whispered, running her hands lazily over his abdomen and tracing the fine, faint line of dark hair down his belly. With small, feathery kisses, she teased his belly. Pouring a thin stream of lotion along each thigh, she commenced massaging it very slowly, gently, into the skin. When that was accomplished, she nibbled his thighs randomly, barely grasping the skin with her teeth. Her hair fell around her face and brushed over his erect penis.

He reached for her but she put his hand aside. "Patience," she told him and continued the massage. When she had finished rubbing his ankles with lotion, she turned first one foot and then the other to press a kiss of her tongue to the tender concavity below the ankle bone on the inner side of his foot.

Faintly, in the distance beyond the open bedroom window, an owl hooted, while nearer the cottage, spruce trees whispered among themselves. Louise nuzzled Ned's groin and, with a hinting, lambent touch, ran her fingertips over his penis before taking it in her mouth.

Twice he spoke her name, the second time with urgency and she pulled herself up and sat astride him, guiding his penis into her.

If she were going to fall in love with him, he must understand that sometimes she would be on top. Smiling down at him, she felt governance and strength and immense tenderness toward him.

Chapter 24

The day of the party both Ned and Tom Benjamin arrived early. Ned to organize the bar, Tom to hang around the kitchen pilfering food and flirting.

"Tom, why don't you fix yourself a plate?" Betsy asked him.

"What! Before the others get here?" he responded with shocked innocence.

"Don't stand on ceremony. Not that you ever did." She thrust a plate into his hands.

"Well, since you put it that way." He began loading the plate from the platters the women were filling. "Did you find me that warm woman, Louise?" he asked, hesitating over a third piece of roast beef.

"I've called your bluff, you old lecher. Suzie Docker is bringing her sister, Jane."

"How old is she?"

"I didn't ask and she didn't volunteer, but she looks a well-kept-up early fifties."

"Single?"

"Yes."

"Must be something wrong with her then."

"You're not only a lech," Betsy told him, "you're an impossible sexist."

"I never said otherwise."

"That's no excuse." Louise tucked a napkin into the collar of his shirt. "It happens Jane is a widow."

"How did her husband die?"

"Does it make a difference?"

"It might."

"Then you must remember to ask her."

Standing before the mirror, Louise appraised the rust colored swimsuit and brown plaid wrap-around skirt. Her gaze traveled to her face. She studied it for a moment. As time stretched away from Jack's death, she was gradually becoming someone else. Someone she could like. Would I have changed, she wondered, if Jack had lived? Not in the same ways, certainly. She was beginning, if only by inches, to take charge of her life, to steer instead of drifting.

"Knock, knock," Ned warned, coming up the stairs.

It was the first time he'd been up here. His presence in her bedroom made Louise feel light and oddly domestic.

"Is there more tonic and club soda?" he asked, standing behind her. "You look pretty."

"It's on the back porch." She turned around. "Thank you." She took a step, eliminating the space between them. Slipping her arms around his waist, she rubbed her thigh lightly against his groin. "Don't wear the bikini trunks," she said.

"Oh? Why?" He smiled beatifically.

"I don't want any of your former friends getting nostalgic."

"Louise, you act as though I'd humped half the town."

"Only the female half."

"You're disgusting," he said. Smiling at her in the mirror, he gave her the finger and left.

Accepting a gin and tonic from MacRae, Suzie Docker explained, "I may have to run into town later. Mitzi and Junior are supposed to come in on the bus today. I put the phone in the window," she told Louise, "so I can hear it if it rings."

"Where have they been?" Ned asked.

"Working at a summer camp near Bemidji." She popped a potato chip in her mouth. "The season's ending now so they're coming home to get ready for school. God, this is good. I haven't had gin and tonic all summer."

"It was nice of Ralph to bring the boat and ski stuff over," Louise told her. "Everyone's enjoying it."

"Yeah, it's fun," Suzie agreed, "and he'll be careful not to let 'em go out if they've had too much booze." She wandered away to gossip with Marie Oster. Louise stood by the bar watching Betsy throw Tom Benjamin and Jane O'Brien together, then strolled over to sit under the birch tree.

Since their lunch at the River House, Donald had spent little time at the cottage. When he was there, he was indulgent with Amy and Peter as always, but remote and civil toward Louise. He'd shown up at the party because it would have been unseemly not to. Their relationship had altered. Louise had no illusions about that. She was saddened and resigned.

Donald stood on the dock talking to Brian Doyle. The young vet's glance strayed to the bar where Ned played host. Annie, his assistant, laughed and chatted with Ned, handing him bottles and glasses as they were needed. It was much the same manner she must use assisting Brian. Eventually she waved good-bye and joined Frank who was going out to water ski.

Brian and Donald parted, Donald ambling up the path to the bar, Brian heading toward Louise. He looked vaguely distressed.

"You seem very pleased," he observed, sitting down in the shade near her.

"I feel benign."

"I've been hearing about your plan."

She waited.

"You're really thinking of buying the Yacht Club?" he asked with an edge of disparagement.

"Yes." She held the cool glass to her temple. "Ned's been talking it over with Bill Hermann. Nothing's set, but I'm serious."

"Whose idea was this—MacRae's?"

"No. In fact, he tried to talk me out of it in the beginning."

"In the beginning."

"What does that mean? What's on your mind?"

"I think it's a bad idea. The sort of idea someone like MacRae would have."

"What's so bad about it?"

"Don't you wonder how Jack might feel about some of the things you're doing?"

"Should I? Do *you*?"

Ralph Docker's boat skimmed swiftly up the channel, Annie Johnson up on the skis behind it. Brian watched until they'd disappeared beyond the spit. He lifted his glass and drank. Lowering it, he looked at Louise over the rim.

"You've been lucky," he said, "to come through things the way you have."

"Unscathed?" she asked captiously.

"That's not what I meant. I meant you're . . . landing on your feet? You're getting on with life pretty smoothly."

She studied his pleasant, freckled face keenly. What did he want? Was he a little drunk? She was angry but it was pointless. There was no meanness in him, only loyalty and maybe a trace of guilt. After all, he too was managing to survive without Jack.

"It might have been more respectful if I could have postponed living for a while?"

"I don't want to see you foul up your life."

"You're talking about Ned now. I can't make you like him, Brian. And I'm not going to try. He doesn't need to be defended."

"Doesn't he? He's a gigolo." He pulled up a handful of grass and threw it aside.

"Oh, Brian." She wanted to be kind. "That's an old-fashioned word."

"He doesn't take things . . . seriously, Lou."

"How would you know that?"

"I just do."

"Why don't we drop this while neither of us is too bloody?" she suggested, squeezing his shoulder lightly.

"How could you go for a guy like that, after Jack?"

"Don't be a damned prick, Brian. What are you trying to say, that I didn't bleed enough when Jack died?"

He saw the pain. "I don't want you to get hurt, Louise." He leaned on the chaise and pulled himself to his feet. "Sorry, Lou."

She watched him shamble away. He was a dear boy and a damned nuisance.

Settling himself on the spot of turf Brian had vacated, Tom put a hand on Louise's knee. "Young Lochinvar been riding too hard?"

"Have you ever heard of a damsel who didn't want to be ransomed from the infidel?" she asked rhetorically. "You have now. Please don't lecture me about MacRae. Or the Yacht Club. Or anything else."

"You going to let Doyle spoil your afternoon?"

"Hell, no."

"Now you're talking Anglo-Saxon."

"How did you get so smart?"

"When you've seen as many bare asses as I have, you get a certain perspective on life."

"Some perspective that must be." Louise saw Jane O'Brien at the bar talking to Ned. "How do you like Jane?"

"Might interest you to know I'm taking her to dinner."

"You're not."

"The hell I'm not. I'm going to blow this place early to get home and change clothes."

"You are some fast worker."

He laid a hand on her arm. "Only kids can afford to waste time."

"I know."

Everyone seemed to enjoy the afternoon except, maybe, Brian. Louise luxuriated in an hour of unclouded well-being. Giving Tom a playful hug, she left him and went to the bar to sweeten her drink. Ned, she noticed, had changed into swim trunks and when she handed him her glass he said, "Let's go swimming first."

The lake was dark green with late summer algae. They swam out fifty yards. Louise turned on her back and viewed the cloudless sky, so pale in mid-afternoon, it looked white.

"Having a good time?" he asked.

"Mmmm."

"You weathered Doyle pretty well. I was proud of you."

"You noticed?" She sighed, "He means well. He just irritates me somtimes."

"Because he doesn't approve of me?"

"You know that?" she asked.

"He doesn't make a secret of it." He was matter-of-fact.

"Did he say anything to you today?" Louise demanded, anger returning.

"No. He wouldn't get into it with me here." He swam around her in circles as she floated. "I've had to spend some time with him on legal matters."

"I'd almost forgotten about that. Of course. The business. Doesn't he like the way you're handling things?"

"It's nothing to do with the business. It's strictly personal. The funny thing is, I kind of like the guy."

"My, you're magnanimous."

"Doyle has his reasons for the way he feels about me."

"What does that mean?" She turned over and swam to him. "You're not messing around with his new vet, are you?"

He laughed and ducked her head under. "Jesus, you're suspicious. No, I'm not messing with his new vet."

"You're a bastard," she told him lightly. "You *are* messing with her, aren't you?"

"No. I wouldn't lie to you. This was something about a year ago. As far as I was concerned, it wasn't important, but it was important to Doyle."

Louise felt forbearance toward Brian. Poor boy, if he'd been part of a triangle involving Ned. Well, thank heaven things seemed to be going better for him now.

"You must think I'm a demon operator," Ned told her, "if I'm supposed to be working, doing six shows a week, seeing you and messing with somebody else's woman. When do I find time to eat?"

"Very late at night." She splashed water in his face and swam away.

He followed her toward the raft. At the moment no one was using it. Panting, they climbed on and flopped down exhausted.

After some minutes he kissed her shoulder and rolled over on his back. "This is some beautiful day."

She ran a finger down his arm, pushing drops of lake water off. They coursed in rivulets to the wood beneath him. She lay on her side watching his body at rest, the rise and fall of his chest, the little twitchings of his eyelids, closed against the sun. She could study him like this for a long time without tiring of it.

"MacRae?"

"Hmmm?"

"I was jealous," she said, bemused.

"When?"

"Just now when we were talking about Annie, the new vet." She was disconcerted.

"Is that so bad?"

She didn't answer. She lay back, closed her eyes, and wondered at herself. From the shore came sounds of laughter and music, but that was far away. Louise felt warm and drowsy, comfortable in every cell, along every nerve. I feel healthy and sane, she thought. Jealous and healthy and sane.

"Louise?" He inched closer, propped himself on an elbow and regarded her.

"Hmmm?"

"I'm going to say something and I don't want you to answer. Do you understand?"

"I'm not sure." She searched his face, puzzled.

He ran a hand along her thigh in a gesture at once sensual and proprietary.

She waited, curious.

"I love you."

"I . . ."

"No. I said you weren't to answer, remember. Don't say anything."

"All right."

"I wanted you to know I'm happier today than I can remember being."

Her throat tightened. "I wish we were alone."

"Louise! Louise!" Someone—Marie Oster?—was calling her from the dock. "Telephone for you! Long distance."

She stood with the receiver in her hand, the line dead, then gave it to him as though she'd forgotten what to do with it. He replaced it on the cradle.

"The dog?"

She nodded.

"What's happening?"

"He . . . ran away. He's not with them."

"When? Have they looked for him?"

"He left three days ago. They kept thinking he'd come back."

"He may still. Don't start worrying."

Nobody understood him as she did. He was coming home. He wasn't done with her.

Chapter 25

Monday's dawn presaged summer's last-gasp heat wave. Dog days lumbered toward September, reaching a nadir during the week following the party. Audiences for the show dropped off. The cast and technical people began to wilt, and noisy backstage comaraderie was reduced to monosyllables.

Donald was occupied with preparations for the fall quarter. Betsy worked to get the winter line out at the shop, summer items cleared, and holiday promotions ready. Everyone pressed toward fall, anxious to have summer ended.

Only Louise was held in the summer. Unsure where the dog was, she couldn't move ahead or make plans. She wanted to sit motionless and wait for him to show up.

She'd been a fool. He still owned her. He was capable of bending her to any design. Alive he'd done it with charm and sex and an uncanny ability to arouse her sympathy. Now he used fear. She couldn't kill him, despite what she'd said. He'd gamble on that. She was trapped. She could continue seeing MacRae until the dog found a way of murdering him. Or she could give in. Mrs. Andrews' dog. So devoted, people would say. Always at her side. He did what he did out of love, she told herself.

Louise made excuses not to see Ned, but he followed her home from the theater Friday night. After putting Amy and Peter to bed, the puppy on the rug between them, Louise collapsed on the couch. She was pale and her head throbbed. Now what, she wondered, watching MacRae make himself a drink.

"Would you like something to drink?" he asked.

"No."

He paced and drank. He looks more haggard than I do, she thought. He did not seem to know how to begin his argument. That was uncharacteristic.

"The dog may be dead, Louise," he said at last. "He may be headed in some other direction, while you wait like . . . like a crazy person, shuddering and sighing and making a damned fool of yourself."

"He's coming." She shrugged, dismissing all other possibilities.

"Well, what if I moved in so I could be here at night? Would you feel safer?"

She laughed impatiently. "I'm not afraid for *me*. You're so stupid sometimes. It's *you* he's going to kill."

He stopped pacing. "This is the damnedest crap I ever heard. I'll shoot him, Louise." He was beside her, grasping her arms roughly. "Do you think I wouldn't kill the bastard?"

"I'm sure you would," she said thoughtfully. "And it would be all my fault."

"Louise, do you hear what you're saying? You're talking as though he were a man."

She looked away.

His anger yielded fleetingly to pity. "I'm partly to blame. I humored you because I thought if things were good enough between us, you'd see the dog for what he was—a sick, dangerous animal who'd taken a dislike to me. He's not your conscience, Louise, and he's not your husband."

"Don't. Don't say those things. You don't understand about the dog. I'm not going to put it into words. Putting something

insane into words can make you insane. I believe that. The
dog isn't my conscience or a figment of my conscience. You
give me credit for a much more interesting mind than I have.
I didn't ask you to believe in him. I'm not asking you to
now."

He shook his head in dismay. "You're so full of guilt you
can hardly breathe. It's making you sick."

"That isn't true. You don't believe that."

"The hell I don't." He was up and pacing again.

"Why would I feel guilty?"

"Why?" he snorted. "Because you're not as liberated as you
think. I don't know what your marriage was like but it must
have been pretty damned suffocating. Jack must have been a
real bastard in private."

"No."

"I don't believe that. I think you were scared to death of
him when he was alive. But after he died, you busted loose
and started getting even. You took up with a man he didn't
like and made up your mind to buy a business that would set
him spinning in his grave."

If she had the energy, she'd be angry.

"But you got to feeling guilty," he continued, "and you in-
vented the dog to keep yourself in line. You're hoping he'll
come back and make you a virgin again, aren't you?"

"Please." Perhaps if she behaved calmly, he'd see that she
wasn't insane. "You think Jack was a monster, that I couldn't
wait to escape, and that I'm feeling guilty now because I *did*
escape—at least escaped briefly." She looked at him for confir-
mation. He stood leaning against the bar table. He nodded
and waited for her to go on. "Jack was full of pain he
wouldn't acknowledge. Sometimes it came out in negative
ways. He could be frightening," she admitted. "I made a career out of giving him his way."

"Why?"

Whatever Jack was, she'd been his accomplice. "Because it
turned me on."

She could feel his disgust from across the room.

"Jack was domineering. But he didn't ... *beat* me. It was easy to let him have his way. I never wanted to punish him for it." With a knowing smile and a caress of each word, she explained, "I may have been a victim, but you have no idea how willing I was or how sweet the rewards were." Because she had to give MacRae up, she wanted to hurt him. Then, seeing her success on his face, she felt remorse.

He sat down opposite her. "I can see that I never had a chance of competing," he said quietly. "I don't even play the same game."

Ignoring this, she went on, "After Jack's death, I began to change. I had to learn to dominate *myself*. I began to make decisions." She spoke of making decisions as though it were a precious talent she hadn't known she possessed. "Sometimes it was frightening, but each time I found out a little about who I was, like an amnesia victim finding clues to his identity." The melodramatic analogy made her smile. Then the amusement dissolved and she was swept by a wave of loss. "Whoever I was going to be—that's gone now. Do you think I don't *hate* giving it up?" She closed her eyes. "I didn't want to play his game anymore."

"Then don't."

"I'm married to him."

"And the Yacht Club? What happens to that now?"

"You can tell Bill I've backed out." She got up, not allowing herself to look at him.

"And us?"

"That's all over." She hurried toward the stairs, steering a wide path around him.

Saturday, Louise sat waiting in the shade most of the day. Betsy was away early seeking the air-conditioned refuge of the shop. Donald was at the university.

When Amy made lunch for them, Louise was touched. After they'd all eaten the sandwiches, the little girl read to her brother from *Charlotte's Web* and the two of them fell asleep on Peter's bed. Beau lay down by the screen door where he could keep an eye on everyone.

Louise remained for some time in the yard, then went upstairs and, from the drawer beside her bed, withdrew the gun case, set it on the table and opened it, merely to look at the gun.

Although it hadn't been with this same weapon, Nell's suicide inevitably surfaced in Louise's mind. Months before the suicide, Nell had spoken of her unhappiness. As she and Louise carried boxes of rummage to the church basement, she said, "Women get trapped in men's lives, Louise." Glancing at the surroundings, she explained, "I never bargained for this. And there's no escape." Setting the boxes on a large sorting table, she brushed a wisp of hair from her face. "Oh, sometimes I escape for an hour or so," she said, but she didn't define "escape."

Louise lifted the gun from the case. While he was alive, she had never considered herself trapped in Jack's life. Staring sightlessly at its cool, smooth surface, Louise turned the gun over several times, running her hands over the surface as though the metal spoke through her fingers of solutions.

Finally she returned the gun to its case and the case to the drawer. She went downstairs and out to the porch where the children were sleeping. Standing in the doorway, she contemplated their soft shapes with a helpless gaze.

Taking up her post in the yard again, she sat, rigid with attention, listening. As the empty afternoon inched along, the dread she'd carried became a prickling fear.

"That's enough to wear to bed tonight," Louise said, stripping Amy and Peter down to their underwear. "It's hot." She lay down with them until they were asleep. The puppy slept on Peter's bed.

Moving quietly from room to room, she turned out the lights, and climbed the stairs. Sitting at the window seat, she listened, back pressed against the dormer wall. The woods were restless with unseen dogs.

Later she slept. And then was drawn upright in bed by the howl. Betsy slept undisturbed in the next bed. He was in the woods across the road.

Chapter
26

Pulling into the heart of New Warsaw, a small community fifteen miles south of Falls Village, Louise and the children were greeted by Polish and American flags, red, white and blue streamers and fluttering banners proclaiming "Polish Day—Welcome!" They parked as close to the center of things as possible, then walked to the square with Beau trotting along importantly on a leash.

When daylight had finally come filtering through the trees Sunday morning, Louise knew, lying exhausted in bed, that one more day of sitting, afraid and waiting, would put her beyond reason. She recalled a notice of a Polish celebration. It was made to order. A frivolous afternoon.

Brightly festooned booths offered Polish food: sausages, bigos, fancy tarts and babka; others featured games of chance and skill. Peter and Amy tossed dozens of jar rubbers at dozens of soda pop bottles and each received a treat from a grandmotherly woman running the stall. There were stalls of Polish imports and others displaying crafts by local talent: wood carving, crocheting, knitting, quilting, even some charming primitive paintings. Louise chose a piece of imported handmade lace "to trim my Christmas dress."

A parade, small but warmly greeted, marched along Main Street on the west side of the square, led by the New Warsaw Consolidated High School Band and brought along toward the rear by the visiting American Legion Drum and Bugle Corps of Falls Village. Riding in an open convertible and giggling nervously as she waved a gloved hand to the crowd was Miss New Warsaw. Town children on bicycles decorated with brilliant crepe paper streamers and farm children on horses and ponies concluded the procession, leaving behind the inevitable horse manure and torn crepe paper.

At the north end of the square in an old-fashioned semidomed band shell, a group of perspiring, shirt-sleeved men, wearing straw boaters, played polkas, schottisches and oompa waltzes. A space was cleared before the band shell and dozens of couples, many in old-world costumes, whirled, laughing and shouting to each other, their faces pink and smiling. Louise was caught up by the lusty good spirits. Her hand was grasped and she was suddenly swept into the dance by a white-haired gentleman with an exquisitely shaped moustache and sparkling blue eyes. She laughed and gave herself to the strong beat and frenzied spin of a fast polka. The afternoon swung past her, green and red and blue, festive and carefree.

Amy and Peter, holding Beau's leash, stood at the sideline beaming and surprised. They hadn't known their mother could do those foreign-looking dances.

The lovely faces of her children in the gathered crowd; the dry, strong touch of the old man's hand; the sky and the checkered light in the trees; and the throb of her own life in her chest began dissipating Louise's humid oppression.

For some reason, she thought of Nell, feverish and trapped. Louise didn't want to give in to Jack. She wanted her life for her own. And she would find a way to have it.

When she returned to Amy and Peter, her cheeks were flushed and she looked young. The three strolled into an adjacent street from which the clatter, clank, and calliope sounds of carnival rides, mixed with squeals, drifted out to them. Louise took the leash while Amy and Peter rode the merry-go-round half a dozen times. They were going to be happy and sane. She was going to take control of life. She was impatient to see Ned, to tell him, if he would listen, that she was going to kill the dog.

Before leaving the cottage that night, Louise took out the expandable file in which she was keeping household accounts. Ned had helped her organize it and she was able to find what she wanted almost immediately.

She riffled through check stubs, beginning with January and extending through May. As she replaced them in the file, her face wore a distant, slightly puzzled aspect. There were monthly checks in varying amounts to Emerson Florist. All made out by Jack.

Though nervous energy alone kept her going, Louise was lighthearted that night. It was the last performance of *Perfect Union*, and the cast was up. Following the final curtain, they would strike the set. Kegs of beer and cartons of sandwiches waited in the dressing rooms for the strike party.

Would she tell Ned at the party or wait until they were in bed? She didn't think she could wait, and the symbolism of the party appealed to her. Clearing away the old, cleaning the stage bare, making it ready. She laughed at the corny figure of thought.

Louise hung up her gingham gown for the last time, and Amy's beside it. When Amy had pulled on jeans and a shirt, she skipped out of the dressing room in search of Peter.

Sitting before a pockmarked mirror, Louise hurriedly cold-creamed her face, humming as she tissued off makeup. When she'd got down to bare, pink skin, she tossed the tissues in a basket and rushed out to find MacRae.

In the hallway between the two dressing rooms he stood with several cast members clustered around. Immediately beside him was an older woman, small and soft, dressed in a pastel print that showed off her white hair.

Louise waited, looking on. He wore faded, close-fitting jeans, and she imagined how she would enjoy removing them later. He looked up and caught her gaze. She smiled and he returned the smile. It was going to be all right.

Leading the older woman by the arm, he parted the gathering and came toward Louise.

"Louise, I want you to meet my mother. Mother, this is Louise Andrews."

Her face was kind and shrewd, like Ned's. She grasped both of Louise's hands. "I'm very happy to meet you, my dear." She sounded as though she meant it and as though she'd expected to meet Louise.

When they'd made polite inquiries of one another and each found the other more than tolerable, Ned took Louise's hand and led her aside.

"Has anything happened?"

"I can't wait to tell you." His face was close. She wanted to touch it but resisted.

"I wish I could stick around for the set strike, lady, but my mother came from Red Wing today to catch the show before it closed. She's dead on her feet. We're going to clear out now." He read Louise's disappointment. "I've missed you," he told her, cupping her face in his hand. "Tomorrow night?"

She nodded.

Half an hour later she was coming out of the women's dressing room carrying hats and other accessories bound for the costume shop.

Frank, headed in the same direction, and bearing men's gear, emerged from the next dressing room. "Shall we open a thrift shop?" he asked.

They climbed the stairs to the loft where costumes were stored. Frank fumbled for the light switch. After making several more trips, they settled down to sort it all out and find the proper box, trunk, or closet for each item.

"They also serve who only sit and sort," he told her, reaching up to a high shelf for several large boxes marked "Hats—Men" and "Hats—Women."

Setting them on the floor, he asked, "Still going ahead with your Yacht Club plans?"

"Yes. Are you going to tell me what a mistake I'm making and how I'll disgrace the family name?"

"No."

"That's refreshing."

"I don't know if you're making a mistake. A thing isn't a mistake until it goes wrong, is it?"

Louise opened a trunk that gave off a strong odor of mothballs and began folding capes and laying them away inside.

"Frank, I've wanted to ask you something for several weeks, but I haven't had the courage."

"I hate to disappoint you, Louise, but I'm spoken for at the moment."

"I've been paying bills since Jack died," she went on, "and I noticed a monthly check to Emerson's that Jack was paying."

Frank listened, nodding.

"Jack had flowers or some type of seasonal decoration placed on Nell's grave every month, didn't he?"

There was a hesitation as though he were debating whether to end this line of conversation before it could begin. Finally, "Yes."

"Ever since her death?"

"Yes."

Louise tossed aside the shawl she'd been folding and sat down beside him. "Were they . . . ?" She was afraid to ask, but if he had the answer, she had to know.

"Lovers? I don't know. I don't think so."

Louise questioned whether he said that to spare her, or himself.

"Nell was infatuated with Jack," he said. "You must have seen it."

She supposed she had, without really concerning herself.

"She threw herself at him. Partly because she was genuinely attracted to him. Partly to punish me."

"She felt very trapped in your work."

"Yes."

He spoke dispassionately enough, but Louise wondered if that were from long experience.

"Jack was my best friend," he went on, "I think I loved him more than Nell did, but who can judge a thing like that?"

"How could you love him under the circumstances?"

Over and over he smoothed the cravat lying on the table, all the time considering her question. "Jack was like an energy source," he explained, setting the cravat to one side. "He was like a sun or fire. Everything was attracted to him. For warmth, for the light he gave off. For the energy one hoped to absorb from his supply. We all used Jack's fire as though he were a natural resource.

"I could hardly blame Nell if she threw herself at him. And I couldn't blame him," he concluded.

Louise stood suddenly, thrusting the chair back. She was filled with turmoil. What she'd hoped for from Frank was a clear-cut case against Jack that would reinforce her decision to kill the dog.

"Why did he place the flowers on her grave, Frank? Why, if they hadn't been lovers?"

"Jack needed to hang onto everyone who was drawn to him. It wasn't a need he could govern in any reasoning way. It grew out of his childhood, I'm certain. Only death could defy him and even then he was going to hang on and claim the person in some manner. The flowers were his way of hanging on to Nell."

And the dog was his way of hanging on to her. Louise paced around the small, hot room.

"If *you* had died, Louise, Jack would have opened the heavens to claim you back." He was unembarrassed by the drama of his words, and they shook Louise because once again she began to feel helpless, up against something stronger than herself.

Below them a counter-mood of laughter and celebration prevailed. Standing, leaning across the table toward him, Louise pursued, "When Nell killed herself, was it because of Jack?"

"Well," he began slowly, "I wouldn't want to say something like that. I think maybe she'd always been ill. Maybe I was attracted to that, thinking I could help her. Her depressions were getting worse. My work was part of it. And Jack may have been part of it." He tilted his head sideways, lost for a moment in speculation. "I always thought it was strange that she would steal Jack's gun to do away with herself, when *I* owned a pistol. I've suspected it was her way of relaying a final message to him."

Bitterly, Louise summed up her own feelings, "If you throw yourself at the sun, you're damned well going to get your wings singed."

Frank smiled sardonically. "Those are not the happy words of inspiration we're looking for, Louise."

As she left the theater lot behind and drove through the warm, humid night, Louise noted the distant flashes of brilliant haze. Heat lightning. Often it came to nothing more than a light show.

By the time she turned into her own drive, the lightning had advanced and grown distinct, the accompanying thunder, no longer muffled, cracked like gunshots, then rumbled angrily. The quality of the air told her rain was perhaps twenty minutes away.

The children were asleep. She carried Peter through the crickety darkness to the sleeping porch, laid him on his bed and removed his outer clothing. Amy, who was much heavier, had to be led and half-supported from car to bed. Louise kissed them and spoke to Beau, who had been at the door to greet them.

Made whimpery and unsure by the lightning and thunder, he ran gratefully around her legs and sniffed at her sandaled feet. She took him outside to run and do his business before the rain came. He wandered reluctantly in a small circle around the step where she sat.

In a few minutes he came back, wagging his tail and shifting his rear affectionately from side to side. Louise petted him and played with him for a while. She was very fond of him. He gave them a great deal of pleasure. And hope. To her he'd become a symbol of healthy change.

A huge, crooked bolt of light flashed earthward across the bay, followed by an ear-splitting crack and roar. Beau whined and tried to climb on Louise's lap. She stood. "Come in now," she told him and opened the door. He fled before her into the cottage. Leaping onto Peter's bed, he pawed at the covers and burrowed as close to Peter as possible. Louise smiled sympathetically. "I'll see you in the morning."

Changing into a light robe, she washed her face and brushed her teeth, then wandered into the kitchen and stood, preoccupied, before the open refrigerator. Were Betsy and Donald sleeping here tonight? She couldn't remember. Outside, thunder and lightning warred and a skuddy breeze whipped the leaves to rushing sibilance. She poured a glass of milk and returned the carton to the refrigerator. As she turned to leave, hand raised to flick the light switch, she heard it.

There was a momentary respite between thunder and imminent rain. Swaying trees muzzied the air, but through the open kitchen window came the faint but unmistakable jingle of ID tags. He had come across the road.

Her heart pounded in her ears. Slowly her hand continued

up the wall to the switch, extinguishing the light behind her. Without noticing that she moved on tiptoe, she went quickly through the first floor turning off lights. On the porch, hands fluttering, she lowered the canvas shades and fastened them securely against the rain. Beau's tail thumped against the bed as he watched her work, but he remained close against Peter.

Large drops of rain began to throw themselves against the canvas as the western wind hurled them at the front of the cottage. Why had Jack waited until now? He'd been ill or hurt, perhaps. He wouldn't want her to see him until he was strong. Where should she meet him? On her own ground. She wouldn't look for him. He would have to come to her.

Mixed into the pelting sound of rain, she heard the soft jingling again. It was at the back of the cottage. No, it moved. It was beyond the fireplace wall. Now, in front. He was circling the cottage.

Neither Beau nor the children stirred. The children. When he came in she mustn't confront him here. Not near the children. She stepped backward leaving her slippers where she'd stood. Bare feet were quieter and she was certain he could hear her, even above the sound of the storm. Not turning her back to the door, she stepped noiselessly across the wood floor, inching closer to the hall and stairs.

Reaching out at last with her left hand, she felt for the stair rail. In front of the cottage the jingling stopped. A terrifying snap of thunder struck not far away, and Louise's ears rang. She strained to hear but there was only a humming in her ears. Her foot was on the bottom step.

One step at a time, close to the wall, up she went, pausing on each tread to listen. Still the battering rain and the thunder were all that reached her. Gaining the top of the stairs, she waited, resting against the door frame. Her eyes burned. She blinked them painfully and crept toward the bed.

The dormer windows stood open and rain slashed sideways across the room. Louise ignored it and the ghostly daylight that filled the space when lightning broke close by.

In the euphoric resolve of the afternoon, she had formulated no more than a vague plan. She would face him. She would warn him. He could run if he chose. He was, after all, her husband and she wouldn't kill him unless she must.

She sat on the edge of the bed, facing the stairway, opened the drawer of the table, and felt for the gun case. Without turning on the light, she removed the pistol from the case and loaded it.

There was a flat thud, like a screen door closing. The wind worrying the boathouse door?

"Donald? Betsy?"

No answer. Minutes passed. The sky and the room went white. The night shattered as lightning struck a tree in the grove. For a moment Louise thought she'd accidentally discharged the gun. She cried out and began to tremble helplessly.

"God help me," she whispered, and could not hold the gun still in her hand. As the thunder receded unwillingly across the lake, another sound, more unnerving, filled the growing void. The clicking of paws on wooden floors.

The lightning that had felled the tree in the grove had been the final volley from a withdrawing enemy. Now, only small splinters of light and low, ill-tempered grumbling accompanied the steady beat of rain. From below, back and forth across the broad area that made up the living and dining rooms, the clicking melted into the other sounds.

It seemed to go on forever. The cadence was hypnotic. Louise's mind blurred. Her body slumped. She caught herself up.

She heard nothing. Had she slept? Drugged by exhaustion and the rain-heavy air, she lay back on the pillow, keeping the gun in her hand. Slowly, slowly, she was pulled down into black cotton.

A room, small and chaste. The walls, the floor, even the ceiling, were lined with white tile, cold, smooth, pure as innocence. Moving to the window, she parted the curtains and was met by a wall, blank and white. She was filled with panic and anger. Beating her fists against the wall, she cried, "Goddamn you, Jack, I'm going to get out of here!" Then hearing his step, she whirled to face him.

He smiled his perfect smile. Didn't he know there wasn't a door or window? He knew. "I like this house," he murmured and drew her firmly to him.

There was pain. Burning, prodding, clawing pain. She felt her body assaulted by his weight, torn by his nails. She groaned, then screamed, "No, Jack!"

Louise opened her eyes. He stood on top of her. From his mouth he let drop Beau's limp, dead body. It fell on her chest.

With frenzied strength, she plunged sideways onto the floor, the dogs falling with her. "You can't do this to me!" He was dislodged momentarily and Louise was on her feet. Where was the gun? It must have fallen.

She seized the small bedside lamp and when he lunged with a tormented yowl, she swung, smashing him across the shoulder. "I'll kill you," she promised in a voice she didn't recognize. He fell back, stunned by the blow. With the lamp still in her hands, she waited. "I *will* kill you."

Pulling himself up, he looked at her but didn't gather himself for attack. Head, neck, and withers went slack as power and purpose left him. From his throat he forced a whine, barely audible. Shaking his head as though to dispel a nightmare, he turned and limped toward the stairs.

After some minutes Suzie was at the head of the stairs, groping for the light switch. "Louise! Louise!... oh, God. What's happened?" she breathed as she caught sight of Louise.

Chapter 27

Suzie's husband, Ralph, took Amy and Peter. He called Tom Benjamin. And Ned.

There was nothing left of the night as Tom finished with her. Sunlight, yellow and almost palpably real, filled the window nearest the bed.

He'd given her a shot to calm her, but she shook with sobs that rose from a well of betrayal extending back through years. "The puppy. The puppy," she cried. Her hope.

Ned sat beside her, trying to comfort her. When Tom Benjamin prepared to leave, Ned rose. Tom would phone the police from town and report the attack, he explained as Ned walked him to the car. Wearily, the doctor climbed into the VW. The dog had to be found.

The voices of the two men rose, muffled, from beneath her window. Louise's sobs subsided, but the tears continued to slip from beneath her lids and it didn't seem possible that they would stop. She heard Ned lock the screen and climb the stairs.

"The kids are sleeping. Suzie helped me put them back in their own beds." He sat on the bed again.

"Do they know about Beau?"

"Not yet. I wrapped him in a rug from the porch and Tom took him away," he told her.

Beau. Anger and sadness filled her chest and threatened to break her ribs. "Beau!"

He held her. The shot was beginning to take effect. Her voice sounded quieter, weaker. "Hope. The puppy was."

He stroked her hair and spoke softly. "He wasn't your hope. Your hope is in here." He lay a finger against her temple.

She lay down. "Please do me a favor," she said to him sleepily.

"Yes?"

"Talk to the police or whoever. Ask them to get him without killing him if they can."

"Louise . . ."

"Brian can kill him with a shot of something. I have to be there."

"I'll talk to them." He stretched out, facing her.

She was very drowsy. "I have to tell you something."

"Not unless you want to."

"I have to. I want to."

"All right."

"I was going to kill him. With the gun. I had decided, Ned, do you believe me? I didn't want to be crazy."

"I believe you."

"He's taken Beau from Amy and Peter." She clenched a fist and covered her mouth with it. She was crying. "He's taken . . ."

He moved closer to her, smoothed back the hair around her forehead, and repeated, "Not hope. Can you hear me, Louise?"

"Yes."

They slept side by side for many hours.

Monday passed. The dog wasn't found. Word circulated around the lake and in town that the dog was dangerous, and it was unlikely he could go for long without being seen.

Louise, Amy, and Peter remained inside with the screens locked. Ned returned to them when he left the office at five. He was going to take up residence, he told her, until the animal was certifiably dead. Louise assented though she wouldn't talk about the death. She knew it wasn't necessary for Ned to stay but there was no point in telling him, because he wouldn't listen. The dog wouldn't return. Sunday night had been the end. If the police found him, she would see him again but he wouldn't come back on his own.

Amy and Peter were stunned, dazed by Beau's death. Louise told them no details, only that Fido had come back and that he'd killed the puppy. She couldn't protect them from that. It was something they had to know.

They were bereft. First their father, then Fido, now Beau had left them. What could they trust? Louise spent nearly every waking hour with them at first. They didn't want her out of their sight. They were willing to be comforted by her. Though still exhausted, Louise was free of fear and filled with calm and it gave her great satisfaction to be the children's comfort.

When she next saw the dog it was Wednesday afternoon. The young officer at the desk rose as she identified herself. "Just a minute, ma'am," he said and went through a door, returning a moment later with a leash and, at the end of it, the Irish setter. "This him?"

The dog stepped across the gray tiled floor lightly, gingerly, as though it burned his feet. It occurred to Louise that the pads of his feet were probably very sore indeed from the hundred miles he had come, the long trek from Worthington. A great distance even for a cross-country runner.

"That's him." Louise had brought a leash which she fastened to his collar, removing the strange one. She unbuckled the shameful muzzle and lay it and the leash on the officer's desk.

"I'm going to take him to the kennel and have the vet put him to sleep."

"All right, ma'am, otherwise you can take him to the City Pound. They'll do it for you there."

"No. I'd rather the vet's."

"Would you sign this release for me and then have the vet sign this other paper?" he asked, handing her a form. "It's for our records."

The dog stood beside Louise, his head drooping. Louise put the form in her bag. "Thank you—for finding him and keeping him for me."

"You're welcome." He looked over the desk at the dog. "It's too bad you've had trouble with him. He's a beauty. The men said he was tame as a kitten when they picked him up. He wouldn't touch food, though. We tried to feed him."

"Thank you again," Louise said and turned to go. She pushed the heavy door and let the dog precede her out. In the parking lot she opened the car door and he stepped painfully up onto the front seat. Still he wouldn't lift his head to look at her. She started the engine, pulled out of the lot and headed the car toward the kennel.

Tears blinded her. She turned the car into the curb and cut the engine. Reaching in her bag, she found a handkerchief. The dog lay a paw on her lap and Louise lifted it to examine the underside. It was raw, hot and cut in several places. She set it down again and ran a hand along his back, petting him, crooning to him. She buried her face in his shoulder, dull, dusty, and full of burrs, and continued to weep. Kissing his head, she murmured to him.

"I loved you." She wasn't going to pull memories apart like someone unraveling a sweater. She *had* loved him. "I'm changing. I'm not destroying you to protect that. I'm trying to set us free. Please understand, Jack."

At length she straightened, dried her eyes and started the engine. As she drove, she glanced at him occasionally and continued talking to him.

When they reached the kennel, the dog got out on Louise's side, accompanying her with resignation into the hospital. I should have called Brian, Louise thought. He may be terribly busy. Annie was coming out of an examining room as Louise led the dog into the waiting room.

"Louise, can I help you?"

"Is Brian here?"

"Yes. Just a second. Sit down and I'll find him."

The dog sat close, resting his head on her thigh. It was all she could do not to scream and run out, taking him with her, running away with him. How difficult it was to be free. Much more difficult than being captive.

Brian was there. Without speaking, he nodded for her to follow. Her fingers on the leash were stiff and cold. With her left hand on the arm of the chair, she got up, feeling old and weak. She followed Brian, moving mechanically down the hall to the last door on the left. He held it for her.

Brian helped the dog up to the table.

"You know—what has to be done?" Louise asked.

"Yes," he told her, preparing a hypodermic syringe.

Before he gave the dog the injection, Louise lifted the animal's head, trying to read in the face, the eyes, any message, any emotion. There was nothing to be read. There *had* been, though, these past months. Hadn't there?

It was over quickly.

She had set him free. She had to believe that.

Saturday was moving day. From Louise's cottage boxes and boxes of belongings must be carried to town. Ned, too, was transferring his things back to the apartment. At nine-thirty Saturday morning, he turned into Louise's drive pulling a small trailer behind the Buick. When the trailer was loaded, they locked the front and back doors and took a last look around the yard and boathouse. It looked forlorn.

The last unloading to be done in town was at Ned's. "Let us

help you," Louise told him. "I've never seen your apartment. I'm curious."

With everyone carrying something, it required only four trips to empty the trailer of Ned's things. The apartment, on the second floor and facing the park, was a living room with balcony, bedroom, small kitchen and bath, the living quarters of someone busy, who spent little time at home—comfortable, tasteful but without any personal touches.

"Mommy, can Peter and I go over to the park for a while?" Amy asked, handing Louise a box of kitchen ware.

"If you take Peter's hand going across the street and don't stay long."

Ned stood in the kitchen doorway watching Louise put utensils in a drawer. Finally he cleared his throat. "We're a little awkward with each other now, aren't we?"

She smiled, knowing what he meant. "Our adrenalin glands are taking a well-deserved vacation."

"We have to get acquainted all over again," he said.

"What if we don't like each other?"

"Impossible."

"No, it's not. We've been living in a nightmare. Awake, we may not be able to stand each other."

"We always have this," he said, pulling her to him.

Louise extricated herself, took his hand and led him into the living room. They sat down on the sofa where they could see Amy and Peter running in the park.

He played idly with her fingers. "I want to marry you."

"No."

"Never?"

"I don't know." Louise watched Amy pushing Peter in the swing.

"Why?"

"By winter your ardor may begin to cool."

"No."

"Mine may."

"And if it doesn't?"

"We'll talk."

He turned her chin. "Am I somebody you couldn't love except when you were crazy?"

"Don't be silly. You're ridiculously self-conscious about your reputation."

"Some women only want to sleep with my reputation. It's all they're curious about. What about you?"

"Did I just want to know if you were as good as they said?" Louise laughed hard and slapped his thigh. "Hell, I don't know why I slept with you, except I couldn't stop myself." She looked at him. "You remind me of a sixteen-year-old girl asking if I'll still respect you."

He grinned.

She hugged him. "It's nice to know you can be childish and human, MacRae. And you know what's nicest?—that you don't mind too much if it shows."

"What you said about your ardor cooling, that isn't the reason you won't marry me now, is it?"

She did love him, but she wouldn't let him sway her. "No. You're right." She kissed the veins on the back of his hand. "I'm not the person I was before Jack died. I've changed and I'm changing. I'm becoming—more free. Until I know what that means, I'm not going to give it up."

"Nobody—man, woman or child—is free, Louise. We all depend on each other."

"I know. I mean I want to be *myself* within that—dependency."

"I wouldn't ask you to give that up."

"I've been someone else's Louise for so many years, I don't know who *my* Louise is. Before I can think about marriage, I want to find out. I feel like a mother looking for the child she gave away."

He held her gaze. "This isn't just continued loyalty to Jack?"

"No. Whatever happens between you and me has nothing to do with Jack. In some ways, the past was someone else's life. What's left is mine."

Peter and Amy, whooshing down the slide, waved in the direction of the apartment. Though they couldn't see her, Louise waved back.

"Let's get the kids and go have lunch someplace," he said. "Then I have to take you home and get to work." He stood up, pulling her to her feet. "You're going to be impressed, Louise. I'm going to become a man of responsibility."

As he held the door for her, she cast her eyes heavenward and strolled past him. "I *respect* you, MacRae. I *respect* you."

Chapter 28

Louise sat gazing at the early afternoon snowfall. Beyond the windows of the Yacht Club, Swan Lake lay, frozen and snow-blanketed, pale and fuzzy as angora. Less than three weeks remained until Christmas.

Today she'd hung lights on the Christmas tree outside the window, and strung tinsel garlands inside. With the new snowfall, there'd been few customers to interrupt the decorating.

From November through April the club didn't open until noon, so Louise came in about eleven and worked until four when Art came on. She was pleased to be able to open by herself and Art was grateful not to work a split shift, as he once had.

The past summer seemed as long ago as childhood and far less real. These days when she thought of Fido, it was with some small doubts. Had she, as Ned maintained, created him? It would be confortable to believe. There had been so much on the other side, however.

Doubtless some mysteries were insoluble and maybe it was a mark of one's resilience and self-confidence that one accepted that and went ahead with life. The alternative was to weave oneself into a cocoon of doubt.

Louise got up and poured herself a cup of coffee. In the kitchen a radio played Christmas music while the cook opened and slammed refrigerator and freezer doors. The sounds reminded Louise that Ned was coming to the house for dinner and they were taking Amy and Peter Christmas shopping afterward.

Ned was good to them all. Louise was greatly tempted to yield to his proposal and the comfort it offered. It wasn't for lack of love that she withheld from marriage. It was because she still didn't understand how freedom and love worked.

She had sold one to buy the other when she met Jack. Never again.

She flicked the switch that lit the tree outside. Tucked away in her bureau drawer was the piece of handmade lace she'd bought last summer to trim her Christmas dress. A small act of faith.

Amy and Peter had each written at the top of their Christmas "wish lists": a puppy. Another act of faith. She couldn't deny them that. Yet, contemplating it, she grew cold and rubbed her arms to warm herself. Jack. Someday he would let go of her or she of him. In the meantime she would buy a puppy. It *was* an act of faith.